ONE

MORE

IRiS

BY

DARCY GRECO

the PeppertreePress, LLC
Sarasota, Florida

Cover graphic design by Kathryn Reina kathrynreina.com
Back page bio photograph by Ash Dudney www.ashdundney.com
Graphic design by Rebecca Barbier.

For information regarding permission,
call 941-922-2662 or contact us at our website:
www.peppertreepublishing.com or write to:
the Peppertree Press, LLC.
Attention: Publisher
1269 First Street, Suite 7
Sarasota, Florida 34236

ISBN: 978-1-61493-723-4

Library of Congress Number: 2020911459

Printed July 2020

*This book is dedicated
to all the real characters that inspired this fiction.*

CHAPTER 1

Tell my heart to hold its pace
To slow this racing pulse.
Closed eyes,
Heavy breath,
Envisioning the potential landslide.
Extracting the wreckage once buried.
Waiting, just waiting.
The second hand on the clock broken like me, who I was.
A tug of war in human nature,
*   going forward while the past becomes present.*
My mind crawling with uncertainty,
Uncomfortable in my own skin.
Relief in tomorrow that this moment will have already passed.
Wishing, aching, yearning till then.
Waiting, just waiting.

~IH

The Meeting

This string in my hand keeps pulling, tickling my arm and catching on my skinny stackable David Yurman bracelets. Shifting with the wind, one yellow balloon attached floating delicately above my head. It may have been a bit much for the occasion. The light physical weight, a stark contrast from the fear and intoxicating beverages that once held my grip. After all, it's not exactly my mother's birthday, but my daughters insisted on the balloon. So here we are, helium included.

Twins don't actually run in either of our families. We have other impelling genes to pass on. The doctors said the chances of multiples were higher coming from mature eggs such as mine. Who knew? Something about a woman's natural last attempt for kin.

Birthdays ... it is sort of close to my mother's birthday, only a few weeks away. She hasn't truly celebrated her birthday in a few years, at least not the last eighteen. No cake and candles. No gifts or vacations. Not even a fancy dinner. My mother or Vera (as my sisters and I grew to call her) was never really a big birthday person anyway.

My girls also requested to bring a bouquet of flowers. Brightly colored tropical blooms, equipped with deep leafy green stems and four birds of paradise. A wide aqua satin ribbon ties the stalks together. The flowers are pretty breathtaking. So is today.

Breathtaking, that's right, keep breathing. I need to remember to keep breathing. The air in this parking lot is thick with earthy hints of dead worms and wet grass in the distance. It's surprisingly humid this morning. We flew thousands of miles to be here and I seem to have forgotten how warm the summer days can actually be, even here in upstate New York. Breathing in and out. In with calmness, out with my concerns. At this moment, I'm so filled with excitement, I'm not sure if I'm going to pass out or throw up.

"Wait till your grandmother sees you girls," my husband says to our rambunctious daughters. Glen is one of the best things that ever happened to me, along with becoming a mother. Waiting lovingly by my side to help, on this highly anticipated day.

"She's going to be so excited," he continues.

"Yes, I'm sure she will be," I chime in. This will be her first time meeting our already five-year-old girls. I went back and forth about coming here alone. With or without all the family, but decided everyone here would be a welcomed joy.

Our charming girls, the little bonus bundle that completed our family. A picturesque image I still have to pinch myself to believe.

"When can we eat? I'm starving," my daughter asks.

"I'm not sure yet, I don't really know how this works. Grab a granola bar out of my bag. Actually, grab me one, too."

It's times like these I could really use more than a bar. On second thought, that would be great. A simple little bar would do. One where I could order a strong clear martini, and another close behind. What would that help? Kind of ironic given the situation. If I were to drink right now, it would definitely be a shot of tequila. The good kind— Patron. The only kind I drink, well, at least if they have it. I mean it's not like I wouldn't drink Jose Cuervo or something along those lines (if that were my only option). I would certainly choose something over a less than equivalent tequila.

Yes, a true drink of choice. The whole experience is lovely. The salty grains scrape across the back of my hand and onto my tongue. Just before a hard glass pushes the most extravagantly burning liquid down my throat, finishing off the experience with a quick squeeze of zesty lime. The pulp still lingers on my lips. Wiping the residue from my face, a few granules push back into my mouth and that yummy salty taste appears once more. Just then I realize that I am fantasizing about my love affair with the old days. I need to stop. I need to refocus. Looking to my husband, "I'm going to give Sharon a call, I just need a minute."

He nods in an understanding way and distracts the kids with yet another YouTube video on his phone.

Walking back to the car, I recite the serenity prayer.

"God grant me the serenity, to accept the things I cannot change, the courage to change the things I can and the wisdom to know the difference." Breathing out, a slight feeling of relief comes over me just as she answers the phone.

Sharon's a charming mature Southern woman who radiates love

and comfort. She's sort of *on call* for me today, understanding the importance. Clearing her entire calendar with promises to simply be by her phone. We have played out so many scenarios—it's hard to believe the day has arrived.

"Hello there, Iris," she answers. Her voice is raspy and deeper for a woman. Tales of parties she's attended from years past.

"Hey, Sharon, we're here."

"Oh." She waits for me to proceed.

"Yeah, I just caught myself romancing salt, lime, and Patron. So I figured I'd give you a call."

"Well, I'm glad you did." Her choices in words are as calming as the way she says them. She never rushes. Pausing widely in-between sentences and sometimes even one word to the next, appropriately of course. Not so long that you forget her original meaning. More like for time of reflection and to cautiously choose what she really wants to say next.

"I believe a good tequila shot was a favorite pastime of mine as well. I loved the excitement. Feeling that fierce flame slip down."

"Yes, ma'am. Perpetual burning bliss."

"Don't you know it, honey? One time at 'Mickey's Bar,' they ran out of salt and somehow we got it in our heads to use sugar. Let me tell you—that was a little different. That sugar didn't help take the bite out of the fire we were guzzling back."

"Yeah," I laugh. "Probably didn't quite do the trick."

"It sure didn't, but you better believe me that sugar didn't stop us."

"Yes, ma'am, wouldn't have stopped me either," I respond smiling.

"You're doing great, you called. Easy does it, honey."

"You're right. Thanks, Sharon."

"I'm here all day by the grace of God."

Hanging up the phone, my home screen picture pops up. One of my new favorites. The twins and some neighborhood playmates piled high. Laying one on top of the other in what was supposed to be a pyramid, each one smooching the one below. My husband attempting to protect me the way he always has, trying to block the stack of children from crashing into us. Glen's arms stretched out, head turned toward mine, his gray hairs showing off. In a stereotypical way, he looks more distinguished. Some may even say it would be to his advantage, being an attorney and all. His glossy blue eyes a little more aged these days, but so are mine. Giving my crow's feet a run for their Botox.

I sit in the car tracing my pale polished fingers over the stiches of the tan leather seat and take a glimpse at my reflection in the rear view mirror. They say not to look back, but today the past seems to be becoming present. And I worry most about what things will become after. I brush my hands through the pale blonde hair that I used to have naturally. People can change. I have changed. I take in another deep breath, fill my lungs, then exhale even slower. My thoughts collected, I let go of my expectations and I head back to meet my family.

CHAPTER 2

Feelings wash over me like citrus soap stinging my eyes,
The water rinsing and laughing behind.

~IH

It was the end of May and ninth grade—our school baseball team had made it to the playoffs, which was highly unusual coming from our athletic department. The Trojans for once assembled a team of good players. Holding an undefended record, our first ever. Unless you count the season before that, which held a perfect score of defeat. Our fair-weather fans of students and faculty packed tightly together, beaming a sea of black and gold. My group of friends and I sat on the top left side of the metal bleachers—the sought-after section mixed with even more popular upperclassmen.

Baseball was drawing huge crowds and even better after-parties. Tonight my girlfriend Katie was hosting the celebratory festivities at her house for our clique of girls, plus our coextending boys, Sean, Wesley, and Rick. Sean was equal parts our guy friend and Katie's boyfriend.

Katie and Sean sat close together, the way couples do, paying closer attention to each other than the game. They were busy discussing their plans for later, in between their make-out sessions. Sean had already seized Katie's virginity, so I wasn't really sure what was left to discuss. But I suppose the exploits Katie whispered in Sean's ear were pleasing nonetheless.

"Gross, you two, get a room," Wesley yelled while he threw a couple of condoms back in their direction.

Gross or not, we were the Trojans. The bleachers were littered with the small square packets. It was tradition to throw them at opposing teams, or in this case, our lovebird friends behind.

"Don't be jealous 'cause you're still back on Virgin Island, Wes," Sean returned laughing.

"Oh, is that what you think?" Wesley blushed while quickly trying to cover his absence of words and sexual relationships.

Rick spoke up, "OK, guys, I can't concentrate on the game with you two girls bickering back and forth."

Wesley was delightful and sensitive—he was also my favorite. With four older sisters, he often referred to his home as "the sorority house." Wes was knowledgeable from his immersion of estrogen and every at-home beauty product on the market from tampons to facial scrubs. I think that was what made him more mindful and attractive. Wesley had tight blonde curls that he hated and fair skin. Clear green eyes and a small dimple on his right cheek when he smiled. Sounding a bit like a woman longing for greener grass when he spoke of the features he would change about himself.

"Wes, tell me again, why do you want your hair straight?" I ask, sitting directly beside him.

"Ugh, look," he said as he pulls one of the springing curls outward between his fingers.

"It looks like I'm walking around with blonde pubes on my head—even Jessica says so." Jessica was the youngest of his older sisters—she was also the cruelest.

"Well, I disagree, you wouldn't look like yourself without your curls. They give you your cute charm."

"So you think I'm cute, hun?"

Now my face was hot. I raised my hands to my hair to pull it back, hoping to cool the blushing heat from my face.

"Oh, you have a French manicure," my hands catching Wesley's attention. "I like it when girls keep up their nails."

"Ha, wow! Yes, Wes, I got a French manicure yesterday. And may I just say you might be the only guy in the stands that noticed, let alone could name this style of polish."

"Please, my sisters are always talking about their nails. It does finish a look. When I see a girl with banged-up nails I wanna say, 'Oh girl, you need to go get your nails done.'"

"Wesley, if I didn't know better, I'd swear you were gay."

"Well, let me show you how gay I'm not by directing that pretty little manicure where to go."

"And he's back."

We both laugh. Neither of us would ever want to ruin the friendship we had, although Wes certainly would make a cute boyfriend.

The Trojans won the game and us girls headed back to Katie's, the boys would stop by later. Waiting for us in the basement mini-fridge, glass bottles of Seagram's exotic strawberry daiquiri and peach fuzzy navel wine cooler (thanks to Katie's older brother). The finished basement was Kate's bedroom and a fabulous hangout. Barely noticing the lack of windows or musty air that basement living provides, we sipped the sweet sugary taste of youth and popularity.

Our boys were running late, the way they often were, but we hardly noticed the clock as we drank our beverages with 3.2% of alcohol. We danced around to hip-hop music, playing dress-up in Katie's mother's old clothes. We made up skits and a few rounds of truth or dare, until we were halted from the sound of a pounding fist on the front door. We feared the boys were drunk and would wake Katie's parents. All of us scrambled upstairs only to find Sean's uncle, and a sobering moment of truth.

"It's really bad," his uncle said as we swung open the door.

"Sean is dead. Rick and Wesley are in really bad shape—they've been taken to the hospital. The doctors aren't sure if they are going to make it."

We froze. Six teenage girls stood like statues in a living room with one grown man at the front door. Everyone incapable to comprehend the statement or details that followed. Sean's uncle poured out with tears and specifics, although I found myself fixated on the word *dead*. Pondering its assertion, past tense, he's already dead. Sean is dead.

Katie, in shock, fell to the floor, as we stood in disbelief. She began screaming. Wailing as she kicked her feet hard into the air as if trying to break into a different universe. The one that she was just pulled into. Although they were young, Sean was the love of her life. The high school sweethearts everyone adored, the guy she adored and loved. She was supposed to be with him tonight, holding him. Not rocking on the floor comprehending his death.

It wasn't until that day that I realized the shortage of words in the English vocabulary. Sure there seems to be plenty when you look at the size of a dictionary, some that I will never use, but in that moment, nothing could describe accurately what I was feeling. Nothing I could say could help my pain or anyone else's go away.

As for Katie, I discovered that there's not really a word for a girlfriend who loses a boyfriend. It is not like a spouse who becomes a widow. There is no cue word to describe the pain you have gone through upon meeting someone that's socially acceptable. Nothing short of trying to explain the heartache you have endured other than going through a long, drawn-out story of events.

My heart ached for her, for Sean's family, for all of us, and especially Sean. I tortured myself with the meticulous details, creating a play-by-play scene in my head. The path, the curves, the tree that got in the way, the road that should have lead them to the house where we waited. Agonizing over the pain and fear that the boys endured.

Sean's uncle broke down in the doorway, half inside, half out. He explained how Wesley and Rick were being held in ICU—that the boys had been drinking before the accident. Pausing to sob, letting out some of the most horrific sounds imaginable from a grown man. And that was the end of our youth.

The guilt *ran*, not walked into our bodies, and a hole was carved into us, never to leave. We all knew better. Our boys were drinking, just like us. Driving to see us, but never made it. Our lives stolen, though Sean paid the biggest price.

An experience we occasionally hear about in the news, but never imagine affecting us. A banged-up car on the corner of a school parking lot, a frightful tactic used nationwide to scare kids from drinking and driving, usually during prom or graduation season. A dreadful point all parents fear and most teens can't understand.

The visual reminder we no longer needed—this was our wreck.

The pain sunk deeper as we made our daily hospital trips to check on our friends stuck in ICU. The hospital, halls, and rooms became a place of desensitization in a weirdly familiar routine. And every ringing phone was filled with fear and anticipation, the way it does after tragedy.

Wesley's head was wrapped with bandages and had grown to the size of a basketball from the swelling. Tubes and monitors came out from the shaved away patches of curls missing above his temples, some by the nape of his neck. Wesley's head injury trumped the rest of his wounds and he soon slipped into a coma. The doctors performed multiple scans and tests that concluded Wesley was indeed brain dead. His injuries were total. He was living completely on life support to function. After watching the regression of Wesley's state, his parents decided it was time to let him go. We were all given a chance to go into his room individually, one last time.

I walked through the door where the window in the opposite wall faced the streets down below. Cars still busy about their day, continuing life as Wesley's was finishing his. It was heart-wrenching to look at his even paler than usual face, tinted yellow and blue with bruises, full of bloat. I spoke only a couple of words softly to him as I stood beside his bed.

"You have always been one of my closest friends. I will never forget you." I pause to catch my breath and the tears. I reached my hand outward to give his cold fingers a squeeze. Noticing my once white-tipped French manicure, the one that Wes liked just one week ago. Now chipped and tinged, a distraught manila color, distraught like the rest of me.

I somehow managed to smile, "I promise to not let my nails go again. I'll keep them polished for you," but continue sobbing once more. I lean over his body and whisper, "I love you, Wesley."

I stand to my weakening feet and pull myself together. Leaving the room and him.

Rick's injuries were improving, though he bore the greatest bandage of guilt. The stitches, cracked ribs, and concussion didn't come close to the mental pain he tortured himself with for being alive. The doctors weren't ready to release Rick from the hospital, but he refused to miss Sean's funeral or Wesley's, which was just a few days behind.

Closed caskets placed in rooms filled with sadness and people far too young to be gathered in honor of death. Most paying their respects escorted by their parents, as many of us were still too young to drive. We went through the motions of losing a friend, not once, but twice.

At the close of the week we held a vigil service beside the tree that was nearly ripped out of the ground. The scene of the accident that was now home to numerous candles, pictures, and flowers. The families were devastated. I watched as Wesley's mother wrapped her arms around his father. Rocking him gently as they sobbed, mourning the death of their only son. All four of Wesley's sisters and us girls held hands with piles of tissues surrounding the grass below. Sean's father and uncle standing lifeless, just staring in anguish, while the strangely appropriate *Free Bird* song played from a nearby car speaker. Kneeling to place our hands upon the broad tree that changed our lives forever. The wood hard, like the lesson we had learned.

> *A child becomes parent,*
> *Not due to matured age.*
>
> *-I.H.*

The dueling funerals were only a year ago. Buckled in tightly now, my stare is jolted forward—back to the glass windshield. Darkness encloses this old beat-up jeep. Naturally, it's dark, as it's quarter past twelve. The gravel is bumpy as the tires race for better traction. Facing the challenging mission of driving down railroad tracks, with a stick shift, at night. I would rather not. I would rather be home, in bed, asleep like most fifteen-year-olds. Maybe still awake finishing up a movie or chatting on the phone, but definitely not here, propelling down these tracks.

My mother is drunk again. Leave it to Vera to be over-served picking up our to-go dinner, needing me to drive us home again. It's fine. I'd much rather drive, than let her get behind the wheel right now, but I wish she didn't insist on us coming over here, to these stupid tracks. I also wish I had my driver's license or even a permit, or that I knew how to drive a stick shift.

She has been slightly more cautious of her consumption and operating motorized vehicles (when I'm present). We have a mutual understanding in our silent acknowledgment, at least since the accident.

My body crawls with discomfort when she races around the streets loaded. Delighted with the thermos of one of her animal prints residing in the center console. She believes her camouflaged cup hides her beverage, usually poured from a cheap aluminum can. The kind of drink I despise and only people with a real problem would pick.

Tonight is an all-time low—even for Vera.

We used to run down to the tracks to flatten pennies and quarters. The tracks are practically in our backyard with just a preserved wooded area and an open field in-between. As children, we raced down the tracks with our change in hand to see whose nickels would be able to stay on the tracks to be flattened. A hand-me-down game played for years with the questionable urban legend that we might derail the train, which never happened.

That was in the daytime though, by foot, where we could jump back into the ditch, and make a run for it, if we actually heard a train. Not driving straight down the line with a steep edge to either side.

The sky is pitch black—not even a streetlight. A perfect plot to A) Roll off the tracks flipping our jeep, crushing our canvas hooded top and make off with a few broken bones or B) We are hammered with metal cars, crushing us to our death, hopefully quickly.

"That's good, turn the car off," she says.

"What? Vera, we don't need to do that. Let's go back," trying to act as nonchalant as possible. My heart races rapidly in my chest. She still manages to hold full power of the driver while traveling shotgun.

"No, turn it off. Live a little, it's not like there's anything coming right now. We'll be able to feel them," she slurs out. Pausing only to sip from her zebra-print thermos.

"Yeah, I don't really want to feel," she interrupts me saying, "Shhh, listen. Just listen. Isn't it great to be out here in the quiet of the night? Only the animals moseying around, no people to worry about. Not really knowing what's around the bend?"

The windows are down—they usually are in her jeep—allowing a few mosquitos to come and go as they wish. Vera doesn't believe in spending the extra money for AC in vehicles. Plenty of breeze with a crank. Also, I think it makes her feel more adventurous. Driving down the road with the wind blowing against her face, whipping her long strawberry hair in different directions, a treat to behold watching her matching locks and red jeep.

"Yeah, kinda neat, Vera," I replied not wanting to upset her or push her into one of her moods. She has a switch that I would like to avoid flipping. Although this is one of the crazier things she's ever physically driven me to do, she seems unexpectedly calm. I can't really tell what the point of this exercise is tonight. If she's truly suicidal and planning on taking me out with her or if she's actually enjoying the pure excitement of this scare. She likes to live dangerously. Me—I would just like to live.

I sit for a few more minutes, trying to keep the sweat from beading up onto my forehead. I make my move and hit the button overhead, turning on the light that almost blinds us.

"Hey, what are you doing?" she mumbles out.

"Oh, my sweater, I thought it was back here. I must have left it at the house. I'm pretty cold—aren't you?" Not actually giving her time to answer the question. I continue, "Let's go back, so I can grab it." Crossing my fingers that she doesn't just say to turn on the heat (a feature she didn't skip).

"OK, party pooper."

She takes the bait. Vera is a smart woman, I know she can see right through my excuse, but she seems to be sympathetically taking pity on me. It's not like she'll remember tomorrow anyway. I know that if I can just get her home, I'll be able to get her into her chair where she can pass out for the night.

I turn the key—I have to get us off these metal tracks. There's not exactly a place to make a U-turn and we drove pretty far down to reverse the whole way back. She continues to sip, while I struggle to find a way off this mound of gravel.

"You're going to have to gun it into the ditch," she laughs.

Strangely enough, she's right. There seems to be no other choice—

the next road to intersect is at least four or five miles ahead, a distance I definitely don't feel comfortable driving in the event an Amtrak should come.

Flipping the stick into fourth gear (I think), I go for it, miraculously and without stalling. Cheap frothy beer splashes above the rim of her cup, all over the dashboard and both of us.

Surprisingly she finds this funny saying, "Thank God, I brought more."

Crashing down onto the dirt ledge, the tires spin rapidly for traction, plunging us forward at high speed. Grabbing the wheel tightly, I steer through the wildly flaying high grass until we get back onto the mixture of dirt and gravel.

"The shocks are going to need to be checked later this week," she says.

I can't talk right now—I'm busy trying to focus on this off-road adventure I didn't sign up for. I can't wait to just get back to the street, so I can be on a real paved road. I know if an officer were to find us down here, we would definitely be pulled over. Seeing that it smells like the inside of a keg, it would not go well for either of us (not to mention the whole 'no license' thing).

Before long we make it to the street and back to the house. Stepping out in the driveway, my beer-drenched jeans stick to my legs. I hate wet jeans—wet jeans from stinky beer are especially unpleasant.

Shutting the old doors, Vera and I circle the vehicle and lightly examine the exterior. Somehow there doesn't look to be much damage, a small dent by the front passenger light.

"Aw, that ding's nothing," Vera says confidently. "Jimmy down at the body shop can probably pop that out in five minutes."

The jeep is old, but right now it looks like it just came off an African expedition.

Long grass sticks out of the front grill and the windshield is covered with hundreds of tiny dead bugs. A small branch seems to have gotten stuck under the right tire cover as well. It's filthy and banged up, but we are safe and most importantly, we are home.

Vera proudly announces, "All and all, it was fun—no one got hurt, right? Let's call it a night."

"Let's," and we walk inside.

CHAPTER 3

Carefully she listens,
Coloring in details of everything, yet nothing with substance.
Skipping over the shadows like a stone grazing across a pond.
The emptiness swallows her, lacking courage to speak the truth.
She hides behind her canvas, swirling circles like the one her life
    has become.
She wonders if she'll ever have the chance to escape.
Though she fears the void will follow her wherever she may go.
Stuck on this dead-end street.

                                                        ~IH

Our group of girlfriends vowed to never drink and drive or get into a car with someone who was drunk. "Never again," we all said with our hands stretched out, overlapping in a circle. Pinky fingers crossed, kissing the back of our own thumbs. Solidifying our words in the form of a teenage handshake.

The first part of the vow was easy for me—I wasn't actually old enough to drive yet. The chances of me drinking and driving were slim to none. I was the youngest of my friends with a late summer birthday, but the girls were already driving, the full vow was important. The second part was harder. I knew I could turn down peers and such as to which vehicles I would take rides, but I was still dependent on my mother. Getting places and keeping my word without a driver's license would be hard to do in my home.

Treading lightly with my mother in awkward conversation on driving safety or the lack thereof. A submissive gene that skipped my older sisters.

"Vera! Where the heck is Vera, has anyone seen her?"

Janus was yelling from the kitchen. Addressing our mother by her given name, the way both my older sisters do. Using her first name for a better response time, unsuccessful at the moment.

"Chill out, she's probably outside—what's your problem?" April, the eldest and voice of reason, moonlighting as a parent.

"I need to get to work and Vera's blocking me in the driveway."

"Just take her car, she's not going anywhere. It's Sunday, she's probably filthy."

"I don't want her car. I want my car! Why is she so irresponsible? She knew I needed to leave early this morning."

I could see Vera out back through my bedroom window. Sundays were for the garden. I decided to leave the comfort of isolation and bed to help my frazzled sister.

Stepping over the paintings I completed from last night's insomnia, I yawn and yell down the hall, "Janus, Mom's in the garden. I'll move her car."

The garden was one of the few places Vera played mother well. Tending to the needs of her precious herbs, vegetables, fruits, and a various spread of flowers.

"Thanks, Iris, at least someone is helpful around here."

A cool breeze blew through the mid-June morning—a cardigan would have helped the thin pajamas I was wearing in the driveway. Exams were over and so was sophomore year. One year closer to getting out of here—I want to go far away. To a place that makes our warmest June days feel like they're cooler winter months. I was researching colleges for my widely accepted liberal arts major. My main requirement was getting into a place with a warmer thermostat—

Texas, Georgia, South Carolina, Louisiana, Florida, and just for fun, California, although Cali might be too far, even for me.

After a game of musical chairs with our mother's jeep, I strolled around back. Vera had her Walkman on full blast with her favorite denim overhauls rolled at the ankle and a tangerine-colored sports bra—Vera's Sunday uniform. She was knee high in tomato plants, only the cyclone wire cages standing between her and the juicy red fruits. She jumps back, startled by my approach.

"Iris, I didn't hear you!"

"You're lucky you can hear anything with this music. Does the volume go up any higher?" (Our usual role-reversal conversation.)

"Oh, Iris, you got to feel the music, live it, breathe it, smell it."

Vera was invoking her nonconformist days. Experimenting long after the era ended, I was just happy we never found anything with five leafy points among the daffodils. Those plants were saved for inside.

"All I smell is dirt."

"You've got to be kidding me. How about the rosemary and these peppers? Look at these peppers—you can't buy peppers like these."

"Actually you can. They have these buildings now—they're called grocery stores."

I grab the second bucket at the end of the row and began to pluck the ripened tomatoes.

"Iris, my sweet little Iris. I remember when I conceived you, I had no idea what I would name you."

"Yes, yes, I know. And you went to a spring, saw a field of iris flowers, fell in love, and named your fetus."

"There was more to it than that, it was a like a rainbow of colors beside the brook. I knew you would be courageous, wise, and adaptive to all circumstances."

"And look at me now." I reach my hands above my head like the first letter to the YMCA song. Smiling in my banana pajamas, the bottoms struggling to stay on my hips, stained brown by the ankle from dragging across the ground.

She ignores my humor—our names are sacred to her. She believes everything happens for a reason and all things crystals. I was her beautiful flower of passion. April, the start of gardening season and first-born's birth month. Then there was Janus. I think she was still high when Janus came along, although she swears Janus is the symbol of dual gates, leading different life directions. Vera was a huge Janis Joplin fan and most of her second pregnancy she was chasing our father home from the bars. Taking more than just a piece of her heart. It's amazing they stayed together as long as they did, that my sisters and I all have the same last name. Vera was full of forgiveness until the day she wasn't. Our father left with another woman and never came back. My sisters remember a few things about him, the tone of his voice, hazel eyes and the way he brushed his teeth with his left hand even though he was a righty. I couldn't tell you any more details than shown in a photograph.

"These tomatoes are perfect for canning—what do you say, Iris? Ready to set some jars?"

"Ready as I'll ever be."

"Oh and remind me to bring some to Mr. Anderson later. He's down to his last jar, and made a point to tell me after mowing his yard."

Mr. Anderson was our kind and highly intelligent neighbor. He lived down the street in the creepy old brick house. I couldn't tell who was older—the house or him. He was a professional appraiser before retiring. Mr. Anderson's antique paintings hung close together inside his home, leaving little room for wall space. Along with unusual trinkets, like stained glass bowls, porcelain figurines, and a full nativity set made from ivory tusks.

"He's such a kind man, I hope he isn't lonely."

I love watching our mother like this, behaving in the light of a new day. Her genuine care for people outshining her faults. Vera gives a lot away, gathering fresh flowers from her garden for the pharmacist, sending meals to families when there's illness, giving rides to friends or co-workers. She's a hopeless romantic, wearing her diamond pendant heart around her neck.

I walk back inside and stand at the kitchen sink, bathing the freshly picked produce. Scanning over the yard through the window as the warm water rushes over my hands, lulling me into a trance from the heat and relaxation of the moment. Our detached garage to the back left, the garden on the right, and the aboveground pool beside the deck. Beyond the line of mowed grass, and our property sits the thick woods on protected land under environmental laws, with only the train tracks trespassing though.

Zoning off as the water pressure caresses my skin almost to my elbows. I was rubbing the surface of a tomato hard, so hard the skin punctured and red pulp burst onto my arms and shirt. My hands were covered in tomato blood. No juice. But I see blood—it brings forward my nightmares, the ones I try to wake from, sometimes when I'm not even asleep.

I can see the blood from our friends splattered across the windshield of the car, on the floorboards with their bodies slumped over. I shake my head and the image away, but last night's dream comes back haunting me further. It's a recurring nightmare that keeps me from true rest. Where I am trapped walking down a long white hall, no doors to escape except into the room at the end, I don't want to enter, but always do. I'm overwhelmed with blinking lights and beeping noises. Pulling the sliding curtain back across the ceiling, revealing Wesley with his swollen head. While Sean stands from the hospital chair, exposing a gaping hole in his stomach, holding the unattached steering wheel, the wheel that supposedly broke through his abdomen killing him upon impact during the wreck.

Images of our friends that can sneak in before I have a chance to push them out. I long for comfort and an escape. I was given prescriptions for a few different antidepressants and was recommended some mild sleeping pills. I don't want them—I don't want to become dependent on substances like my mother. Late one evening, however, after lying awake in bed for hours, scared to sleep and scared not to, I walked into the empty kitchen and poured myself the smallest glass of red wine. I had read in a magazine that red wine was helpful for your heart and could be good for your nerves—both of which could use relief. I entertained the settled feeling that came from a few sips, a peaceful sense that rested my anxiety. I went back to bed and slept quickly and soundly through the night. No disturbing images. I began welcoming a small glass that added to my health and calmed the nightmares, a much-needed relief while dodging the dependency of pharmaceuticals.

I decided to take a four-week long *Young Artist's* class over the summer, filling my days of July with paint and clay. The elective class was a promising distraction and the additional credits folded nicely into my college resume—the resume I was banking on to get out of here. The teacher was known for her work with ceramics—something I always wanted to try. Encouraging us to insert blurbs of poetry to coincide with our creations. Poetry was an unexpected welcomed point of interest, although I wasn't quite as good with the uncooperative clay. Not like the paintings I developed with my oils, but I enjoyed the expressive writing. I thought of my friends often while scripting out poetic lines, forming an artistic foundation over tragedy. In addition to my new writing interest, I found the only thing on earth that was better than poetry—Allie. It was there that I met her.

On our first day of class, she sat properly in the plastic chair among the misfit artists. I could tell she was taller than me even sitting, long dark-brown hair graced her shoulders with one side tucked back behind her ear, exposing a simple pair of garnet studs. A beige knit sweater hung over her olive skin with light makeup on her face, although she didn't need any. It was cool in the classroom, keeping it heavily air-conditioned with all the art supplies during the warm summer days. I wished I had also brought a sweater. She was soft-spoken as we said our names going around the room.

"Allie, from Hillside,"

Hillside was in the suburbs, a small town about twenty-five minutes from here. Vera always says "It gets country quick!" and it was easy to see when we drove out to ZIP codes such as Allie's. She was kind and genuine from the moment we met.

I had to act fast when the teacher told us to partner up for our first project. Allie had the same idea. We quickly locked eyes and moved into a conversation. She must have noticed the strange characters surrounding us as well, like we had landed on our own deserted craftsmanship island. Waving little white flags of clay to retreat.

There was something deep about Allie, something deeply hidden. Like she was pretending, pretending to be fine. Her eyes held unnerving scenes behind them, but instead, she put on a hopeful face. Trying not to let anyone on to her damage. It was something I'd seen before, the secretive pain kept from the world. I saw it almost every day in the mirror. Allie was only half a year older than me, with her January birthday, though it was her maturity that struck me. Carrying an old soul from wisdom that hardships can bring.

Allie's father was diagnosed with MS when she was entering middle school. Through the years, his failing health set a domino effect in their suburban lifestyle. A jealous uncle took advantage of his situation and further complicated the family business. Taking matters a step further

27

when he became a prime suspect in a fire that took Allie's home. The final straw of cruel acts that literally burnt down their home, the fire she came home to three days before her birthday.

She was able to save her golden doodle inside, returning to the driveway while she watched. Waiting for the fire rescuers and her family to arrive. Her younger brother's window burst first with flames and smoke, the remaining windows following close after. She said it sounded like thunder mixed with breaking glass. The sounds echoed off the barren trees and snow-covered yard, amplifying the noises with perfect acoustics. By the time help had reached her white, one-story home, most of it was gone from flames.

What the fire didn't destroy was smothered beneath soot and smoke damage. The home in which she grew up filled with memories became just that—a memory.

Without a home, they spent the first few months shuffling around between family that hadn't betrayed them, friends' houses, and an extended-stay hotel. Allie clung to the one pair of jeans and a hoodie that she had on her body at the time of the fire. Along with two sweaters, one dress, and her high school cheerleading uniform that was salvaged from being inside the washing machine downstairs in her basement.

By the time I met Allie, she was just moving back into their finally rebuilt house. She wanted to create a few art pieces for her uninhabited bedroom. Pottery to place upon her freshly hung white shelves. A welcomed bright change from the dark soot that once clung to her walls.

Allie and I quickly became inseparable. Keeping right up with all my household action, not minding in the least. She was more than familiar with family dysfunction. Finding comfort between the closeness that I shared with my sisters, and even wild-hearted mother. All of us girls together made quite the impression. Lacquering the town red, along with our toes. Allie slipped into our mix easily, like a lost slipper found under the couch.

It was late in the day and July. I had just finished marching new cans of tomatoes up and down the stairs that my mother and I prepared. Thirty-eight jars of sauce waited their turn in the dark cellar beside Vera's other domesticated trophies. The basement looked like a bizarre science experiment, clear jugs of homemade wine from our grape vines, including dandelion and cherry (my mother's favorite).

Janus and April had a group of their girlfriends hanging out in the kitchen while I worked. I could hear the doorbell ring and I knew it was Allie. She's the only one who uses the front door besides the pizza guy, and tonight Vera was cooking spaghetti from the pile of tomatoes we didn't can.

Janus answers the door. "She's in the basement."

I charge upstairs, forgetting my aching calves.

"Allie, you made it!"

"Like I have anything better to do."

The sweet smell of basil and garlic was radiating from Vera's sauce on the stove.

"Come on, I want to show you the picture I was telling you about, with the birds."

We were passing by my sisters' friends in the kitchen.

April yells, "Iris, when you gonna come hang out with us? I was just telling the girls about your mixology talents. She can swirl more than paint together."

Ugh, so many girls tonight—as the day progresses, so do the amount of friends.

"I wouldn't say that."

"Of course, you wouldn't, that's why we do!"

"Allie, tell her she's too modest, too shy. Please tell me she's not always this way."

"She's not always this way." God, I love the way Allie keeps up.

We continue towards my room, but then Janus calls. I have a hard time turning down Janus.

"Come on, Iris, make the espresso martinis?"

I peered back to the kitchen. All six dining chairs occupied, a couple folding chairs, two bar stools and one La-Z-Boy—that was brought in from the living room.

I hadn't responded yet, though Janus was already giddy.

"You guys are going to die, they're so good!" She knew I wouldn't say no to her—Janus is the typical middle child, longing for reassurance even with her successes.

"I've got to change first, I'm disgusting,"

I was working in the garden and canning all day, wearing tiny blue mesh workout shorts, a once white tank top, and dried sweat.

"You're fine, no one's here you need to impress. Except maybe with your drinks. See we went shopping …"

Janus walks over to the counter with fresh picks from the liquor store. I grab a pitcher, shaker, and shot glass from the cabinet, then begin mixing equal ratios of vanilla vodka and espresso vodka, eyeing a long splash of Kahlua (Kahlua is the special ingredient to kick it up a notch). Vera walks in grabbing another Natural Light from the fridge. Light in quality and price, natural in nothing. She returns an empty can to the counter waiting with the others for their five-cent deposit.

"You girls better not be bothering my little girl. Tell them to make their own drinks, Iris!"

"It's fine, I don't mind. I'm hoping some of the dirt falls in when I shake."

I smile back at the girls.

"Whatever, Iris, don't be gross—make it right."

I continue shaking, while Vera handles dinner and the boiling water for the pasta. She's prideful in her dinner contributions, and as hostess to the group of girls. The line of my sisters' friends or hers blurs. Vera tells jokes, drinks her Natty light, and stirs the sauce.

"I don't get it …" Janus exclaims, "I make this exactly how you do, but it never turns out like this. The kitchen goddess, both of you."

I can appreciate the enjoyment Vera gains from being acknowledged, there's something about entertaining. The excitement of pleasing people, something I do naturally. I like to make the drinks—a bit sweet for me, but I like that I make it the best.

My mother, wrapped in her kitty-cat apron calls out, "Ladies, you know where the plates are, Parmesan's in the fridge. Come and get it."

While everyone was busy going through the assembly line, Allie and I finally make it to my bedroom to look at the painting I made for her.

"It's beautiful, Iris. I love it, there's something special about humming birds. I can't wait to see in in my room."

"Thanks, I'm a fan of them, too. I think it will look good with your new curtains."

She held the painting up, admiring my work. I felt proud and hungry.

"I'm starving. You're staying—right?"

"No, I promised my mom I'd be back in an hour. My dad's having a good week, so she made his favorite dish, artichokes French."

"Yum, I won't keep you, although I'd like to with the mob of girls in my house."

"You could have awkward silence at mine?"

"No, thanks, I'll probably just stay in my room and paint tonight."

We were walking back down the hall when we ran into Jake, my mother's repulsive boyfriend. Complete with his seventies mustache grime and red A&H air-conditioning monogramed shirt. Vera must have invited him over to show off her domestication and bountiful dinner.

"Iris, Allie, nice to see you. Looking mighty fine this evening I must say."

Looking down to the skimpy shorts and top covering my body, wishing for more fabric, thicker fabric, less translucent. I say nothing.

"You girls dress up for me or did I catch a lucky break?"

"Vera's in the kitchen, Jake."

"I know, but I need something from her bedroom."

He's revolting, I can't stand even listening to him breathe. I know he's getting pot or money from her not so secret stash in the treasure box. I don't know why she keeps him around. Why she doesn't just leave him alone after they break up. My sisters and I hate him, but Vera can't.

"You know you girls are pretty enough to work at Moxies—I think they're hiring. I'd be happy to get you an interview."

Afraid to speak and thrown off from his comment, I don't know how to respond. Scream, cry, smack him across the face, but I do nothing. I just stare like a helpless child. Moxie's, the adult strip club off Main Street, housing the upper crust of naked women. I feel as though my stomach's going to come up. His inappropriate comments and possible fantasies of me parading across the stage, sliding up and down a pole.

He laughs and heads to the bedroom. My stomach tightens, I'm not hungry anymore, and I can't think. I feel sick.

"Iris, are you OK?" Allie asks with concern, but she already knows the answer. I can hear the girls still praising my martini from the other room and I attempt to numb the anger with vodka.

"I need a drink, come and get a drink with me."

We walk into the kitchen where everyone's eating and talking over each other. I pour a shot of vodka and swallow quickly. It's sour and cheap.

I turn to Allie, "Want one, right?"

"Sure, Iris. You want to talk about it?"

"No."

I pour vodka into an orange juice glass this time, minus the orange juice, but sip as if there is.

"Should we tell Vera?"

"Tell her what? Nothing happened. He's gross, but he didn't do anything. She would probably find an excuse for him or say he was just messing around. Plus, she's already drunk."

Vera's getting antsy, deeper into her eighteen-pack, pulling out the hard stuff from the cabinets and her spirit. She talks louder as if wearing hearing aids and the volume is turned down. As the time slides later into the night, her voice commands authority.

"Where the hell did all these dishes come from? What do you think I'm some kind of maid service?" My mother's tone is sharp.

April tries soothing her, our babysitting shifts have officially begun, "Vera, relax, I told everyone to leave the dishes in the sink. I'm washing them when everyone's finished."

Vera's heated and loses clothing as the night progresses, her hot temper and body streaking around the house in her boy-cut panties and bra, leaving her dignity and clothes on the floor.

"Don't tell me to calm down, you need to calm down."

"You don't have to stay, Allie. Your parents are waiting for you."

Allie looks uneasy, we all do.

"I don't mind—you might need my help. My mom will understand."

"No, we can handle it. Sometimes Vera's easier to manage with less people anyway."

"Call me if you need anything."

I walk Allie to the door, Jake's comments still torment me.

I pass Janus in the kitchen. She's trying to shuffle their friends out of the house—the party is over.

"I'm going to jump into the shower. I think we have a long night ahead of us."

"OK, Iris. Please don't use all the hot water, we've got a lot of dishes."

I turn the knob to heat the water, cautious of my time, then quickly slide off my shorts, top, and hair tie. I grab a towel and place it on the sink vanity across from the tub. I step inside and watch the water turn a sandy brown at my feet. I don't know if I want to cry being wrapped in the comfort of the warmth or scream into the noise of the water. The showerhead pelts droplets onto the ceramic tub and me, washing away some of the tension and dirt.

I lather my hair with shampoo when I hear the doorknob turn and someone enter.

"I'm in the shower," I yell, as if the steam and noise couldn't give it away. It was him—Jake. Even with the noise of the shower, I could hear him breathing before his response.

The soft yellow shower curtain doesn't seem strong enough to keep Jake's head from peeking in my direction. The curtain is wet with a see-through glow, making out more details from our shadows than I would like. I could see Jake's large Timberland work boots step across the matching bath mats.

"Get out, Jake," I scream, a cry that would be muffled outside the bathroom walls, but plenty loud enough for his ears.

"Sorry for you, I have to wiz, baby."

I want to die. Contorting into a human twizzler, my limbs lock in place as I attempt to cover as much of my body and privates as possible. Bowing my head as the water trickles over my naked skin. My gaze stays focused on the plastic shower curtain, willing it to not to move with my eyes.

I can hear the toilet flush and his feet move closer toward the shower, he stops at the sink directly across from me. He takes his time to wash his hands and laughs. He loves this, the power of his mischievous behavior, pushing my limits of security.

"Sorry I flushed the toilet, hope the water doesn't change and make your nipples hard."

I can't speak, internalizing the disturbance and frustration.

"I can see you, Iris. You are a sheep, and I the fox. You know what will happen one day."

He walks out slamming the door behind. I wait a few minutes before I have the strength to pull the curtain back to confirm his absence. I fear he hides inside silently, uncertain how far he would push. Looking to the fogged mirror, I can see that I am alone.

I fall to the floor of the shower and weep, hoping the water would wash the words and dirt from my body.

By time I dress and get back to the kitchen, the dishes are clean and everyone is gone, including Jake. My sisters off to their bedrooms, while Vera sits alone with a full bowl of spaghetti.

"Iris, where have you been, sweetie?"

She's loaded, past the fun, and even angry phase. She's entered the totally wasted and insecure phase. A side of vulnerability not many get to see and for some reason right now, I'm thankful for her depth.

"I was taking a shower."

"Did you eat? Come on, you're going to waste away—get a plate."

She orders and I follow her directions, the submissive daughter. She longs to be comforted and so do I.

"Is Jake still here?" Wanting confirmation.

"No, that bastard left. I'm done with him."

But I knew otherwise. He'll be back—he always is.

"Why does everyone hate me so much? I'm a good person."

She asks, but I know it's rhetorical. She means well. She's doing the best she knows how, a product of a wild childhood herself. Giving us girls more stability and love than she was granted. Which seems shocking, but true—our grandmother confirms her absence and regrets during the younger years.

"Just be nice to people, Iris, everyone struggles. Don't be mean, just because you can."

"OK, Vera." I sat down beside her with a bowl of pasta and a glass of wine. The vodka was gross, not that the box wine is much better, but technically, it pairs better with the dish.

Instead of arguing a pointless fight, tonight I join her. And just like that, she switched from my mother to Vera. I know she's tired of hearing all her faults from my sisters. April and Janus remind her of all her wrongs, including the quantity she consumes. I figure by the time she got to me, she was tired and if she wanted to stop, she would have done so already. Instead I listen. Patient and gentle with her, taking in her advice, which at the moment isn't bad. She's right about people having struggles—everyone does.

My appetite returns and I eat my dinner at the table. The TV angled to us airing an engaging romance chick flick. I didn't notice Vera quieting. We both sit at the table in silence with the film's distraction.

April walks into the kitchen "Iris, you're up—we thought you went to bed. You OK?"

"I'm fine, I was just talking with Vera," I look over and see Vera, at the head of the table with her head in her plate, passed out. Her cheeks stained red from rotating her face in the sauce.

April rolls her eyes, "She needs to go easy on the rouge."

We stood from the table and wiped her face. Sandwiching her between us with her arms draped over our shoulders, carrying her to her bed.

"Goodnight, Vera."

CHAPTER 4

"People need second chances, a break to get back on their feet."
~ Wisdom from Vera

A fair shake for everyone except our grandmother, that wall will never come down.

~IH

O ur house could have a hotel sign out front, with vertical lit words stating, "VACANCY." Vera took everyone in from distant friends to a stray cat, letting people crash for weeks or months. Until the squatters could rub some pennies together and find a place of their own, getting back into the rhythm of life. Liberally offering opportunities to everyone, but to her own mother. Vera would argue that her mother wasn't on her second chance, and no one could argue with that.

Cleveland ... home to the Rock and Roll Hall of Fame, the Museum of Art, Lake Erie, Ohio State University, the Drew Carey Show, and my grandmother—Vera's first maternal influence. Our grandmother was once wild, but changed drastically after our grandfather's death. He died long before I was born, but I've heard plenty of their crazy stories. My grandmother explains with a heavy heart the burden she carries from leaving Vera, starting around the age of seven. Vera would stay alone, so my grandmother and grandfather could go out drinking at the bars. Leaving barely heated frozen dinners for young Vera to eat, sometimes without electricity, forsaking food options for a stale loaf of bread. The only thing worse than their absence was their return home, where young Vera witnessed physical abuse first-hand. Vera would hide under her bed, hoping it would stop. Our grandmother would find Vera asleep many mornings beneath her mattress on the floor, passed out from fear and exhaustion.

Our grandmother regrets the choices she made as a mother, the kind of mother she was to ours, Vera's prime example. Making excuses for Vera's disconnect, a trait she grieves to have passed down. Grandmother found God and herself through Grandfather's death and struggles to redeem herself with us girls. Unfortunately for Vera, she feels she's too late.

Vera moved to New York when she was eighteen and continues to make a point of keeping her distance. My grandmother has always respected Vera's wishes, attempting brief phone calls or cards in the mail. Very few opportunities arise for us to be together, with the exception of two fabulous weeks every summer at Grandmother's house in Ohio.

Not by chance do my sisters and I visit our grandmother during my favorite art show of the year. The Lakewood Arts Festival is held annually on the first Saturday of August. Like Christmas in July, but it's August, with Grandmother, not Santa. Lasting more than one day, like Hanukkah, then plus an additional six days—so same, same but different.

Grandmother examines the parking situation along the streets "Where should we start, girls?"

"Where we always do, we can head from Belle to Elmwood." I point with my finger from the backseat. "Look, there's a spot."

"As long as we stop at Mallorca for dinner when we're done," April adds.

"Oh, clams casino and chicken marsala!" Janus and April love the restaurants more than the art show. Mallorca offers a taste of Spain and Portugal dishes, a staple after all the shopping. It's incredible, like nowhere we ever go with Vera.

White tents with vendors stretch along Detroit Avenue, displaying creativity from over one hundred and fifty painters, photographers, printmakers, sculptors, and more.

Janus stops at a jewelry stand with lattice fencing. Necklaces, bracelets, and belts hang down from small s-hooks.

Janus lifts a gold pendant with a triangular-cut stone, "Is this a blue topaz?"

"Tanzanite, although the blue is very deep," the jeweler informs Janus.

"I don't think I've ever seen such a dark blue tanzanite—how rare!"

Grandmother turns the tag over noting the $685 price tag saying, "A little steep for me."

Embarrassed, Janus sets the pendant down, "Yeah, maybe too rare!"

Janus looks over a tray with mismatched bracelets and stones finding a blue tourmaline ring with a $25 price tag. She tries the size seven ring on her finger.

"It fits perfectly."

"And it matches your eyes, I can't wait to borrow it!" Janus and I have always looked the most alike—close in height, blonde hair, and apparently blue tourmaline eyes. April resembles Vera more, with her strawberry blonde hair, greenish eyes, and vomiting reflex when she drinks. Janus and I tease April in all their similarities—nothing pissed April off more.

"Not a chance, Iris! Beside your scrawny fingers wouldn't fit."

"Maybe on this finger?" I raise my hand to table height, but below observation for everyone else, lifting just one specific finger in the middle.

"Iris, that's enough," April mothers.

We continue walking along, stopping at every tent. Grandmother doesn't skip even one, and I follow close like a puppy wagging its tail. Janus and April spend more time taking in the sunshine, music, and people watching. Janus occasionally admires her new ring. We come to a station of metal work. Normal household items twisted into funky yard ornaments, wind chimes, and other unique objects.

"Here, we go, the best spot on the block." Grandmother scans the display with care for her next creation to take home. She always gets something for her yard or garden—Grandmother also owns a green thumb. One of the few traits she's happy to have shared with her daughter.

She finds a double-hooked planter made from a rake, painted brightly like a house you'd find in Key West.

"This one, girls. This is the one."

My sisters and I take interest with oooh's and ah's over her new treasure, although I secretly wonder where she'll put it. Her small yard already crawls with oversized marble globes, rose bushes, two lilac trees, and one miniature Japanese tree, a sunflower water feature, a jumbo frog, ladybug metal objects, a wooden carved bench, and decorative flagpole. Not to mention the other plants and random recycled odds and ends she adds along the way. Her yard could be featured on Hoarders for the Outdoors—at least she doesn't have to mow.

I stop at the display of mailboxes with magnetized artwork that snaps onto just about any shape postal box. With my interest in paintings, I find the interchangeable designs delightful.

"Guys have you ever seen these before?" I practice pulling the art magnet off as if being introduced to the world of attraction for the first time.

"Those are something, what a fun idea!" Grandmother would encourage any of our interests.

"Neat, Iris. Now you won't have to complain when we tell you to get the mail." Janus pokes still with her feathers ruffled.

"I was thinking for Vera."

I couldn't help but feel bad that I would be leaving next summer.

As much as I was looking forward to getting out, I still worried that I wouldn't be there to help Vera through her life, the buffer to my sisters' honesty and her own wrongdoings. You can't stay to love someone to health. Soon I would be gone. I would be calling and sending letters—the same way our grandmother has always done for us. Cheer at the mailbox, our new place of correspondence.

"They're beautiful, Iris. Which one should we get your mother?"

I flip through a collection of famous paintings by Van Gogh, Picasso, Vermeer, and Monet. Stopping at the recognizable, *A Sunday Afternoon on the Island of La Grande Jatte* by Georges Seurat. The recognizable image made through pointillism captures a feeling of both relaxation and energy.

"This one is for Vera. Sundays are her best day."

On the thirteenth night we were back home in New York sharing with Vera all the stories from our trip. Vera attempts enthusiasm to our adventures, although she places more enthusiasm to her booze when we talk about Grandmother. The rows of empty cans on the kitchen counter are longer than her interest in stories with her mother. The phone rings and Vera disappears to her bedroom while April, Janus, and I continue chatting.

"That's not how the song goes! Please tell me you haven't been singing *Running Down a Drain* the whole time—it's Tom Petty! How can you mess that up?"

"April, you're killing me, and we thought you were just tone deaf. Turns out she's actually ..." I stop talking as we all turn our heads to the side door that Jake just helped himself through.

"You could knock, Jake." April addresses him with her strength.

"I could do whatever I want, young lady."

"Nice, Vera, your creepy boyfriend's here," Janus interjects also full of confidence.

"Watch your mouth or I'll wash it for you."

"I'd love to see you try." Janus stands from the table, while I sink deeper into my chair. I want to hide. I wish they didn't even talk to him, egging him on. I would, but I can't.

"How 'bout I start with you, Iris?"

I open my mouth, but nothing comes out. I sit lower in silence.

"Leave her alone, she isn't the one talking to you," Janus demands.

"That's what I like about her, she's submissive, the way your mother …"

Vera chimes in, "What the heck is going on here? Can't everyone behave themselves for one minute?"

"Come on, Jake, it's back here."

Jake passes us and walks to Vera's bedroom, a devious smile plastered across his face.

"What a fucking douchebag. You OK, Iris? You don't have to let him talk to you like that." April tries comforting me.

"Yeah, I'm fine. I'm going to go to my room."

"You want to sleep in my room tonight? Janus offers

"No, I'm good—really. Thanks though."

I lay in my yellow enamel twin bed with the sheets from my childhood love for little ponies. The cartoons distributed across the linens with bright-colored hair from the ponies' manes. I can't help but think of Vera hiding under her bed as a child. I wonder what color sheets she had, what she stared at. The ponies look to be jumping bursts of rainbows. I wish that was all we had to jump in life—rainbows. The bright colors reminded me of a time in my life when I was more vibrant, colorful. Before I realized the mugs declaring "World's Best Mother" wasn't really fitting for my own. Before our friend's lives were stolen from our stupidity.

I try drowning out the arguing that comes from Vera's bedroom with my pillow, all the noises of chaos. Next summer at this time

I will be leaving, somewhere warm. I don't know what I want to do with my life yet—the education doesn't matter as much as the distance. I toss and turn until I can no longer resist the urge to get up for a small glass of wine. I didn't need one glass while I was in Cleveland and I wasn't haunted with any nightmares. A geographical change is going to do wonders for me.

I walk to the kitchen and pour my red wine. Turning back from the refrigerator I can hear Vera and Jake again. The louder she screams, the more aggressive he becomes. My heart races in my chest and a warm surge rushes throughout my body. I don't know what to do, check on her? What would I do if something was wrong? Rip him off her with all my strength, but what if they're having sex? So gross, but sometimes it's hard to tell the difference.

The banging noises escalate and her body pushes open the bedroom door. I can hear her fall to the floor with an elbow or knee, I can't tell from here. But some body part definitely crashes through the wall, I know there will be another hole. I run to the hallway to help. Jake has his hands wrapped around Vera's neck. Looking up to me from the floor, she struggles to say, "Call 911!"

I panic and scream, "Jake, stop it! You're going to kill her, she can't breathe." I'm crying in fear and anger. Vera stretches her arm out with the cordless phone in her hand. Her face is red from the lack of oxygen, "Iris, 911!"

They'll never get here in time, I have to save her, but I don't know how—he'll probably kill us both. For a second, I consider killing him to save her, to save us, but with what? The tears are coming faster.

"Stop it!" I yell again and grab the phone from her hands. He has her pinned to the floor, but he manages to rip the phone away from me before I can dial.

I am completely helpless, no phone or courage.

"A bunch of pussies in this house," Jake yells as he releases his grip on Vera's neck.

Vera coughs hard with choking sounds as she tries to regain her breath. He stands from Vera with the phone still in his hand and exits the house. He pulls away in his car, taking the cordless phone with him.

CHAPTER 5

Oh, the places you will go, sometimes more than once.

~IH

Anticipation of leaving this town built, counting down the weeks, days, and checking off final exams. Like many eager teens, I was ready to start life in the real world or better yet college. I was overjoyed when I was accepted into Tulane University in Louisiana. A warm southern geographical change was promising.

The morning started off strangely perfect, sunny but not hot, the skies painted chalky blue and even the birds seemed to be singing praise from the trees. A postcard setting highlighting my black graduation gown and gold tassel draped from my cap. I was especially proud when I saw Vera on her best behavior, with my grandmother at her side.

Grandmother was overjoyed to be invited to the ceremony. I was happy she could make it and that Vera had gone along with my request for her to be included. My sisters left shortly after the handshakes and mandatory photos to set up for my party immediately following.

Long tables filled with trays of salads, pastas, and plenty of drinks— soft and hard. Pop-up tents sprinkled across the back corner of the yard for friends to crash.

"Safer here than on the streets," Vera insisted and I couldn't argue with that.

Vera, my grandmother, and I pulled into the empty driveway—my sisters must have run out for some last-minute items. Holding my cap and rolled-up diploma in hand, I went back to my bedroom to officially read and admire my diploma. I didn't get a chance to look it over at the ceremony. I wanted to make sure everything was spelled correctly and give myself a second for it to seep in. I started fantasizing about the future, how soon I'd finally be leaving.

The phone rang breaking my daydream—it was my sister, April, but I couldn't make out what she was saying. She was struck with panic and screaming.

"We're at the hospital, Janus was in an accident."

"Wait, what? What kind of accident, where?" I yell into the phone.

"She was swimming, we finished the decorations and she was swimming. She was playing around in the pool when she dove in, it was too shallow."

"What, dove into our pool?"

"Yes, she was trying to jump through the inner-tube but it was too shallow and she hit the bottom."

"Janus dove into our aboveground pool?" I ask again with confusion, as if it would change the outcome.

Yes, concentrate, Iris. She couldn't move after she hit, she took in some water, and floated up to the surface."

Unable to grasp the information, I become silent while the sensation of shock ran through my body, a process I remember all too well.

"She tried to yell, but the words were muffled."

I stare out the window to the aqua blue aboveground—our pool filled with chlorinated water and fond summer memories, looking peaceful and calm as glass. Coming back into the moment, I can hear April still talking.

"She managed to scream for help, but we thought she was playing a bad joke." April chokes up, pausing just for a second to power through. "When we realized she wasn't kidding, Samantha jumped in to pull her out. Her right leg was still dangling off the deck, submerged to her thigh in water. We yelled for her to lift it out, but Janus just cried.

She couldn't feel the water." April's voice escalates, "She couldn't feel her legs, Iris, either of them! She was coughing up water and numb."

My chest tightens, thinking of my sister struggling for oxygen, unable to move her legs. The air feels thin in the house, I can't breathe. I have to breathe, but I can't and I can't speak.

"We called 911 and they sent a helicopter to pick her up in the backyard. Paramedics in blue jumpsuits ran out to her."

Needing fresh air, I move through the house to the outdoors. I have to see for myself. The backyard, the same yard April's talking about—with the screams and the helicopter. Like being told of a séance from a movie, but this was real life.

"They moved her on a board, strapped her in, and took off just as quickly as they landed. It was so loud, Iris. We were so freaked out—all I could think of was getting to her. Everyone jumped in their cars to meet at the hospital."

"Wait, what?" As if waking from a trance, the tears were pouring out of my eyes onto the phone and dripping down onto my shirt. "What are you talking about, what are you saying?" I couldn't process the information—details from a story beyond my wildest imagination, supposedly about my sister. This was a far cry from the encouraging limitless possibility speeches still echoing in my ears from graduation.

"Iris, it's true. I'm so sorry."

"I can't hear you, April, where is Janus now?"

I scan the yard closely as I step outside, every blade of grass appearing un-scuffed, no sign of such commotion. *This couldn't be true, this couldn't be happening.*

"She's in surgery now, Iris, they took her back as soon as she landed. We don't know anything else yet, we're waiting for the doctors to come back out. They said the severity of her injury is great. They don't know if she's going to make it. Janus is paralyzed, Iris, our sister is paralyzed, she might die."

And then I lost it. The screams reached my lungs with forceful high pitch. The sounds complimented with tears that streamed out of my eyes. I sobbed and tried not to hyperventilate. I attempted to put one nonsensical word in front of the other.

"What?" The tears were pouring out so fast, the top of my shirt was actually wet, soaked.

"You need to get here, you need to get Vera here, it's bad, Iris. It's really, really bad."

As I hung up the phone, I see Vera and my grandmother, on the deck behind me, also crying. They could hear everything as I walked through the house to the backyard. Which was good, I would not have had the strength to reiterate all the horrific information just depicted. Vera grabbed the keys and we rushed out the door.

By time we reached the hospital, the doctors had finished stabilizing Janus and they had moved her to the Intensive Care Unit. We were sent upstairs to wait and get a formal update. The doctors explained that Janus' life could go either way, not helping our minds or her injuries.

The Intensive Care Unit, the same fucking hospital, in the same fucking unit my friends were in just a few years ago. A familiar place I never wanted to see again. The waiting room was also the same. The layout of chairs, two rows in the center with additional seats along the perimeter of the walls. The same old box TVs mounted in three corners of the room. The same stupid pictures fastened on the walls, a kitten playing with a yellow ball of string unraveling, and a generic waterfall seen in a light purple frame, still crooked. It was the same, the feelings, and the uncertainty of life, all of it. Except this time, we were here for Janus. This time, it was my sister and she seemed to be in worse shape than my friends were, if that was even possible.

Following the briefing regarding her weakened condition, we were allowed to see her, one person at a time. I braced myself before walking through the double electronic doors, exposing the circular nurse's station. Preparing myself for the worst visions I could fathom. *What were the odds, the exact fucking room Wesley had only a few years ago, second door on the left.* Images of Wesley with tubes and patches of hair missing pop into my mind. I shake them away. I tell myself I can do this, *I've seen horrible things before, I am prepared.* I think this before entering Janus' room.

I walk inside and a flood of emotions wash over me. It was Janus anchored to the bed with tubes, wires, and numerous machines. She had straps that restrained her wrists and ankles, allowing for her body to stay put like a real-life Frankenstein as the bed rotated slowly from left to right. Helping to increase circulation of blood flow with her lack of mobility.

I collapse. Nothing could have prepared me for this. I find myself being lifted back to my feet with the help of a nurse who walked in immediately behind me. The nurse points, "Take a seat in the chair by the bed."

I did as she said, without taking my eyes off Janus. My sister, my strong and loving sister, white as paper and completely immobile.

I tried to come up with something to say as she struggled to get out the word, "Congratulations," from behind the oxygen mask. She was awake.

Tears stream down her face and her whole body, strapped to the bed. It was still my graduation day. I stand back on my weakened legs to wipe her tears. She wouldn't have been able to dab them, even without the arm restraints. She was actually paralyzed from the neck down.

I could barely speak, I knew this would be horrific. The hospital bed let out a beep, as it does every thirty minutes, startling Janus and me. The few muscles she could control in her face cause her eyes to open wide as she lay trapped to the slow rotating bed. The slowest of movement, so as not to cause any more harm.

"I'm so sorry, April," I manage to get out, with more tears falling down my cheeks. Her eyes fill, too. She blinks as if to change the subject and faintly whispers, "I got to go in a helicopter."

A smile curls my lips, thankful she still has her personality.

"Yes, I heard. One of these days you'll have to tell me about it."

"Not much to tell. I only got to look at the ceiling, plus I was kinda out of it."

The nurse walks back into the room and explains that they were going to be doing some more testing, that I needed to wait back in the lobby. The nurse speaks without looking up from her computer, there's not a second to lose, Janus' life is incredibly fragile.

"Yes, of course."

"I love you, Janus, you're going to get through this." I find it hard to take my eyes off her as I leave, uncertain if this would be the last time.

Walking through the door, the lightheaded feeling returns once more. This time I steady my hand to the wall. Bracing myself, while the feeling of disbelief brings physical weakness. An image of my sister being pushed in a wheelchair jumps forward. If she makes it out of here, she will have to learn to walk and run all over again—first, she has to stay alive without machines. Tears fall again as I ponder the thought of her being paralyzed forever, or not making it. I save myself the torment for the moment and head to find April, Vera, and our grandmother. I can't be alone right now.

Janus shattered her C4 and totally crushed her C5 vertebrae. After a few weeks and surgeries, the doctors were able to fuse a cadaver to her spine, allowing her upper body to regain some motion. However, she remained weak with little strength in her arms and fingers. Her lower body appeared helpless. The roller coaster continued when Janus went into a severe case of pneumonia. Her inability to come up for air following the initial dive had flushed her lungs with water and a trach was put in to aid in breathing, further complicating her ability to move and communicate.

We got into a routine of learning her cues, but the trach brought us to a whole new level of challenges. Vera came to visit sometimes, but it was too much for her. She couldn't cope with seeing her daughter so helpless. Janus had good days and bad—we all did.

"Janus, they have a new watermelon Jell-O in the cafeteria and it's freaking awesome!" I pause for the natural flow of dialogue, although I know this is a one-sided conversation.

"I'll ask your nurse if you can have some this week. I'm not even kidding, it really tastes like watermelon."

Janus lies in the bed, the only way she can—with straps over her body, keeping her from falling off in the event of a seizure, another new obstacle.

I sit in the chair beside her bed and pull firmly on the handle, shifting it a little to the right, because it sticks, and the footrest pops out. It's weird what you can get used to when it's the only way.

"Well, what should we watch today? The news, PBS, Jerry Springer—god, there's just so many options, it's hard to decide."

I glance over to see Janus struggling for my attention.

"Shit, I'm so sorry. Are you OK? What do you need?"

But she says nothing, she can't. It sucks trying to have a conversation with someone who can't move and can't talk. Her head is strapped in place as well, so shaking for yes or no is out of the picture. I put my hand over the hole in her throat, but she is too weak today. She doesn't have the strength to even whisper out words. Fuck, this sucks!

"OK, it's OK. Can you blink?"

I look closely at her eyes, they struggle to close, then open.

"OK, yes—good, blink for a yes. Do you need your nurse?"

Nothing.

"OK, no nurse. Do you want some ice chips?"

Nothing.

"Are you tired, is the room too bright?"

Nothing.

"Want me to change the TV channel? Is it too loud?"

Nothing. Nothing. I can see her eyes fighting the tears and so I fight, too.

"I'm sorry, Janus, I'm trying to think. Do you want the door shut?"

Nothing.

I want to die, I can't take it—my sister needs something and I have no idea what. The pain and guilt from not being able to help is unbearable. I continue to participate in the saddest game of charades for almost twenty-five minutes.

"Are you cold, do you want the fan off?"

Her face changes and she pushes hard to blink.

In lieu of crying, I poke at her "Gosh, I wish you could have just said so. Let me stop the wind from spinning, princess!"

I look back as her face lightened—if she could have laughed, she would. So I did for her, to keep from crying. I waited until I got in my car that night instead to cry. I cried all the way home and into my pillow long after visiting hours ended.

Janus' health stabilized after six weeks of being in the intensive care unit, an unusual period of time for most ICU patients. They moved her to a recovery floor in the children's wing of the hospital. Janus was older than most of the "kids" at twenty-three, but the new setting was a welcome change. The children's floor was pleasant, lively—even the hallways were painted in cheerful colors. I was happy she was more comfortable, but I was nervous about the summer coming to an end. College would be starting, I never had a chance to move so far, yet want to stay so bad.

Janus recovered from pneumonia and the trach was taken out.

"Take off your first semester? I think not. That's ridiculous!" Janus yelled from her hospital bed.

"I can't leave you like this, not right now."

"Why? I'm just going to be lying around here. It's not like I'm going to be able to jump out of bed, because you're staring at me." Janus is confident as she switches into her authoritative big sister role even from the hospital bed.

"That's not fair."

"Iris, a lot of things aren't fair. Besides there's a new girl down the hall—she's almost twenty. We have a lot in common, even some mutual friends, so she'll keep me company."

"It's not going to be the same."

"A lot of things aren't going to be the same." Looking down to the floor, her words sink deep into my bones. Janus still isn't walking.

"How did you meet her, what's she in for?"

"We have a couple physical therapy sessions together—which is kind of my new excitement for the day. And she fell off a horse or something like that."

"That sucks."

"Yeah, she'll probably be fine … and so will I, but you need to go. You can't just sit here with me forever."

"I would though, I would sit with you forever." I look at her sincerely, holding back the tears that come so quickly, even all these weeks later.

Janus breaks the tension, "Yeah, but you talk too much and I like my quiet time. Go! Go start your life, get to school—you've been waiting a long time for this."

CHAPTER 6

Bonjour, salut, merci
A woman's gentle voice pronounces clearly,
Sounds from my car speaker.
Attempting to adjust to my upcoming French-influenced
    environment
With a distraction from reality
Navigating my thoughts and roads as I drive.

~IH

August was unraveling fast. I stayed as long as I could, soaking in time with my sisters, but my first class started in less than a week. Janus was adamant that I didn't miss even one day. I finally had to pack up my car and take the drive down to Louisiana.

I knew I was nearing the South when I could see the Waffle Houses and firework stands popping up. Handing out explosives with a side of bacon and grits is a sight not so popular in New York. There would definitely be an adjustment period. Figuring out the major differences of living below the Mason-Dixon Line and becoming a college student.

The dorms were small, as to be expected and I shared a room with a foreign exchange student from Holland. Our looks were similar, but that was all. I didn't share the interest she had toward math or Star Wars, but she was polite and we mostly kept to ourselves, concentrating on our studies.

I was still coping with Janus' situation back home. I was miles away from home, but all the nightmares managed to find my new address. Tormented while I slept, watching Janus run around with her legs strong beneath her body, sometimes playing tennis. Occasionally Wesley and Sean made appearances as I slept. I'd find myself wandering the halls of the hospital and finding them at the end, covered in blood. I'd startle awake in sweat—it's just a dream. Though sometimes reality felt worse, Janus was still paralyzed in the hospital. The nightmares shedding light on the depths of my pain, confirming neither distance nor time has lifted the shadows from my subconscious.

October and pumpkin spice arrived in New Orleans and I began working two part-time jobs. Trying to fill a void, plus I needed money, I found work at a little art gallery and a college bar to keep myself distracted. I enjoyed being around the art, although I haven't painted since Janus' accident. Bartending was an easy fit as well, I certainly knew how to make the classics. The carefree style of The Cove forced me out of my shell and dorm. Pushing me to interact with people and learn how to become a college girl.

I set a goal to earn enough money to live on, and to be able to fly back home for Christmas break. Though I couldn't bear the thought of not being with my sisters until the holidays, I was happy to hear Janus was making improvements in her recovery. The doctors and nurses all loved her—she was like a local celebrity in the children's wing. Gaining strength with a promising outlook to be sent home before the holidays.

With a small bit of weight lifted from my shoulders, I was finally able to enjoy the vibrant city that was now home. Halloween was near and ghost tours, fortune telling, and three-for-one vodka ads filled the windows and balcony overhangs, although the French Quarter didn't need a reason. Skimpy costumes and parades filled the community and streets, extra tarot card readers with folding tables and chairs sprinkled in-between starving artists, and street performers throughout Jackson Square. Beckoning the bystanders and tourists to become entranced by their performances. I was. I was captivated with the culture in a city far different from the one I'd known, I was finally embracing New Orleans and all it had to offer.

The clouds parted and down flew a dove like the dewfall,
Anchoring into my mind and heart.
A new permanent presence
With whom I was pleased.

~IH

On the corner of Blossom and Magazine Street in the *Warehouse District*—that's where the little art gallery was located, my second job. It was there that I met him—Glen. Walking through the glass door on that cool breezy Saturday afternoon. Slender, charming, and definitely the most beautiful man I had ever seen in person. Wearing a white-pressed collared shirt tucked neatly into his light-washed denim jeans. His hair tapered in close along the sides, while the top was a smudge longer with a slight wave and perfect lips. No jewelry, but the simple silver Tag watch that lay on his left wrist.

He moved through the gallery with care. Standing a bit longer at a few that drew in his attention. He was sophisticated and well-mannered. Yet his leisure blue Sperry shoes alluded to someone more relaxed and gentle. Calm and collected in his domain as he gazed at the paintings.

"What are they asking for this one?" His voice is strong and deeper than I expected.

"That one is $935. She's new, we just got her last Thursday," I manage to say without my voice cracking. My legs wobble as I stand from the stool behind the front desk and straighten my cotton dress with my hand.

"She's beautiful—you, too."

"I'm sorry?" My face flushes and I'm taken back that someone dressed like him would be so forward, or maybe I just imagined him calling me beautiful.

"I'm sorry. I meant, are you new here, too?"

"Oh, yes. A week, two of them." Holy shit, I sound like an airhead. I haven't had much interaction with such an attractive man—well, ever. He moves closer to me, I could smell his sandalwood aftershave and a hint of espresso. I could have breathed him in all day.

"Oh, two weeks, guess I've missed you here."

I missed you, too, and then pray that I didn't say it out loud. He is seriously beautiful.

He continues, "Breathtaking, this one. I love the way she is turned to the window, almost as if she's looking for someone to come back for her."

"Good observation. The artist titled this one *Waiting.*"

"*Waiting,* huh? I wonder what she is waiting for? If it were me, it would be for the bistro to get my order right. A medium black coffee is pretty self-explanatory."

"I'd say so." I knew I could smell some kind of coffee. He turns and faces me, with his hand outstretched toward mine for a formal shake.

"My name's Glen, Glen Hawthorne."

"Iris."

"Iris. Just Iris?"

"Yes, just Iris," His hand feels strong in mine and my stomach tightens as I look upon such a gorgeous specimen.

"Well, just Iris," he has a grin. Shit my last name! *Just Iris.* I'm not used to such formalities. I don't even think my college professors have asked for my full name. Concentrate, he's still talking, and what is he saying? His lips are perfect, they're as exquisite as the rest of him.

"I apologize for being intrusive."

"Oh you're not." I would like for him to intrude. Shit, who am I, where is all this coming from? My cheeks feel hot again and I pull my hair to a low pony to help cool my face.

"I enjoy it here."

"Me, too. The people have been very friendly here and at school, the whole city. I go to school here, in New Orleans." *Stop talking, Iris, stop-talking-Iris.*

"You go to school? What are you studying?"

Shit, he must think I am an idiot, why is this so hard? Normally people don't chitchat this much or look like him.

"I'm studying liberal arts. Well, not studying liberal arts. I'm a liberal arts major, I'm kind of figuring it out." *And I am an idiot.*

"I hear you. I'm trying to figure things out myself, that's why I like to come in here, clear my head. It's relaxing being surrounded by the beauty from the paintings."

"Yeah, I know what you mean." *He is perfect* and he continues, "A little escape from the harshness of reality."

It was as if he could read me and somehow think the feelings I felt. The way he studied the faces and the structure. A real appreciation for the arts, the same one I had.

"Do you paint?"

"Oh, no, Iris," he said, "I leave that sort of work to the professionals. Do you?"

"Paint, yes, but I'm no professional."

"I have a feeling you're being modest, I bet you have a lot to show."

I can't talk, why did I even ask? Asking questions only keeps us talking longer ... but I want to.

"Well, just Iris ... "

"Oh, please, Iris Hunt. Hunt is my last name." Embarrassed that I even had to clarify.

"All right, Ms. Iris Hunt, I stop in here often, I hope to be seeing you around."

"Looking forward to it, Glen," I shift my body weight to my left leg and cross my arms in front without falling. Hoping to appear more confident than I feel.

Glen indeed began visiting the gallery frequently, at least more consistently when I was working. He worked nearby in the business district—money, guns, and lawyers. Well, he came from money, was born in Texas, and was working freelance at a firm while studying to become a lawyer. So *same, same, but different.* I loved it. I loved when he came by the shop. I loved the feeling I would get, after talking myself down as to whether or not he would stop by. The feeling I got when he did. My stomach tightening hard every time I saw him as he walked through the door. Strolling around together, we'd interpret the work, making up our own stories to all the pieces that hung so carefully on the white walls behind.

One day he showed up in a charcoal suit and a grin that made him even more irresistible. He was carrying a small collection of dainty irises. They were perfect and an obvious choice.

He hands me the flowers, "Would you join me for dinner Saturday night?"

"No," regretfully I said. "I have to work my shift at The Cove. I have the bar every Saturday night." He looked disappointed. "But I'm free Friday evening?"

"Friday it is," his face brightens. "You're quite the busy lady, school, two jobs? I think we share the same over-scheduling problem."

I smile awkwardly, not sure if that was a compliment, plus, I still feel completely nervous around him. It's like looking through some kind of real-life soap opera filter.

"I'll pick you up at eight, if that's OK for you?"

"Yes, perfect." I manage to reply without bursting into dance, although I was happy-dancing in my head. I couldn't wait to tell my sisters and Allie—I'm going on a date with Glen!

CHAPTER 7

Tossing and turning upon this old stiff bed
Not much of one to begin with
A sheet of metal with a thin foam pad
A poor excuse for a bed
More like a cot, though I've had softer cots
The pillow is flat, at least I have one again
The blanket is thin, too
A sheet of strings barely hanging on, like us
Once more through the cycle and we may break
At least I don't have a roommate anymore
I'm a light sleeper, they always snore
Still the guard's pace, checking us through the night
After the shouting back and forth has subsided.
After the bartering of objects—the fishing slows to a halt
Waking early for chow
The early hour doesn't bother me though, no earlier than I woke
    for work most my life
Waiting to be more than halfway through, that's a big deal
    around here
I look forward to that
Not everyone gets to say that
I've been counting down the days at night
You never really get used to it here.

                                              ~IH

The Meeting

I slide on a pebble beneath my foot. I kick the loose stone, it brushes across the chipped white-painted lines. Similar to the first time I came here, though I imagine the lines have been retouched a time or two since then. Carved into my mind as if it were yesterday, the luminous pink cloud clearing just in time for my ninth step, my amends.

Driving up the long straightened blacktop road, after miles of winding hills and curves. Set high into the mountain, only the depths of the pines trees surrounding. It's in the middle of nowhere. Where they tend to put these places, for good reason. It's not like you'd want them close to heavily populated areas. Or more like the general population would want to live near them.

Enormous concrete walls sixty feet tall tinged yellow from age, a container for lost hopes and the fate of the lives inside. Overgrown roots sporadically climb along its base, the only living thing trying to get in. Sitting close to the road, giving it an even more intimidating presence, missing just a fog machine and eerie music. Stretching down the street built into the mountain with giant square towers stationed periodically, while even larger covered watchtowers finish off the final four corners of its campus. Armed guards or COs rather pace back and forth while scanning the grounds for mischief, crowds that become rowdy. Waiting from their perch with loaded rifles, like special ops to swoop in with firepower.

Turned right into the driveway of the worn-out parking lot, and parked in-between the faded white lines marked "Visitors." They have a few designated parking spots for people of distinction, Sheriff and Warden. Otherwise, it's first come, first served. Five women wearing hunter green polos mow the few patches of grass.

I'm almost certain they are inmates taking care of the grounds and an uneasy feeling comes over me.

How could the guards be so trusting? Letting these women roam around unattended. Surely these criminals could escape, running in different directions, increasing their odds of success, capturing visitors like me as hostage. I look to the tower, they are being monitored, maybe more so now with me in their proximity. The women must be on honor block, holding excellent records to house such privilege. Maybe I've watched too many crime shows. It makes sense to save on expenses for maintenance of the grounds, taking advantage of the manpower from within, or women-power—just the same.

I knew I would be seeing criminals, I wasn't expecting them on this side of the barbed wire walls when I arrived. Maybe the women are in some kind of community service group, maybe I'm jumping to conclusions. One woman turns, pushing the lawn equipment away from the street, back towards the woods and I can see her black numbers running across her shirt like a football jersey. My first observation was correct, they're inmates.

I walk through the heavy double doors and wait in a small corridor until buzzed through. Now past the three rows of chain-link fencing with barbed wire circles along the top, a tall concrete wall and freedom to my back. I am inside. I enter the lobby and approach a window, like an old-fashioned bank with a glass-enclosed counter. The guard barely looks up, "Your purpose?"

"I'm visiting," I say into the tiny cutout circular holes, speaking with clear pronunciation. As if showing off my English skills would make me less threatening. They probably hear a lot of slang.

"The sign-in sheet is on the counter in the back. I'm going to need your driver's license, make and color of your car, along with your plate number."

Stumbling through my purse I begin to assemble the items requested. I hand them over and say, "I'm so sorry, I need to run back out to get the license plate number—it's a rental," I tell the guard with a smile, a big pearly one. Attempting to break the cold energy radiating off of him. He's unamused, and as if I requested the most inconvenient task, he motions with just his head to the front doors, buzzing me back out.

Soon I am back inside filling out the paperwork required to go further. The visitor sheet reads "Name, ID Number, Name of Inmate, Relationship to Inmate"—the last one gets me. What do they think when they see the Relationship line? The assumptions or questions, who else reads this, where does this information go? I'm sure the Relationship line is filled with all sorts of people-boyfriends, girlfriends, fathers and mothers, sisters and brothers, caseworkers, and clergy.

I sign my name Iris Hawthorne, daughter.

Thank God I don't have the legal rap sheet of my mother, they probably wouldn't let me in. Walking my forms back to the front desk, the guard returns my license along with adding a key.

"You can put your belongings in the lockers around the bend. You don't have to take off any real gold jewelry." Concentrating upon the word real. Clarifying the accessories worn here by people.

"Don't worry, sir, if my earrings set off the alarm, my husband's going to have bigger problems." I joke, but he's got nothing. I suppose he's not in the laughing mood.

"Metals from belts may trigger the detector, so they do need to be removed."

Good thing I'm not wearing a belt and I came prepared in my sports bra. I already read that underwires can trigger the alarm and I wasn't looking for a private exam, nor did I want to go free range in a locked room full of sexually deprived criminals—female or not.

"You can keep keys, wallet, and any other items inside the locker, if you would like." Continuing his charm robotically, "We're not responsible for any lost or stolen merchandise here or in the parking lot."

God with a promise like that, it's a wonder people don't come here more often. Besides, if your shit isn't even safe here among the highest of security, where in the heck do you find a trustworthy spot? Seeing that my guard friend had not been playing along with my antics thus far, I opt out of further humors.

"Yes, thank you."

He looks back down to some papers, forgetting "You're welcome." This guy is in desperate need of a cookie. I wonder if they intentionally put the personable guards up front, greeting everyone with such a *warm* welcome. I contemplate if it's natural or a learned behavior, the monotone of his voice.

"When you're done with the locker, you can head down the hall to the left—that's where you'll be checked over."

"I can't wait." I cheer, egging him on.

Just before the guard sweeps me off my feet with chivalry, the room is filled with intense commotion. I look through the square windows of the solid front doors, glued to the production going down outside.

A white Ford prison van with two long blue stripes and the word *Correction* pulls up. The windows covered with caged screens, attached at hinges worn from harsh winters past, leaving a rust residue down its paint. Three guards shuffle out of the van wearing full body gear, black vests (surely equipped with metal inside). Gloves cover the guard's hands, although not for warmth, with masked helmets and security bars crossing over the eyes and mouth area. Like a scientist unable to breathe from the same air as a dangerous chemical compound, the gear protects them from risk of exposure to evil.

The side door of the van swings open and with extreme precision, just one high-risk inmate steps onto a metal side rail, then down to the blacktop. A massive woman stands tall with her feet now on solid ground, the ground in which she will probably call home for years to come, or like many others here, life. She scrapes her feet across the concrete like a welcome mat to her shoes' soles. Built with a broad neck and shoulders, she could easily be mistaken for a man. Her GI Jane body screams steroids or testosterone replacement. The woman is a living example of intimidation, she looks like a nightmare, latching a face to the definition, fear. I am reminded as to where I am.

I was surprised that the inmate would be paraded right through the front doors like the rest of us. Although this is no performing arts center, I suppose there's no need for a secret back door. My once lifeless guard is quick to his feet, rushing three other visitors from the lobby along with myself into a separate room. Rounding us up like sheep to our pen, with our gate locked behind. Possibly an afterthought for safety, housing a double-paned mirror facing the lobby, five plastic chairs and musty cold air, were all trapped inside. Now with the lobby clear, my fellow visiting friends and I stand shoulder to shoulder as we wait invisibly, holding the best tickets in the house to a show we didn't want to see. The doors are buzzed and the inmate proceeds forward with now four armed guards circled around her.

I stare, frozen as if breathing could potentially set her off or give away our hiding spot—we are merely a foot away from her body. I could braid her hair, if it wasn't for the glass or her shaved-off strands. She looks into the mirror, catching a reflection of her image. An image she may not have seen for a while, depending how much of her sentence has been served, the inmates have no access to mirrors. Instead they rely on foiled coverings inside bathrooms, keeping with facility's safety. She looks intently to the mirror, suspicious of people behind it. Sniffing us out like prey, as if we wore the yellow Star of David on our outermost clothing. She could feel us. She and I engaged in a staring contest without her knowing, or maybe she does. I forfeit the game only to take note of the four teardrops below her left eye—one of them not filled, just an outline. Markings from a tattoo she could have skipped and could easily be implied.

Looking away from her tatted tears, expecting a full pond at her neck, observing a few fibers sticking straight off the sleeves of her old school black and white striped jumpsuit. The prison system allows inmates to wear designated colors such as hunter green, gray, orange, and navy—this gear is saved for the most offensive and dangerous transfers. Relatively speaking, at a place like this, they're all bad. But this one is different, she appears to be among the highest ranks for sinister level at a maximum-security penitentiary.

Her calloused hands are cuffed in front of her colossal body with a wide leather belt wrapped around her waist. A thick metal chain attaches at the belt and to links stretching down to her ankles, which are also shackled. Thin wiry hairs sprout from her over-grown buzz cut, the hairs on the back of my neck stand straight after closely examining hers. She is the real deal—the guards take no chances in this transfer process, a task their jobs and lives may depend upon.

An evil grin of pleasure presses to her face, pleased with the ruckus and commotion she has created. As if she was saying, "All this fuss for me?" She loves it—the attention. She smiles wider now, showing her top row of teeth as she looks into the mirror. She would probably eat her young, I imagine the heinous crimes she has committed, though I don't want to.

At last a guard calls out, "Clear," and the next door is buzzed open. With her bulging arms stretched in front of her body, the guards proceed walking forward to the next corridor down the hall. A few more minutes pass, the same guard once more yells, "Clear," and our secret hidden room becomes unlocked with a click, our door swings open.

"You may proceed," the guard announces to us visitors. The situation hits me hard, the malevolent woman could be my mother's neighbor. Killers surround my mother, but then again, she's one, too.

CHAPTER 8

Boats passing through the districts
Both his early, full days and my long, later nights.

~IH

I stared from the window of the dorm building, refraining from squalling out loud as Glen walked back to his Silver 5 Series. He had wooed me with dinner, drinks, and an appropriate kiss on the lips at the close of the night. His lips were soft, but full of hunger for more, the same as me. Our date was incredible and so were all the others that followed.

Our busy schedules left little time for us. I was occupied with school, both my jobs, and Glen's schedule was tighter than mine. Glen attained an internship that grew into a paid position at a high-end law firm. When he wasn't engrossed at the office, he was finishing his studies in criminal law. Tackling the demanding balance of working and law school. He was planning to take leave from the firm after the New Year, so he could concentrate solely on the bar for a couple of months. Glen was an overachiever, a trait he claims to have gotten from his father.

Although our time was scarce, we found odd moments to share. Glen continued to drop by the gallery to visit or grab a bite to eat at The Cove. The Cove wasn't exactly the kind of place he would normally venture, and he certainly wasn't there for the fried food and beer. But it was the best we could do for the time being and I loved the playful banter that developed, just like our relationship.

"What can I get for ya, handsome?"

"Scotch, the best you have." I could feel the stress coming off Glen as he sat up to the bar—his shirt open two buttons lower than normal, and somehow even more attractive than ever.

"Scotch—my kind of drink," I attempt to lighten the mood, this was an unusual choice for him. "You must be having a heck of a day."

"Yeah, you could say that." His hand rests on the counter as he draws his fingers up and down, rolling them from pinky to pointer finger with a tapping sound.

"What's going on?" My mind races—*what if it's me? What if he's breaking up with me?* A band of heat rushes through me.

"I wish you could! I'm afraid no one can help, not unless they can get through to my father."

"Oh, your father." And the heat disappears from my face, relived with the antagonist. "So you have a difficult parent, too?

"You have no idea. It's complicated."

"Oh, I have an idea about complicated parents." Although we shared the same feelings toward our parents, I dare say we did *not* share the same issues.

"He's impossible. Always his way, not caring about my interests or anyone else for that matter. He's so stubborn."

"I'm sorry to hear that." Trying not to pressure him into any details. "Well, this is the best difficult father Scotch we have in the house, which doesn't mean much, coming from here."

He laughs.

"See, it's already working."

He takes a small sip, before swallowing the rest in one long gulp.

"Whoa there, killer, you know that Johnny Walker—goes for $14 a shot, you're supposed to savor it."

"My father wants me to move," Glen blurts out. "He wants me to move back to Texas, and work at the family firm after I finish school."

The oxygen is pulled from my breath. I now, too, dislike his father.

"What, move? I thought you were going to stay here to work at the Brown offices after the bar?"

"Yeah, that's what *I* want to do. He has other plans, his own."

I can't believe it, I might be losing Glen after all. There's the long distance thing, but that never works out.

"What are you going to do?"

"I don't know—I want to stay here. I need to convince him that this is the right place for me. I love this city."

Me, too, but keep it to myself, while I process the information.

"Right now, I think I'll just take another drink … if you don't mind?"

"Coming right up," less perky than when he first sat down. *This sucks.*

"Could I entice you to join me in a shot, Iris?"

"Just one? I thought you'd never ask." Flashing my best fake smile, while inside my heart ached.

We sip the Scotch in silence and watch over the people. The people in and out of the bar, the ones on the street, dancing, mingling, and working, the entertainers and the entertained, all the people that make this city so great.

"Oh, Iris, I almost forgot. You have a nail in your tire. I saw your car when I was walking in."

"Shit, are you for real?" *This night sucks.*

"Don't worry—I already called Triple A. They're towing it to a shop near me, I'll have my buddy take a look at it in the morning."

"Wait, seriously?" I yell louder then I was planning. Glen looks surprised with my frustration, "One—I can't believe there's a nail in my tire and you didn't tell me as soon as you walked in. You've been here for over an hour!"

Glen's face is blank as he sits nervously, like waiting for the principal.

"Two—thank you!" I can see a smudge of relief in his face, but still some confusion. "I can't believe you already took care of it for me. That may be the kindest thing anyone has ever done for me. Normally, I'd be freaking out right now."

"So you're not freaking out right now?"

"No!" I shout. Maybe the shouting is throwing this off. I take a deep breath. "I'm just not used to people doing things for me. Here you are worried about where you're going to live, and you stop to take care of my flat tire!"

"I like to take care of you, I'd like it if you'd let me take care of you more."

"Well, let's not get carried away, but thank you—really." I pause, taking in Glen's sweet gesture. "And Three, since when do you have buddies in car repair shops?"

"Ha, Iris, I've got friends all over."

"Well, aren't you full of surprises."

"Oh, I have surprises all right. This was pure luck getting to play your knight in shining armor. But there is a catch."

"Fire away with the catches."

He pauses for just a moment, and then his eyes light up.

"You're going to have to come home with me tonight."

Now I pause, pretending to consider my options before saying, "I think I can handle that, but you might have to buy me another shot first."

Glen's apartment was incredible—actually, it was a condo—well, house. Downplaying his status in lifestyle per his usual. His parents had decided to purchase the property for the duration of time Glen spent in law school. Insisting that there was "no sense in throwing money away in rent, not when you could gain interest." Which was true and I could see their point. Only I had never known anyone who

71

could make such a "wise investment" as they liked to put it.

It was built like a fortress with a stone wall that climbed high with wrought-iron spikes pointing to the sky. Crushed glass purposely rests in between the daggers awaiting any brave intruders, daring anyone actually to attempt to climb that tall wall.

Beyond the wall was a quaint garden with one large statue in the center, followed by a massive wooden door and two huge sconces that were lit with real burning flames. A long black iron balcony ran across the exterior of the second floor with complementary greenery from the garden below. The entrance to the building was impressive. The inside also did not disappoint.

Inside were more dramatic fire-lit sconces, all the way down the hall and up the winding stairway to the right. Joining three apartment-style units together, one upstairs and two downstairs. Glen's was up.

Climbing the stairs, I had a strange sense of déjà vu come over me.

"Weird, I feel like I've been here before."

"You must be thinking of your other boyfriends," Glen laughs.

I can hardly contain my excitement or maybe it's the scotch. I refrain from running up the stairs with my newfound burst of energy.

"Yeah, how could I forget, all my other boyfriends. Really though, there's something, something familiar." I have no idea what could be so familiar—I have never been inside a home in the French Quarter or anything like this before.

"I got it!" I turn around standing face-to-face with him on the stair below. In my deepest, most serious voice, "You may go anywhere you please, but never enter the west wing!"

Expecting Glen to be fully amused, but he just stares.

I repeat, "Never enter the west wing! Get it?"

"Get what?"

"Oh come on, the castle? *Beauty and the Beast*?"

Still nothing, his face is blank.

"Did you live under a rock, never have a girlfriend?"

"Are you quoting a Disney movie?"

"Yes, of course, I am—it's like the greatest line of all times! My sisters and I would joke about Vera's bedroom, I mean my mother's. Stay away. Never, ever enter the west wing."

"Wow, I am flattered that you're comparing my apartment to your mother or *Vera's* forbidden bedroom."

"Well, when you put it that way … " An uncomfortable feeling creeps in—my mother.

"Why is it y'all didn't want to go to your mother's room anyway, isn't that where little girls play dress up and stuff?"

"Not really. She would drink—a lot and then when she finally went to sleep, we didn't want, well—actually never mind." I can feel my buzz fade away and my mood shifts.

Glen must have been able to tell by my face, "Let's not talk about our parents tonight, OK?"

"You got it."

The apartment, as he calls it, is staged with mostly masculine elements, like dark hard wood floors and exposed beams in the rafters. A hand-crafted brass fountain runs down the length of one wall, at least nine feet tall, creating the most peaceful sound of continuous trickling water. Only a few feminine details like oyster-shell coasters and a cream-woven blanket that lay diagonally across the back of the leather sofa. Maybe it's his mother's touch or some kind of interior decorator? I have a hard time accepting a single straight man could whip something up like this, and Glen is both single and very straight.

I've never been in any house, apartment, or place like his in my life. Allie's rebuilt one-story home, was one of the nicest houses I'd ever been inside. This was a whole different level—magazine worthy. The kind of magazines I can't even afford and look through quickly in check-out lines.

"Iris, can I get you something?"

"Sure, water, please."

"Flat or sparkling?"

"Are you serious right now? I don't think I could handle any more sparkle. Flat, definitely flat."

"What sparkle?" He smiles, attempting to become more appealing than ever ... successfully.

I let out a deep sigh and plop myself down onto the metal barstool in the kitchen.

"Do you really keep sparkling water in your fridge?" I couldn't resist.

He pulls out a bottle of sparkling Pellegrino "Yes, ma'am!"

"Remind me of your flaws again? Oh, that's right, you can't quote lines from the Classics."

"Classics! You're not still back at *Beauty and the Beast*, are you? How about Hamlet or ... "

I interrupt, "*Beauty and the Beast* is most certainly a classic and, of course, you would vote for *Hamlet*."

He grins, biting down onto his lower lip. Ugh, those lips. He lifts the glass liter of flat Acqua Panna spring water to the counter, with two champagne flutes.

"OK, OK, OK, now you're just showing off."

"Aren't you funny, Iris? I have plenty of flaws and we shall have a plethora of time together for you to figure them all out."

"Yes, the plethora of time that we both have, I almost forgot."

"No really. Tomorrow's Sunday, well, kind of today," the clock confirms reading 4:45 am, "Let's take the day off."

"You take the day off, from studying—you wouldn't?"

"I would, if I know I could spend it with you."

"Let's! I'll call out of the studio—I never call out." We both raise our champagne flutes of fancy water, clinking them together in cheers.

"How shall we begin our holiday?"

I laugh at the thought of a holiday. Glen is definitely well-traveled. I went to high school with a girl from England, she moved to the states in the tenth grade. She was the only person I'd ever heard use the term "holiday" in that context.

"Actually, I have an idea. Iris, come with me."

Glen takes my hand and walks me back to his bedroom, but proceeds further through … into the master bathroom. It's just as beautiful as the rest of the home. A white marble counter and double sinks stretch across the wall with exposed pipes below. Polished nickel finishings and two vertically hung mirrors add in style and function. A glass walk-in shower with a small door to its right, leading to the private toilet (the privacy for which I was thankful). Not so private was the oversized white claw-footed tub in the center of the room.

"*This* is a bathtub," I find myself saying out loud.

"Yes, it is. And I believe it is the perfect way to unwind after a long day's work."

A bath sounded lovely. A bath in this tub was going to be angelic!

He began to draw a bath with the two levers, directing hot and cold, creating the perfect temperature. Pouring in an incredible concoction of sea salts and scented oils into the water.

"What, no milk to soften my skin?' I tease. He smiles, but remains quiet while he prepares the tub. Wasting no time, I slip out of my musty smelling bar clothes and into the picturesque tub.

"Enjoy, I'll be right back."

"Where are you going?"

"Relax, I'm getting a surprise."

"Thank God, I was wondering when the surprises were going to start coming." Delighted, I reach for a rubber band, pulling my hair high to my head before any strands could get wet. Sinking into the tub still filling, the warmth grazing just over my thighs as the water rushes.

Glen returns with two new flutes and a carafe of …

"Fresh Bellini, Iris?"

"Bellini's, hmmm … so you're trying to revive me?" and he laughs.

"OK, Glen, let's see what your bartending skills are made of."

He's confident, "I think you will find them up to par."

I think I may find everything about him and his drinks up to par.

"OK, now for the surprise," he says before pulling a medium-sized wooden box from the closet.

"I thought the drinks were the surprise?"

"No, the drinks are our beverages." I'm shocked. He has a real purchased gift and I'm equally filled with curiosity as to what would be inside. I reach my wet hand out, grabbing the handle like a brief case. I undo the two brass buckles at the top. Inside is an assorted collection of 120 ml size tubes of acrylic paints. All the hues in artist grade quality, equipped with a gorgeous set of synthetic brushes.

"Glen! I can't accept this, it's too much."

"You must. I spent way too much time in that art shop, more than I would like to admit. Besides you're always talking about how you want to get back into painting, I thought this might help."

I look over the case in disbelief, but say nothing.

"And I'm dying to see what *thee* talented Iris Hunt comes up with."

"Oh, well, no pressure?" I didn't dare tell him, but I'd never had a set like this before. Just student grade paints back home. "This is incredible. How long have you had this? You didn't even know I was coming here."

"Well, I didn't know you were coming here *tonight*, but it was just a matter of time."

"What am I going to do with you?"

"I have a few ideas." Holy shit, this is it, my stomach tightens with excitement. I set my new treasured art box down and try to play it cool.

Taking a sip of my Bellini, Glen joins me in the luxurious bath. He leans in close and kisses me. His lips plush like the times before, but I know this time will lead to more, the more we've both been wanting. Slowly, I open my eyes looking directly into his.

"You're beautiful, Iris."

I was just thinking the same thing, but about him. But I can't speak, not even to say thank you.

"Come here," he proceeds to turn me around, and I lay back onto his chest, tilting my head even further onto his shoulder. Reaching his hand to a washcloth, he soaks it and raises it to my chest, still somewhat exposed above the water.

"May I?" he asks for permission. Not wanting to ruin the moment, I ponder what he may do, may he what ... bathe me? I've never been asked before, but I don't think there's much I wouldn't let him do.

"Yes," I whisper.

He raises the wet cloth above my collarbone and climbs up my neck with the cotton cloth. It grazes the sides of my face and the warm water drips into my hair. I don't even care that I blow-dried my hair earlier—I would dive into the deepest ocean to feel his touch. I am wrapped in his body, while he pays close attention to every detail of mine.

"What did I ever do to deserve you?"

"Iris, I am the one who is unworthy of you."

CHAPTER 9

Raw.
Pure.
Passion.
Hopes and dreams encompass my body.

~IH

I woke before Glen the next morning or shall I say, later that day. Glen was like a fantasy. I was wrapped next to him, enjoying the touch of his body. He slept peacefully as I reflected the evening and events before. I scanned the room until my eyes reached the wooden box sitting in the corner. I slid out of the bed so as not to disturb him and walked carefully over to my surprise.

I opened the box quietly, one buckle at a time. Then I ran my fingers across the goodies inside—I couldn't wait to start. Looking back toward the bed, I know exactly what my first project would be. I grabbed a canvas from the small stack he also purchased and began sketching with pencil first, tracing the lines of Glen's head and the pillow that lay underneath. His strong arms stretched out across the sheets down to his fingers. The same ones he used to grip my body as he pulled me in close just hours before. Sketching lower, the arch of his exposed back, more sheets followed with one fabulous leg dangling out from the misplaced comforter.

Perfection. Happy with both my model and draft, I twist open a few jars and fill a cup of water. Dipping the brushes into the containers, mixing the paints on the pallet into their desired hues. Satisfied with my humble beginnings, I start. Caressing the canvas slowly, intentionally. The subtle shifts of taupe, creams, and white with a few streaks of blue—all in different highlighted and contrasted forms. The image left the real world to be savored in time, frozen for repeated enjoyment. The sunlight peeks through the cracks of the curtains, casting the perfect depth of brilliance. I fill in the shadows surrounding the bed and an unintentional, yet appropriate floating-like feeling encompasses the bed on canvas. I am drawn into the likeness of the picture.

I hear movements from Glen from across the room, the real one—I'm not that lost into my work. He wakes slow with a yawn and stretches his arms overhead, completely changing the shape in which I have just studied.

"Good morning, Ms. Hunt," he says in a raspy voice before clearing his throat.

"Good morning to you, too," I say with a laugh. He even wakes with proper addressing!

"Like a kid at Christmas."

"I was going to wait, but then I couldn't sleep any longer, so … "

"I know the feeling, What do we have going on there?"

"You," I reply confidently.

"Me? This I have to see."

He walks over to the window adjusting the curtains, as well as his boxer shorts. Then proceeds back towards me.

"I'm not done yet." A bit conscious of what he might think of his self-portrait. "I still need … "

"Wow, Iris! How in the world? This is incredible! How long have you been up?"

"Oh, I don't know, not long. Maybe an hour, tops.

"You did all this in an hour?"

"Once I get in the zone, everything kinda flows together pretty quick."

"I always knew you were talented, but I had no idea like this."

I am relieved, I knew he would be kind with my work, but he seems genuinely impressed.

"This is what you need to be doing. You have a gift—this should be shared."

My cheeks blush the way they always do. The extra light from the window shines into the room, showing off my canvas. It is pretty great.

"What are you going to do with this?"

"I don't know yet, probably just hold onto it for now."

"You should do more, you should sell these, Iris!"

"Maybe. I don't know. I don't even know where to start."

"We can get you into an art show. I'll even help you set up."

Feeling both excited and nervous. I could tell from the way he was asking, he wanted a commitment. He wanted me to agree and if I did, there would be no backing out.

"Come on, what do you have to lose?"

"OK, I'll do an art show."

"Great, I'll talk to a friend and see what shows are coming up. I'm sure he can get you in—he's like an event guru."

I laugh, "You really do know people everywhere, don't you?"

"Oh, shit, yes, and we need to check on your car."

Ugh, my car, that's right! Here I am committing to an art show and I can't even drive home.

Glen is still admiring the painting, the same way he does when he's at the gallery. Happiness fills every corner of my body. It really did turn out great, quality paints, and model seem to have aided in the presentation.

"You know, I think I will keep this one for good." I speak back up.

"That's fair, but you still have to give it a title. All artists name their work."

Hmmm ... I think for a moment staring at the painting of a muscular man, completely vulnerable in rest. "I'll call this one ... *Beast gets her Beauty.*"

CHAPTER 10

Oggi Domani.
May your todays reflect your tomorrows.

~IH

The Cove had become a second home, the way jobs do. Splitting meals in the break room with co-workers, sharing stories, jokes, and lots of shots with customers. It's the kind of place that you know the regulars' names and the bartenders knew their drink.

"Iris, we need another round of Jamison and two Bud Lights."

"You got it, Mickey."

"Iris, six shots of lemon drops, four cosmos, and two apple martinis."

"Sure thing, but Casey, there's only five in your group, did someone want a double or is that your vision?"

"I'm not seeing double—one's for you!"

"One of what, your liquid candy bars? Casey, how many times have I told you, I don't drink, my sweets."

"But you have to have a drink with us, it's always so much more fun. Pour whatever, but we're not taking no for an answer!" Casey's bottom lip curls down like a puppy begging. A look that might work best on her mother, if she was three, but I take pity on her and grab six glasses.

"Then, yes to tequila." The bar is better when I join—they need me. Plus my tips are better when I do.

I line the shots, cocktails, and beers across the counter. The shots are raised and Casey says "To Iris and her debut Art Show next weekend."

"You guys, I can't believe you remembered!"

"Of course, we remembered, you're going to be the one forgetting us when you make it big. We'll be saying, *we knew her back when …*"

"Let's not get too carried away.

I revert to the bar like a gardener over her flowers, keeping the patrons' glasses watered and full of care. I spot Glen and his friend from the office, James, walk in, my stomach tingles and my heart beats a little faster, I love when he meets me here. I have a hard time containing my smile and motion for them to come over to the only two seats left.

"Looks like you have a fan club, I might be one of them."

Any strength left to hide my excitement dissipates and I grin a big cheesy smile.

"Oh, Glen, you suck up. Is he always like this, full of compliments and dreamy?" I look to James.

"I don't know it's been awhile since I've dreamt about Glen. He's usually trying to boss me around, even though he's still my bitch, until he passes the bar."

"Don't you worry about that, I'll be ready in a few months and then I will be *your* boss."

"Probably, Hawthorne, but for now … Iris could you get us a vodka tonic and an old fashioned?"

"You bet."

I turn to mix the drinks and pick up a few empty glasses down the way. I fill fresh beer from the tap with my left hand and mixed drinks with my right. Then walk down the line, dropping off the replacements to happy consumers. Finishing my patrol with James and Glen, as I slide Glen's drink, his hand reaches mine. His fingers feel smooth and warm and I picture them caressing me.

"I don't know how she does it, remembering or even figuring out what some of these drunken people want."

I turn confidently away from the touch of his hands. "I speak their language."

Glen didn't know I'd been taking orders from my drunken mother my whole life. I wanted to share everything with him—everything, except Vera.

"So Glen tells me you're a very talented artist," said James, "I look forward to seeing your booth."

"Glen is exaggerating, I'm not a *real* artist."

"You seem pretty real to me. Besides, once you sell one of your *masterpieces,* you'll be a professional."

"I'm more of an amateur."

"Actually when money is exchanged for work, you do become a professional, that is, by definition."

"Leave it to the lawyers to recite the dictionary."

"Hey there's only one attorney at this counter. Only one of us has been paid to represent the fine people of this city."

"Well, get out your business cards, boys, your customers are all around."

I still couldn't believe Glen was letting me keep my *masterpieces* (as he calls them) at his place. He came up with the idea and insisted that it was safer than my dorm. I couldn't argue that my four feet of space in a shared room was adequate, so I went with his request. He had taken it upon himself to set up a corner of his guest room for my work, equipped with a drying rack and a wooden easel for me to paint. It was overwhelming to be showered with such generosity, but that was Glen's style—a learned trait hard for him to turn off.

I had quite the collection prepared for the show and my work spilled over to the hallway next to Glen's collection.

"So people really collect wine?"

"Yes! Of course, Iris." He laughs, looking at me as if I'm from a different planet, but the concept is mutual. I have a hard time understanding where the idea started.

"And then what, people stare at the bottles? What good is it to have all these fancy wines, if you're just going to look at them?"

I could not wrap my head around the idea of saving unopened beverages, a wine collection for eyes to consume. The bottles lined up neatly like soldiers in a row, labels out with a precise degree of regulation. This concept would never work back at my home. Waiting patiently like male penguins for their eggs to hatch through the long winter storm called the days of the week.

"Iris, wine collections are very common, I didn't invent them. This is nothing—you should see my parents' collection."

"It's not common where I come from."

"Well, then how about we pop open a few bottles and try some out? You can taste the difference between toasty oaks, hints of cherry, citrus blends, and sweet after-dinner ports."

I turned on some music while Glen went about selecting the chosen ones from the cooler. He returned to the living room with half his glassware from his cabinet and four bottles.

"Are you expecting company? Why so many glasses?"

"You can't mix the wines into the same glass—it could ruin the flavors."

"Oh, yes, I wouldn't want to hurt their feelings. Seems like a lot of dishes."

"It's worth it—you'll see."

And it was. The flavors were powerful, intriguing, and intoxicating at the same time. I found myself impressed, as Glen taught me to swirl and let the wines breathe. Apparently they also have lungs. The smells and tastes of well-kept liquids filled my senses, as a sexy blues band plays from the speakers. I felt overwhelmingly inspired and found myself with a strong desire to paint. I stood from the couch.

"I have to grab my brushes, I need to put this on canvas."

"And the creative wakes from her chamber."

"I must—do you mind? I'll still try whatever you want, but I …"

"If you must!" He laughs and grabs his glass, following me to the guest room. "I'm not surprised, the experience of really tasting wines can have a strong impact. Many great artists have been known to create with mind-altering substances. Going back centuries with musicians, Indian tribes—even the oracles."

I felt a visionary of movement from my soul, I needed to express myself through color. My innovation had been awakened. I could get used to working like this.

My shifts at the gallery felt like a vacation compared to the hectic hours of the rest of my life. The owners of the gallery were kind and laid back. Maria and Luigi, a charming older Italian couple. They were often out of the Country traveling, but they called New Orleans home, as they loved the way the city was rich in culture. Maria took notice of my uniquely stained hands.

"What is this—paint, Bella? Doing some room updates?" Maria usually called me Bella, as if it were my given name. Possibly overusing the expression and meaning, although it was warmly welcomed with her broken English. I look at my hands covered with paint.

"Oh, no, Maria. No HGTV in the dorms, although it could use it! I've been doing my own paintings."

"You paint? You never mentioned it."

"Yes, well, I used to in New York, but I'm just getting back into it again."

"That's wonderful, Oggi Domani!" Maria was always bursting into random Italian phrases, usually in a context that I could follow. This one was not one of them.

"I'll bite, what does that mean?"

"Today's actions reflect your tomorrow's outcomes. Or at least that's how our famiglia always used the expression."

"Cool, I like it, Maria. I might have to steal that one."

"What do you like to paint?"

"All sorts of things. It depends on my mood, although I am usually driven to people. Near or far, one or one of thousands, I love the emotion." Maria's eyes were big with pride as she listened to me speak. Not many things made her happier than art. I actually wondered why I waited so long to talk with her about it.

"Glen even helped me get into *The Jingle Art Fest.* I'll be at Booth 179, if you should stop by."

"Bella, I wish to see, you must bring me something before—a sneaky peaky!"

And just like that, I remembered why I never shared this information. I loved working at the studio and I would hate for her to feel pressured into telling me she liked my work.

"OK, but this is my first show and some of my work is a bit dark. I'm not sure it's going to be your cup of tea."

"Bella, you know I don't drink tea. Besides we are often most enlightened while in the midst of darkness."

I brought a sample piece by the studio the next day, but to my disappointment Maria was not around. I left it with a note …

Maria,

I hope you enjoy your sneaky peaky!

Always, Iris.

To my surprise, at my Saturday shift, she had hung my work directly behind the front counter. The first painting you see when walking through the doors. Maria said that it had great energy and she wanted to showcase their very own local artist. I loved being considered an artist, the way it sounded.

The feeling was short-lived, as the following week my front-runner spot had been replaced with a different canvas. Discouraged, I walked back behind the counter thinking Luigi must not have enjoyed "the energy" as much. A swift feeling of doubt creeps inside and the art show is this weekend. Dropping my confidence before entering the ring.

I sat down at the front desk to find an envelope sticking out from the bottom of the register. My name was written in blue pen on the outside. I tore it open, and found seven one hundred dollar bills with a note that said …

> *Dear Iris,*
>
> *A woman took interest in your work yesterday and wanted a price. We never did set anything up and I scrambled to give her a number. I hope you find this to be a fair amount for the sample.*
>
> *Amore, Maria*
>
> *P.S. Please bring in another canvas to hang soon, this time include a price!*
>
> *Ciao Bella!!'*

I almost fell out of my chair! Seven hundred dollars, for *my* work—and on a Wednesday! If Glen wasn't so crazy at the office I would have sworn he was the buyer, but then I remembered I never did mention my canvas was at the studio. I had a real sale. My confidence was reinstated and I went to the art show that weekend knowing I was a *professional.*

⁓ஃ

Glen sat arm in arm with me in our folding chairs under the white tent. Distracting me patiently while spectators openly made comments, admiring or not with my ears just feet away. Most people seemed to enjoy my work, but beauty is in the eye of the beholder and you have to have thick skin when you put yourself out there. Luckily I was from New York—both my skin and blood were still thick. I found great irony as I sat at *The Jingle Show* in a pair of cut-off jean shorts and a thin long-sleeved sweater. The long sleeves I regretted with the heat.

Not avoiding sunshine or reindeer in December, still a pleasant change for the beginning of winter. The warmth I'd never experienced at this time of year, but the red and green holly was a reminder that the holidays were nearing. I had been looking forward to December and going home to see my sisters and Allie since I first left for college. Although I found myself a bit wistful that Glen and I would be apart for the first time in our relationship. I held comfort in our soon to be fonder hearts rendezvous with the ball drop on New Year's Eve, an evening I already longed for. But first, back to New York for eggnog—I can make an exception to sweet drinks for bourbon.

CHAPTER 11

Astronaut's go through a pressurization chamber before walking
back into Earth's atmosphere.
I was home in New York sitting in my 747 chamber.

~IH

It was no surprise that my anxiety increased as we climbed closer in altitude and distance heading northeast. It was the whites of my knuckles as I clenched the armrests that caught me off-guard. I had flown twice as a child and didn't recall it bothering me, but the fear of death comes quickly when you're by yourself with no one to distract you.

One of the girls, Jessie, from The Cove previously told me how she liked to pack travel-sized Listerine bottles full of liquor. The size works as a carry-on and you don't need an ID to add cranberry juice or Coke, both convenient features for an 18-year-old on a plane. Initially, I thought Jessie was being dramatic, but it seemed convenient to have a small stash being in such close proximity to Vera. I was thankful for the tip, but disappointed that I only packed two.

As we sat on the tarmac waiting for the plane to deice, I wished for another mini-tequila to add in my tonic. Tonic is my favorite, if I do add a mixer, but I could have sworn I packed another mini-bottle with Patron. Sucking the melting ice from the clear plastic cup, I watch as the flurries float by the fogged oval window. It's weird this late in the evening, the deep black sky being mixed with white from the snow. I take note of the color and wonder how it could be painted dark white.

I can barely see the airline men a few feet away wearing fluorescent yellow jackets, working hard through the blizzard. One more drink would have been perfect. Besides, my Christmas vacation had officially begun, I was on holiday. Crossing my legs, I hear a clinking sound from my cramped nook. I rummage through my purse and discover one last bottle stashed in the cell phone pocket, I thought I grabbed three! Thank God.

I continued watching the men work with long gray hoses in hand, pressure-washing the locks with antifreeze, while my hands held close the inconspicuous tonic water. The doors frozen shut like my many emotions, protecting myself from dealing with life and what has become of my sister's.

Janus was recently released from the hospital after her six-month stay and we were all fighting with acceptance. Janus would likely never walk again. Her new accommodations, the once detached garage now—Janus' small house. It was made wheelchair-accessible and looked as permanent as her immobility. Janus and I arranged to meet in the morning. She was still adjusting the kinks of being home and her aide's early evening routine, making visits easier by day.

The cabin let out a cheer, waking me from my thoughts. I must have dozed off into the white blur from the window, because forty-five minutes later, the frozen seal of ice was melted from the plane and my glass was nearly dry. I took a final swallow of the Patron droplets while gravity set in.

The frigid air hit my face hard like scissors as I walked through the connecting hall. Hello, New York! We have been spared the harsh weather conditions in New Orleans so far—this was a strong dose of reality. I look down at my phone, the weather app screen is lit with my current location and Eastern Time Zone automatically adjusted. The partly cloudy sky image is displayed with the number nine in the center. That's it, just nine. Nine degrees. Shit, I forgot how much I hate winter.

April was picking me up, but had to finish her shift at Flanagan's before we went out to celebrate.

"Sorry, we don't have time to drop off your bags at the house," April said as she drove.

"No big deal, I'm excited to be back."

I attempt enthusiasm in my voice, but find myself withdrawn as I looked out the dark passenger window. Passing familiar streets and buildings, sights I used to know and drive by regularly. A wave of emotion fills me, my cheeks flush, and a gust of sweat heats my neck and hands. The unexpected sadness feels strong, like the heat blasting out of the dashboard air vents. I should have stuck with two bottles of Listerine, and reach my hand out to adjust the vents.

"I don't have to close, so it shouldn't take long. I have to make sure the new girl can handle the bar before we head out."

Trying to hold in the emotion, "I totally understand. I'm just happy to be together."

"You OK, tired?"

"Yeah, tired." I lie, not wanting my sister to think I'm upset or boozed.

We arrive at Flanagan's and I drag my suitcase through the unplowed parking lot. My fingers freeze without the protection of gloves, which I forgot, but I knew we were taking a taxi at the end of the night and I didn't want to be stuck without clean clothes in the morning. The frostbite would be worth it. She practically ran the bar and grill with her seniority, only the manager had been on staff longer. Flanagan's was old stomping ground for a decent burger and a well-used arcade golf game, one of the two sounded good with my rumbling stomach and could aid in sobering me up.

"All right, Iris, time to wake up, we have a long night ahead of us. I'll grab you a Red Bull."

I try to snap out of it, "Make it a Jager bomb and you got a deal?" Sober up or keep it going.

"Nice try, kiddo, but you know that won't fly here. I'll buy ya one later."

My perfect ID falls flat for use at Flanagan's, everyone knows Janus here. At first I felt uncomfortable using Janus' ID, but we do look a lot alike. She insisted before I left for college saying, "Someone may as well enjoy the benefits of being twenty-four." Like an heirloom passed on through the family, mostly colored with white, red, blue, and black letters. Like a key to the city … every bit of information memorized by heart.

I sat slouched at the bar from my faded buzz, it's not much fun sitting at a bar un-served. Attempting to redeem my energy, I devoured a bacon cheeseburger with a poppy seed bun. The luggage at my feet felt anything but natural as I wait for April to finish. It was fine, soon enough we'd be going around the corner to Washington Avenue. Allie was meeting up with us at Mex—she was home on Christmas break, too.

Washington Avenue is a bustling street of bars and nightclubs geared for young adults and college students. Festive Christmas lights dangled along the lamp poles. Windows frosted with white spray painted borders and advertisements enticing patrons to stroll inside. The crowds seemed heavier with people home for winter break. Not even this winter storm could keep the bars empty, business as usual, like Vikings trekking out for bread.

I dragged my rolling luggage that didn't actually roll down the snow-covered sidewalk, like a lost person in the airport, but downtown. I knew what Mex would be like before we even walked in. The doors marketed with a festive sign reading, "Feliz Navi-Cheers." The new favorite hot spot, minus the hot.

"April, how do you always find the tackiest bars?"

"I'll have you know this place is the new Crowbar. Everyone goes here now. Besides you should talk. You're so trendy with your swamp-themed Mardi-Gras bars."

"Yes, April, all the drinks in the south are served with 'gator-bites from the Bayou."

"Well, the comment box is by the door, you can leave your complaint there."

"Two hours home and already at it," I grin.

April pulls me in for a squeeze as we take our seat at the bar. "Aw, I missed you, too, sis!"

I look around the room dumbfounded. April and I definitely have a difference in hangout spots. The walls are painted in a screaming shade of tangerine, which helps none in keeping the wooden panels hidden behind. Staying with the Mexican theme, there's a hand-painted desert scene by the staircase, a bad one at that.

Waiting for the bartender to take notice of us, I shout over the crowd, "If I were to do five jumping jacks, spin around seven times, take four promo girl shots, and squeeze my eyes, really tight, I still wouldn't believe I was south of the border in Mex."

"How 'bout that Jager bomb, smarty pants?"

"Na," clearing my throat, then shout to the bartender, "Presidential Margarita please."

"Make it two," April yells. She may have poor judgment with décor, but she's predictable, if someone orders her favorite drink.

"Make it three," I hear a familiar voice yell from behind me. I turn my head and jump to my feet, almost in one motion.

"Allie!" We squeeze each other tight.

"Ahhhh, I'm so excited! I wasn't sure you would make it when I said we weren't going out till midnight."

"Me not make it to see you guys ... never!"

"Well, you're just in time. This calls for shots, ladies." I yell back toward the bartender, "Could you add in a round of tequila shots, Patron, please."

Allie and April laugh, "You and your Patron."

We chatted through the night catching up on new and old gossip. Filling in details that get overlooked during phone calls. Discussing everything from college classes, work, living in different cities, and my first art show. Sipping from the salt-rimmed glasses during the short pauses. I do love a good margarita—they sit pretty in the wide inverted triangular-shaped glasses. I gushed away with sappy details of Glen making a corner art spot for me in the guest room. Allie worried that Glen and I were moving too quickly, but I rationalized the act with my lack of space in the dorm. She approved, but insisted that I pace myself, which was fair and important. She's a pretty good judge of character and was glad I found someone like Glen.

"So Janus is home. How's that going, April?"

"Good, well, she seems good. She's adjusting. We still have some logistical things to figure out."

"Like what?"

"Oh, like the furnace. It's not keeping her studio very warm and we've had such crazy weather. I think we just need to get a space heater or something."

"I can pick one up tomorrow. I'd love to help while I'm here."

Allie interjects, "How's Vera?"

"Who knows? She's drinking more, which I didn't know was possible. It's hitting her hard that this is the new normal. It's hitting all of us."

"I know I'm happy she's home, but I would of loved for her to walk through the front door."

We sat there quietly for a few minutes, the sobering moment

holding our words. I hold the drink closer to my lips and take a few big swallows, recalling the year before when all of us were sitting at the kitchen table.

"Remember last Christmas when Vera wanted to give what's his name that horrible sweater?"

"Oh, yeah," April says "Vera thought it was so amazing and … "

"Tim, his name was Tim," Allie pipes in.

I continue, "Right, Tim, from her boyfriend of the month club. She thought Tim would love it!"

Vera had Tim's sweater folded neatly on the kitchen counter. The red knit had a large navy blue stripe and yellow collar, it was a cross between Mr. Roger's and Freddy Krueger. Vera swore that it was a fine sweater of distinction. Janus asked if they were going out on Elm Street. And Vera got embarrassed. "You girls have no concept of quality."

She held the sweater up to prove her point, but began laughing at second glance. Janus grabbed the hideous sweater, pulled it over her head and with one arm did a cartwheel and landed in a perfect split on the linoleum floor. Using impeccable acrobatic form, Janus stayed in her split and began petting the sweater saying "Oh, yes, darling, this sweater is just delightful!" We all busted out laughing, Vera the hardest. She loved hanging with us girls and on a night like that one, we enjoyed her, too.

Allie spoke up, "God, Janus was so flexible, I would kill to go back to that night."

"Me, too," I chime back in.

Then April, "Me three."

Before we knew it, the bartender was giving the last call.

"You girls can really hold your own," the bartender slides the tab over the counter.

"It takes practice," I grab the bill and laugh.

My bedroom has been empty since I left and the blinds of my window were drawn open. The sun's brightness charges through early the next morning. I reached my hand to turn the long plastic handle to dim out the light. Barely opening my eyes, I see April snuggled in bed to my left and Allie wrapped up in a comforter on the floor beside us. Just like old times, everyone crashed together in my room.

With heavy eyelids, I fall fast back to sleep. Suddenly the most excruciating sound rings from across the room, coming from inside my purse. April's raspy voice cracked, "What the hell is that? Make it stop!"

Scrambling to my feet, I rustle around for my phone to turn off the firehouse bell. I couldn't grab it fast enough. "Sorry," I whisper, sliding my finger over the OFF button.

"What was that? Please tell me that's not how you wake up every day." Allie's voice is muffled from blankets.

"No, I thought I turned it off last night." My voice is also dry and cracking. "I must have hit a new ring instead."

Allie clears her throat, "God, that was awful. I think I can still hear it, I'm going back to sleep."

"Good night," April pouts.

Seconds later or what felt like seconds, Vera's alarm rings from her bedroom.

"What does a girl have to do to get some sleep around here?" April shouts.

Vera, amused, walks into my bedroom with cheer, "Good morning, ladies, did we stay out too late last night?" Vera's used to a hangover in the morning, and loves to point them out when they're not her own.

"Iris, what did you do to me? I think I'm going to be sick," April complains and continues, "I'm definitely not twenty-one anymore."

"Yeah, me either," I add.

"No, Iris, that only works when you're older than twenty-one, not younger."

"Excuse me, I almost forgot how terribly old you are at twenty-six. Your AARP card should be coming any day now."

"Shhh ... let me sleep, I feel like I'm going to be sick."

April pulls the covers further over her head.

I lay awake in bed after all the commotion. Strangely, I don't feel hungover. A little tired from flying, and thirsty, very thirsty—my mouth is so dry, my tongue seems stuck to the roof of my mouth. Too lazy to stand, I wait for the energy to come, glad I don't usually get sick. Vera always gets sick, Vera and April. Janus and I liked to mess with April that she's just like her mother. One of the few features she can't deny, although she tries.

I could hear Vera turning the water off from her shower through my bedroom. April and Janus' bedroom connect on the other side of the house, lucky to have a private wing. Mustering up the strength, I head to the kitchen to get my glass of water and a cup of coffee. I was actually excited to see Vera.

Vera walks into the kitchen wearing her favorite bright-red robe with the rhinestone-words "Santa Baby" on the back. She loves that robe, pushing the envelope as to when it should appropriately be worn. With Christmas a few days away, it's actually practical. Her hair is still wrapped in a towel on her head, "Iris, you're home!"

We embrace for a long overdue hug, I can smell her beloved cotton-candy lotion freshly applied. It's strong, sweet, and strangely comforting in this moment.

"God, I'm so happy to see you. I've missed you so much," she continues. Looking up to her face, I can see tears filling her eyes. She means it.

"I missed you, too, Vera." I hold her close, the feeling was mutual.

"My big college girl! How's it going, how's life?"

We chat a few more minutes as Vera attempts to pull herself together before running to work. She made herself busy by the sink wiping the countertops off with a paper towel and occasionally her eyes. I have a feeling her emotions catch her by surprise, but enduring to see her love in clear light.

"Iris, I'm so glad you could make it home for Christmas."

"Me, too."

"Look at the time, we'll catch up tonight—OK, hunny?"

"You bet, Vera."

I gaze out the window toward the snow-covered grass, extra white and fluffy from last evening's storm. I can see four metal planter stakes sticking out of the ground, where Vera's garden waits for spring to be revitalized. The trees are bare of leaves, allowing me to see a great deal farther in distance. Past the pond and clearing, almost to the train tracks.

To the back left of the yard sits Janus' remodeled studio apartment (the once detached garage). A better fit given our multi-level raised ranch without hallways or stairs, but a larger dose of privacy. The redesigned wheelchair accessible bathroom was a nice addition to the half-bath that used to be in place. Most of which was possible from successful fundraising and a loan from the bank.

I look to the previously shoveled pathway to Janus' front door—it's filled in with new snow and fresh footprints leading straight inside. Janus' aide must be here! I scan closer and notice shadowy movements from behind her closed curtains.

"Janus is awake!" I catch myself saying aloud to no one. Racing for my oversized hoodie, boots, and tote bag, I run to the backyard.

I run up to the door just as the aide opens it, she jumps back in surprise.

"Sorry, I'm so sorry! I didn't mean to startle you." Embarrassed, I apologize.

"Goodness, it's OK. You must be Iris—I've heard so much about you."

"Yes, that's me. Sister who scares people at doors!"

"No, I just recognize you from their descriptions—you're just as beautiful as they say."

Her voice and words are kind and I find myself humbled again this morning. First, my mother tears up in a hug, now I hear of my sisters referring to me as beautiful.

The aide continues, "You're all the girls talk about, it's a pleasure to meet you."

"Likewise. Thank you for taking care of my sister, she's everything to me."

"Funny, she says the same thing about you. Enjoy your visit, and Janus, I'll see you tonight at eight thirty."

"All right, don't rush if you're running behind!"

"OK, how about I do my other stops first tonight, ten o'clock sound good?

"Perfect, thank you!" Janus yells as the aide walks out.

I restrain myself from jumping onto Janus' lap. I wrap my arms around her body and some of the wheelchair with a giant squeeze.

"Janus! Goodie, goodie, goodie!" I shout in excitement. "I've been wanting to do that all night. It was so hard not to run back and wake you, so close, but so far!"

Janus laughs, "A bit dramatic, but I'll take it. How was last night, did you guys go out in that storm?"

"Oh, yeah! April's still recovering inside, I think she going to be sick."

"Aw, just like her mother."

"Yup, curled into the fetal position in my bed." We laugh the way we always do when comparing their similarities, pleased that the two of us have less.

"Well, I'm glad she went out, she's so busy fussing over me. I hate that I can't help, I'll never be able to repay her."

"She's not looking for anything, you just concentrate on you."

Breaking the tension I change the topic.

"I love the color in here, it's so relaxing."

"Thanks, I was watching an interior decorator on Oprah and the guy was explaining the importance of colors. Green is supposedly the most calming hue in the color spectrum. I figured I could use some calm in my life."

"It's a perfect choice and on that note. I made a little something for you to put in your new pad."

I turn around with my canvas held high for Janus to see.

"Iris, it's beautiful, I love it. I'm so glad you're painting again!"

"You don't have to put it up, if you don't like it."

"Don't be ridiculous, it's exactly what I need. Make sure you sign it, so I can sell it for big bucks when you get famous!"

"Don't you know it, but really—you don't actually have to hang it."

"Yes, Iris, it's terrible. I'll be sure to have someone hang it only when you visit!"

I laugh realizing how absurd it sounded.

"You need to be more confident—you're really talented."

We caught up for a while until it was time for Janus to rest. Some of her meds make her drowsy. I was noticing a late onset of sleepiness come over me as well, possibly the product from last night. But I needed to push through and run some errands.

I stepped outside from Janus' studio. The sun seemed especially blinding with the light bouncing off all the white snow. I reached for my sunglasses, while I found a slight bit of queasiness. Leave it to the sunshine to prove your lack of radiances. Hair of the dog, I decided! I stocked up at the liquor store and powered through some other shopping necessities, including Janus' space heater. So far, so good, but I know this could still be a long week.

I sat filling in Janus about our evening, along with Allie and April—who were still recovering. We were all taking it easy after our adventures last night. Allie and I sipped wine, while April nursed water and Janus her Mountain Dew. Vera missed out on the excitement from the night before and took it upon herself to make up for it.

I normally only drink on weekends, but the rules don't apply on vacation. Sometimes a shot or two when I'm working the bar, but I can stay level-headed. I rebooted my system earlier today with some tonic and a splash of tequila, just one—it can help smooth over the day-after funk. Watching Vera is difficult. She came home from work with bloodshot eyes and lots of energy. Starting long before her double shift ended at the diner. She was past her comedy act, gearing up for her domesticated tending.

"Girls, I didn't get a chance to wrap your gifts yet this year. I'm going to look in the cellar for paper."

"Vera, you don't have to get us anything anymore—we're all adults."

"No, I know, but I wanted to give you guys a little something to open."

She disappeared with her beer in a cheetah-print koozie, checking in occasionally and replacing the contents inside her animal-print drink.

The girls and I ate dinner and told stories until at last, Vera graced us with her presence—she joined us at the table. "This is nice. All three of my girls home at last—well, four. You know you're like one of my own, Allie!"

Allie smiles politely, Janus chimes in, "She's probably glad she's not."

"Oh, Janus, don't be so pessimistic."

"I'll work on that, Vera," Janus calls from her wheelchair.

We know what's coming next—technically, I do feel bad for Vera.

She unsuccessfully parents a daughter who is better at playing the mom, missing a daughter who lives thousands of miles away, while one daughter sits paralyzed. You can almost see Vera's regrets popping above her head, hitting her as we gather for Christmas holiday, a time that should be filled with joy.

Janus sits uninterested and annoyed with Vera. Scribbling a grocery list of items she needs for the week. She does this wearing a bracelet around her wrist in which a pen slides through an attachment. It's helpful, given her lack of strength, but still cause for a hard adjustment. I fill another glass of cab and notice Allie's glass still almost full. I swallow down a sip and tension.

The room is calm for a moment, as we all stare off to the TV, watching a Hallmark holiday special, the one where the guy gets the girl in the end.

Vera stands abruptly from her chair and yells, "Where the hells the laundry soap? April, how much soap did you use? I just bought a container last week and it's almost gone."

"What are you talking about? The soap is above the washer, where it always is."

"It's nearly gone—what, do you think I'm made of money?"

"We did have extra loads this week. I washed and changed Iris' sheets and towels, plus the laundry from Janus, now that she's home."

"Well, you don't have to pour the whole container in for each load."

"Vera, calm down, I only pour it to the line."

"Don't tell me to calm down, I am calm. I just don't think we need to be wasting money on laundry soap, because people don't know how to do laundry."

"I'll buy another container of soap, Vera."

"That's not the point."

Janus interjects "Ok, well, I hate to interrupt, but I have to head back. My aide will be here soon."

Sympathetically Vera cries, "No, wait, stay—I was just saying we could conserve some soap, make it last longer."

"I know, but I got to get back to meet my aide."

April stands, "I'll walk you back."

Allie also insists on getting home and the kitchen is quiet with just Vera and me remaining. The only sounds in the room come from the TV. The television screen displays the closing scene of a family surrounding a Christmas tree, holding hands and smiling as the lights twinkle.

Vera sits in her chair beside me, switching over to her calmer and venerable self. "I'm not trying to be so hard on everyone, it's a lot. A lot of changes right now."

"I know, Vera."

"I'm a good person, good people always get shit on. Don't be shitty to people, Iris"

"I'm not."

"God, I love my kids, I wish she wasn't stuck in that damn wheelchair. I love you, Iris. I want all my girls to know I love them."

"We know."

She pauses with her head slowly drifting forward onto the table, but startles awake and stands.

"I'm heading back to bed, don't stay up too late now."

"I won't, Vera."

"Merry Christmas, Iris."

She yawns and walks down the hallway to her bedroom. I think to myself … *and to all a good night.*

CHAPTER 12

Communications and the great misunderstandings
Dysfunction in the secrets we shelter
Hardwired from birth by our patterns
No different than blood or DNA
Characteristics we claim to avoid, to prove we will be different
Pulled together anyway, in a pretty little bow.

~IH

G len and his parents were saying their goodbyes when I arrived back down in New Orleans. Missing them by a few hours at the airport, I was grateful I didn't have to jump that fence yet. I didn't know much about them, only the controlling hold his father held on the family. Including his persistent attempt to lasso Glen back to Texas.

I saw them in a TV commercial, twice. His parents' faces personifying the family-owned firm that includes hundreds of other attorneys with offices in many of the southern and western states, not including Louisiana. The national broadcast showed a man dressed in a black suit and tie with a monotone voice talking about the millions of dollars the firm has retained for clients. Glen's mom made a quick cameo at the end with the family brown retriever, stroking the dog saying, "Call today."

Glen told me about their dog, Winston. Winston often joined his father on hunting trips with colleagues and friends, confirming my original accusations of Warren Zevon's *Lawyers, Guns and Money*. I wondered if Glen their prodigal son was to return, did they plan on adding another HAWTHORNE to the title. HAWTHORNE & HAWTHORNE already seemed a bit redundant. Maybe HAWTHORNE SQUARED or maybe they would let it slide, assuming people could gather there were many Hawthorns at the practice. Luckily Glen was an only child, so HAWTHORNE CUBED would not become an issue.

Glen enjoyed law, which I found fascinating coming from a home where my mother was mostly trying to avoid breaking it. A close second was Glen's love for New Orleans, a place he claims to have an unexplained connection. With the blues rolling from the uneven streets, to the history of the people who walk them. A feeling of comfort that equally energizes and relaxes his soul.

His Texan family roots were usually described in generic brief sentences. A topic I, too, avoided—no need for formal background screenings. I was mostly thankful his parents' law practice didn't hold ties up north, where they could have represented my own family members.

He didn't want to leave New Orleans—he took specialized classes for Louisiana with its complex legal system that falls under "Napoleonic Law." A term some would classify wrongly, but unique none the less. It's very interesting, Glen would explain. I entertained having enthusiasm towards Glen's passion the way he encouraged mine. One evening after work, I looked up all the specialty legal jargon. He was right. It was fascinating how different some of the rules were—before the third paragraph, when I fell asleep.

Cleansed, dried and ironed with vanity.
Powders brushed on her cheeks and the lids of her eyes.
The eyes she will use to entice and seduce her lover.

-IH

My day was filled with pampering activities—I wanted to make sure the Iris that Glen was missing looked as good as or better than the one he remembered. Keeping good on promises, I got a spa manicure—Wesley would be proud. I was also getting a way overdue highlight with a girl named Rachel. I hadn't had my hair highlighted since before graduation. I wanted to get in before Christmas, but apparently the rest of the city had the same idea. New Year's Eve was a great runner up, glamming for my date later with Glen.

The salon was inside a traditional one-story shotgun house with an added-on second floor in the rear. Like a long funhouse hallway equipped with mirrors, passing one station after the next. I was told to hang right at the back stairwell. The old steps were narrow and steep, Rachel's chair was located in the camel back upper-level. Along with one male stylist, whom I found out later also performs occasionally down the street in drag shows.

The dark wooden panel floors were worn from the great volume of traffic. High heel scuffmarks scattered across its surface. Tall narrow windows tucked tightly into the wide baseboards and ornate crown molding at the top. The walls were painted a buttery gold with a few pieces of eccentric art by local artists. Strategically hung for flair, including the popular George Rodrigue and his blue dog.

I was happily surprised to see the salon was offering wine at the coffee bar upstairs.

A girl with shoulder-length platinum-blonde hair walks over, filling her green mug with hazelnut creamer and a splash of coffee. She looked about my age, wearing a black apron that tied in the back.

"Sorry to keep you waiting, you must be Iris. Can I get you anything else?"

"This is perfect, thanks."

"It been a crazy day, week, month … I lose track—it's still December, right?

"For a couple more hours, yes." I respond.

She lifts the bottle of wine high into the light, examining the low contents.

"I wish this wasn't coffee—I could use a glass of this."

I laugh, but wonder if this girl is really going to drink before she does my hair. I'll stand out with Glen all right.

"I don't mix business with pleasure, but I like to add pleasure for my … "

The man standing at the front station interrupts, "Girl, who you kidding?"

His voice is surprisingly feminine for a guy with a twelve o clock shadow. Disguising his flamboyancy well beneath his Nirvana graphic T-shirt. The drag makes more sense hindsight.

Kurt Cobain shirt continues, "Pleasure and business is all you know. How 'bout your ex's Michel, Tristan, Chris? And shit, what's that one guy's name—the one with the weird overbite?"

"Max, for your information, his name was Keith and he happens to be an amazing kisser. And I meant I don't mix certain pleasure with business."

Nirvana, who is apparently named Max, looks back down to his client, who seems completely unbothered by the bickering pair "Oh sorry, sugar, my mistaking your definition of pleasures."

"Besides Max, this here is a new client and I don't need you going off scaring her before we even start."

"Well, my apologies certainly, to you Ms … ?"

He looks to me as I timidly respond into this conversation, "Iris."

"Well, isn't that lovely. You're in good hands with my little Rachel here."

I was occupied with equal parts intimidation and enjoyment. The energy from the two stylists was intriguing, a ying and yang.

Max continues "I offer my deepest apologies, Ms. Iris, for giving you such a harsh first impression."

"No problem, you're going to have to do better than that to scare me." Finding my confidence.

"Feisty thing, well, all right, sugar."

Rachel stirs her steaming mug of Coffee Mate. "Are you sure I can't get you anything else before we start?"

"I'm good, thanks." I take a sip, "You have no idea how badly I needed this." referring to my straggly wisps of hair. "I just got back from Christmas break with family."

"Family, say no more." Rachel reaches back for the wine bottle and pours the remaining remnants filling my glass to the rim. I guess she'd never heard of the whole let it *breathe* rule.

"We're out of white—is red OK?" she asks with my glass completely full.

"It's great, thank you."

"Good, I'll grab another bottle."

"Oh, you don't have to do that, one glass is fine and I'm your last."

"Don't worry, Max and I can finish it up after close. You've got big New Year's Eve plans, Iris?"

For the first New Year's ever, I was happy to say, "Yes, my boyfriend got us tickets to *The Drop*."

"Well, hot damn! If I had tickets to *The Drop*, I might even get dazzled up for amateur hour. Big shots."

"Ha, no! Well, he got the tickets—I've never been to anything like this before."

Rachel strolls across the room to her station. "Well, fancy pants, come and sit down with me. This chair here is where we change the world and as a bonus, I'll make you look good, too."

I sat filling Rachel in on the details of my life, while she continued to fill my glass and hair with a magic potion of different sorts. Slicing each section with care and hundreds of silver foils, listening and joining in occasionally. I found myself regurgitating stories of my family's dysfunction, the long drunken evenings with my mother. Rachel was interested and could relate, I could tell she wasn't judging me with a similar dynamic in her own family, but with her father. She was inviting and she knew my tales well, like they were her own, because she had plenty. For the first time since living in New Orleans, I felt as though I had made a connection, aside from Glen. A friend, a girlfriend that understood exactly what I was like. She was just like me.

It felt like she'd done my hair for years. Rachel was a true southern girl, mixed in with a bit of creole charm. It was exciting to listen to her choice in words, many words and southern phrases that I would never string together. The connection felt mutual—she promised to come visit me at The Cove sometime for a drink.

"Tonight's going to be good, to fireworks and new beginnings!"

We toasted to our new friendship, my wine, and her now cold creamer.

I went with my new little black dress by Alex and Olivia. Glen and I had already exchanged our Christmas gifts before I left for New York. I knew right away I would wear it tonight—I believe that was his intention. A girl can get away with less than appropriate amounts of clothing but twice a year, Halloween and New Year's Eve.

Skinny straps hang over my shoulders, clinging over my hips. Stopping nicely above the knee, not a minidress. But convenient to balance out the low plunging neckline and my completely exposed back. I paired it with a dainty silver necklace that vanished beneath the dress and shiny black pumps, checking off either expensive or an S&M goddess.

My new blonde locks smelled like Hawaii from all the lotions and sprays Rachel used. I was feeling sassy and a little anxious. I notice the time—Glen would be here soon. It's been almost nine days since we saw each other last, which isn't that long, but it felt like an eternity factoring in the flying, the distance, and Christmas. I decided a tiny ounce of Stoli would help keep things moving and my excitement in check.

A knock on the door sounds precisely as I swallowed my second shot. Go time. The hallway was filled with busy dorm shenanigans and Glen. I cracked the door open slowly, revealing just a hint of me, while I take in a dose of him. His mouth grew wide and he pauses to speak, I had literally taken his breath away. I jump on my opportunity to lead.

"Good evening, Mr. Hawthorne."

"Iris." He breathes in, after a few seconds of starring. "You look incredible."

"Oh, this old thing." I slide my hand down my hip pinching the fabric where it grows loose past my thigh and twirl around slowly like a queen at her début. His eyes scan over me, entranced.

I take the liberty of surveying him and his beautiful physique. Standing before me in his Hugo Boss black sport coat and white button-up shirt. The jacket curves over his broad shoulders, the shoulders that I have used to grab for better leverage. He looks delicious in his white shirt beneath. He almost always wears a white shirt. I harass him that it's some kind of unspoken uniform. He looks good in white, he looks good in black, and he looks good in nothing at all. The shirt tucks into his tailored pants and leather belt. There's something about a man with a belt that makes me want to take it off.

I walk forward hitting the lights and take extra care in locking the door behind. I can feel him gazing me. I love it.

He groans under his breath "I don't know how I'm going to make it through the night."

His hand reaches for my waist, but mine intercepts and I hold it tight into my palm. If he touches me now, I fear I wouldn't have the strength to hold out. Instead I proceed forward towards our activity and keep the ball in my court with my act of discipline, at least for now.

—⸙—

The Drop Party was being held at one of the more exclusive hotels and the guests matched. Expected to be the best in a city that knows how to party. New Orleans' most affluent socialites roamed through the halls, from athletes to their team's owners, attorneys and judges, actors and actresses—everyone of importance. Glen showing a side of his ranking that he usually kept hidden. His mother and father's firm held a great deal of representation among the guests—Glen was but a peer to the elites.

We walked up the stairs through the main entrance.

"We have a room here for the evening. Whenever you are ready to leave, we can head upstairs."

I nonchalantly nod with his hand gracing the lower part of my back. I was giddy with excitement and we have a room! By the way things were going, it wouldn't be long till we went there.

The lavish party was held on the second floor inside a giant grand ballroom. Up lighting glowed across the walls, while opulent chandeliers trickled romance down from the ceiling. Large arched glass windows were dressed with heavy fabrics pulled back, framing the sides like a picture. The massive windows enticed the guests' attention outward to the evening sky and Mississippi River. Where drifting boats passed under the moon's glow.

A nine-piece band pumped current songs with a jazzy twist. It was an enchanting sound that made even the raunchiest hip-hop song sound like Mozart.

"Can I get you a drink, Iris?"

"Why yes, sir."

We spot one of the bar stations and make our way over. The heavily crowded scene pushed Glen and I tightly together. Building the already heightened energy between the two of us.

"Cheers!"

We sip Vue Clutch, the house champagne of the evening. The bubbles danced along my tongue going down. The dry, carbonated beverage was delightful. Sitting well in my preference for unsweetened drinks. It went down smooth, like the music floating through the air.

We brushed elbows with many people that I didn't recognize and a few that I did. Glen was often spotted and sought out for hellos. He'd shake hands and firmly introduce me to the company as his girlfriend. I loved the sound. He was polite, but never lingered, as if he longed for my sole attention most.

We stepped outside onto the grand balcony that placed us just high enough to see the crescent bend at the water's edge. It had gotten cooler as the night progressed and my bare back fills with goose bumps. Glen slides his hand along my spine and notices my raised skin, graciously offering his jacket.

"Iris, put this on, you'll freeze to death."

Clearly, he is from the south, where it was cold at fifty-one degrees wearing almost no clothes—I doubt I'd freeze to death.

"Thank you," I politely respond without correcting his statement.

You could hear distant sounds of drunken festivities echoing, taking place down in the streets below. Breathing in the wild energy of a New Year's evening and the smell of freshly rolled cigars.

Glen speaks up, "Looks beautiful at night."

"Yeah, the water seems extra captivating with the darker black shifts."

"I meant you."

I turn around to face him with my back to the water, pressed between the balcony and him.

"I missed you, Iris. More than I imagined."

"I missed you, too."

"I've never felt this way before, there's something about you." I have chills down my legs, but this time not from the cool air. I cross my legs and squeeze my thighs tightly to hold back the uncontrollable sensation to let him take me right here on the balcony.

I attempt to throw him off with wit, "Must be my personality."

But it doesn't affect him and he leans in toward my neck whispering, "Must be."

His lips tap alongside my ear and down towards my shoulders. His kiss is intoxicating. Shit. My body aches for him. I reach my hand to his shirt collar and hope that I don't rip it off. It's too much, the feeling. I find myself craving him and his touch, but I want this night to last—there is so much to see and it's not even close to midnight. I force myself to slide my head away from his and turn back to the water. He laughs, I think he knows it's all I can do to delay the gratification.

His arms stretch over mine and I can see his cufflinks for the first time with his sport jacket removed. Simple Brass Squares lock his sleeves together and I wonder how I will take them off when my opportunity does arise. I haven't had any interaction with that kind of men's accessories. Hopefully he won't mind if I break them when I free him from his shirt.

He presses into me with all his body and I can feel his strength hitting hard into my lower back. Fuck, it's hard. I want him deep inside, but I have to wait. A breeze flows past my face and I regain my composure.

"Shall we head back inside?"

He moans but complies with my request. "You're killing me, Iris."

"The night is young and so am I."

I hand him back his jacket. Once more revealing all the skin not covered by my skimpy dress, proud to be in control of a man who is used to having it all.

The wait staff passes trays of oysters on the half shell, bacon-wrapped scallops, and a few other hors d'oeuvres. I spot some kind of ice sculpture with people gathered around.

"What's that?" I question close to Glen's ear as if he had been given some secret road map to the party's amenities. He takes my hand and we move in closer.

The ice sculpture was brilliantly carved into the body of a woman and man engaged in a kiss. With swirls of hearts curled around their bodies and down over to the opposite end of the table where many of the guests were congregating. Two waitresses stood on stools and poured liquor down the slope of the sculpture into ice shot glasses. It was majestic, the grandest allurement towards alcohol that I'd ever seen. The waitresses cheered, "The quicker you drink, the quicker you can set the glass down."

Glen and I stood in line for our chance with the ice, I didn't care what we were drinking. Something this spectacular has to be sampled.

The double pours filled both Glen's and my glass at the same time. We look each other in the eyes and drink. The frost sticks to my fingertips like superglue and the liquid entered my mouth. Tequila! And not just any tequila, Patron! My pompous ultimate beverage swirls around in my mouth, mixed with tiny bits of ice crystals.

"That was incredible!"

"I'm not normally much of a tequila drinker, but it's better with the ice."

"Glen, we have to do it again!"

"You go ahead, I think I'll switch to a beer."

It's hard to say how much I was drinking—not that I needed to keep track. The punctual wait staff filled my glass without my noticing. Technically, I only ordered one glass of champagne, two Stoli martinis, and three fucking amazing Patron ice shots.

The *real* ball drop was happening and the countdown began. The crowed watches as the broadcast projects over a large white curtain against the back wall. Live shoots from our very own Jackson Square and Canal Street, layering the screen with marching bands and carnival style performers.

Three, two, one—Happy New Year!" Everyone shouted before leaning in for his or her long and *extra* French (in New Orleans) kiss. Including Glen and I. Our mouths lock in a slow smooth embrace before pulling away. I tug slightly on his bottom lip, as if holding onto him, as though our mouths could sustain me. Sending a shooting sensation throughout my body, longing for more. Turning his head close to mine, Glen whispers in my ear, "Ready to head upstairs?"

"I thought you'd never ask."

We briskly walk back through the hotel lobby. Loaded on champagne, liquor, and lust, I didn't even mind the strap slipping from my shoulder. Or the way my once appropriate length dress inched higher up my thighs. The rising dress instigating Glen, he cups my bottom cheek. Apparently, I wasn't the only one drinking more than usual.

"Mr. Hawthorne, fresh for a public setting, was somebody overserved?" I turn back to Glen, but my smile proves I don't mind. Throwing my inhibitions out, I wanted it, him. I press the elevator button with my onyx-painted fingernails. The color entitled *Midnight* seemed festive and very appropriate. I turn back toward him and walk my fingers down his torso, pressing into one button at a time, like walking across a stone path of a garden, stopping at his belt. I tug at the belt from behind the pant line, not to remove it, but to draw him inward. I can feel his mass at the tips of my fingers. I need to stop— we're in the lobby and I push him away to restrain myself.

His head falls back as he looks to the square screen above the doors, "Why is this elevator taking so long."

I laugh, amused in the pleasure of his torture.

At last the bell dings as we proceed further into the elevator. Both up the hotel floors and my dress. Continuing just beyond where we left off in the lobby. I stabilize myself with one hand on the wall, while the other grabs for the back of his neck. His mouth encloses mine and I find myself short of breath. I kiss deep into him as if he were my oxygen mask, but it only makes me grow weaker. He slides his hand down the opening of my low cut dress and the curves of my bottom. He traces his fingers down to the centermost point of my panties. The chemistry from his touch throws me into a hunger for a man like I have never felt. The elevator continues to climb and so does he. He slides my panties to the side and slips a finger inside. I let out a moan and my breath draws in. Fuck, I want more—I want to come down onto him while we go up. But the fear of the elevator door being opened is greater.

"We have to wait," I manage to say, although I don't mean it. He pulls his hand away and I immediately regret redirecting him. The elevator dings and with my wobbly legs, I fall into him.

"Someone overserved tonight," he teases.

"Never, it was the jolt from stopping abruptly."

"Was it abruptly from this?"

He turns me backwards and pulls me in, I can feel all of him from behind. He slides his hand down, opening the back of my dress, towards my front and plunges his fingers in me. A cry escapes my mouth and I lean my head back onto his chest.

"Your key, get your key, Glen!" I can't wait any longer, the night has been stretched out long enough.

He pulls his hand away as chills shake through my body. I recover from his touch and step forward. Attempting my last press of power before succumbing to his and my desire.

"I hope you can handle more than that tonight."

"Don't you worry, Iris, I do just fine with my handling."

The electronic key grants us the green light and we finally step into our room. Proceeding further than the restrictions of an elevator or hallway, although technically we had already gone far beyond those public standards.

CHAPTER 13

Nine down, seven across.
One comes from a region in France, the other often follows.
Champagne Regrets.

~IH

My head fit nicely into the crease of Glen's chest. Our naked bodies cling together like foam bath toys to a porcelain tub, our skin locking us together like a seal. My ear presses into him, I can hear the beat from his heart while his strong legs remain tangled in mine. I was careful not to let even one sock stay between us and lucky enough to be preoccupied below his waist when he removed his shirt and cufflinks.

"I could stay wrapped here with you all week." Glen whispers into my ear. The tone of his voice and the words were deep and powerful, like the love we just made. Passionate energy pulsed through me and I didn't want the evening to end.

"But it's the first day of the whole year! Look at this place, we should get up, take advantage of such luxuries."

"Get up? Crazy talk, I have everything I want right here."

"Yes … but we should explore. This is the finest show of people watching and I don't have a carriage turning into a pumpkin."

"People watching, you mean go back downstairs? I'd rather not. I see all the people I need right here."

I can feel my cheeks warming, blushing from his words and maybe some of the liquor. I've never been to an event like this before. Now that my hormones aren't ruling me, I want to take it all in.

"We should at least order some room service."

"Now that sounds perfect."

I unfolded the cushioned menu resting on the end table. My eyes search over the categories in black font with bullet points to the left and prices at the right. The list was extensive, especially for late night.

"Definitely blueberry pancakes and sausage!"

Glen laughs adding, "Breakfast sounds awesome."

I reached over to the phone and dial. Glen points down to the menu, gesturing for the biscuits and gravy and whispers, "Ask if they can add a side of bacon."

Listing off the requests, I continue with a small order of truffle fries, a bucket of champagne, and fresh strawberries. Glen's head turns my direction, with a slightly awkward expression.

"Glen, want anything else to drink?"

"Not champagne. See if they have Dr. Pepper."

"Great. Yes, that will do," I say back into the phone. "Well, hang on one second. Glen, are you sure you don't want a beer or a shot?"

"No, thanks, Iris, I don't know how you could still want to drink," he laughs. "I need food to soak up the damage I've already done."

"Amateur," I tease. Thinking back to Rachel's words earlier, she was right about New Year's rookie drinking.

"Maybe, but I'm not the one who's going to feel sick in the morning."

"I never get sick," I say smiling back.

Morning was painful. My head pounded with great force, it pulsated over my temples and eyes, persuading me to close them quickly. My body was covered in sweat, sweating out the alcohol from the evening. I lay in the hotel bed just a few feet away from the bathroom trying to collect my thoughts. I could hear Glen in the shower. The door was ajar and the steam was pouring out, hitting me, fighting over my body's boiling temperature. As though my blood could actually mimic the shower, and steam its way out through my skin. I wanted to join him, but first I needed to get my bearings. I opened my heavy eyelids again to scan over the room, attempting to piece together the night before.

I couldn't remember anything after coming upstairs. An empty tray sits near the door. Room service, we ordered food! But then there was nothing, zero. Blackouts have never been my thing. I've had little experience with bits and pieces missing, but not the whole night. My memory eventually pulls together, as I find items scattered about like a beginner's crossword search that's almost complete. It's strange not to remember, no recollection after ordering food, and a strange sense of malaise accompanies the void. This crossword feels advanced and it doesn't even come with the boxes to guess.

How could this happen? I can handle my liquor and wine—it's a talent that I've mastered, even more as a bartender. A champagne flute sits on the end table beside me. Crap, it must have been the champagne. That shit sneaks up in full disguised camo.

The room is a mess and the precarious feeling deepens within me. I pull the fluffy white duvet over my head, drawing out the light, while causing my body to sweat more. I sift through my thoughts, trying to recall any events. The neurotransmitters are shooting, but nothing is connecting, only the heavy weight of a black hole. I don't know why, but I can tell it wasn't good, whatever happened. We must have gotten into a fight. No, not Glen and I.

I'm so confused from the lack of information. My head pounds hard when my thoughts are interrupted with a knock at the door. I peek my head from the blanket and wait to see if the sound continues. Once more, I hear the knock. This time Glen emerges from the steam and bathroom to open the door. He's dripping, with a towel wrapped tight around his waist. He opens the door revealing a man holding a tray with a pitcher of water, a coffee press, and cups.

"Thank you," Glen offers and he turns around to see me awake. Sheepishly I sit up, holding the comforter like a child's blankie.

"Good morning, a little under the weather?" His tone is firm.

Daringly I respond, "What happened last night?"

"I don't know, Iris. I was going to ask you the same thing." He pauses briefly, just long enough to confirm the uneasy hunch tugging at me.

"It was like you flipped a switch, Iris. You popped the champagne and recharged. The bottle was nearly gone when you insisted on going back out."

"We went back out?" The strange uneasy feeling I had was shame.

"No … *you* went back out! You said you wanted to grab one more drink from the lobby bar, specifically—*one more for the New Year.*"

My hands run through my hair, it's unexpectedly pulled back into a tangled ponytail with a rubber band. I feel gross from his words, the ones I apparently spoke. *Why the fuck did I drink so much and why would I have gone back out?*

He clears his throat, "After forty-five minutes, I came down to find you telling jokes with complete strangers. Everyone was laughing and cheering as you slammed down shots. When you saw me, you shouted from across the bar, "Everyone, this is Glen, the man I've been telling you about!"

The shame was amplified to mortification. I sounded like Vera. That thought even without the hangover would make me sick.

"I wasn't sure what you had been telling them, but I politely excused you from your act and we went back upstairs."

My head was sinking low and I wanted to crawl out of my skin and this room.

"Luckily, I got you back just in time to vomit on the floor."

"I threw up?" I yell in disbelief, "I never get sick."

"Yeah, you said that last night, too.

I breathe out a weighted sigh, noticing the acidic sour zing permeating from the back of my throat. I'm appalled at my actions.

"I got you into the shower and put you to bed."

I was disgusted. I loathe sloppy drunk people, I can't believe I was one of them.

I struggle to form the words, "I'm so sorry, Glen. I don't know what came over me."

"I'm not sure either." He stands tall, while pushing firmly on the French press, his now dry biceps flex.

I can't believe I went back out and telling jokes at the bar—how embarrassing—what is wrong with me? I could have been holding onto him and his beautiful body all night. I was so inappropriate. I'm completely disgusted. Glen would never want to be with someone like me—I don't even want to be with me. I should have stopped. I should have just eaten my fucking pancakes and gone to bed.

"I'm not sure what to say Glen. I don't know how I'll make it up to you—last night was incredible and then I ruined everything."

"I enjoyed being with you, tremendously—until room service—I don't know what happened after that."

"How were your biscuits and gravy?" I ask, trying to break the tension.

"They were awesome," he smiles, "best I have had in a while."

"Glen, I am so sorry for my behavior. I understand if you never want to see me again, but you have to let me make it up to you. I can't stand the thought of us ending on bad terms."

I have no idea what I could do to make up for my ridiculous actions. I'm still so foggy I can barely think. But my stomach yearns for food the way I long for Glen to not be disappointed with me.

"Glen, let me buy you breakfast?"

"We already had breakfast, last night."

"Well, how about lunch?"

"You don't have to buy me lunch."

"No, I want to. I'd feel better about turning into such a jerk last night."

"Iris, you're not a jerk, I enjoy being with you. Technically everyone downstairs at the bar seemed to like you, too. You're funny, you have charisma. But you left and didn't bother to come back—I don't even know why you wanted to go downstairs."

"I don't know either. I can assure you I'm regretting this headache right now."

He grins and looks amused.

"Oh, you like that—you like that I have a killer migraine?"

"Kind of," he laughs. I'm happy to see him not as angry, and I'm appreciative for my unwanted headache.

"Well, good, because it sucks, my head really hurts and I need something to eat. Trust me, I won't do this again, I don't ever want to ever drink again!" In this moment, I mean it. I didn't want to see or smell any form of alcohol.

"All right, all right. Iris, you don't have to swear off alcohol forever, just not so much at one time. How about a burger at Stanley's? They're the best in town."

"A burger sounds perfect. With a chocolate milkshake," I add.

"As if you can have it any other way." His lips are gorgeous when he smiles. I would love to be able to kiss them again. Fuck, he's hot—so am I, actually I'm still sweating. I pull the warm covers off my body, exposing my barely-covered skin from his white undershirt that he dressed me in. I look like a disaster.

"First, I need a glass of water, one of those fancy cups of coffee, a shower, and some clothes."

"Oh no, Iris, you didn't know? Stanley's is clothing optional."

"You got jokes? Why don't you walk that towel over here and show me your definition of optional."

CHAPTER 14

Glen works to pass the bar, while I attempt to raise mine.

~IH

Not drinking *forever* maybe was excessive. But I wasn't going to drink until Friday, February sixteenth (aka the evening after Glen took his bar exam). We made reservations to go out to dinner, regardless of his pass or fail. About six weeks of anticipation, proving I was capable of leaving it when I wanted.

I was working at the Cove the night before Glen's big test, while plates were passed of fish and chips, po'boys, and calorie-packed nachos. Our pub food fought hard to bring an aromatic fragrance to the room to overcome the smell of sweat and cleaning agents. An aura of arrogance and low inhibitions, lit mostly with the fluorescent lights of alcoholic propaganda. Tonight was packed when I saw a familiar face through the crowd. It was Rachel, my hairstylist. I was delighted to see her visit, and she brought some friends.

"Rachel, you're here!" I yell from behind the bar.

"Sure thing, doll. I know a good time when I hear one. I want you to meet Beth and I believe you remember Maxine." Maxine's dressed in a black cut-off sleeve Madonna T-shirt, while Beth's breasts are pulled into a crop top, just longer than my sports bra, kinda like Madonna.

"A real pleasure, what can I get for you ladies?"

"We'll take the house favorite and four blow job shots."

Taking the quick head count, I repeated back, "You mean three shots?"

125

"Nope, one for each of us, and you."

I contemplated the ways to pass, but I couldn't say no. I was still on my drinking leave, but I didn't want to be rude. This is the first time Rachel's ever come to visit, plus she brought friends. I suppose Glen and I would be celebrating tomorrow, what's one day? Might even be good for me. I wouldn't want to embarrass myself again with such a low tolerance. Like New Yorkers getting a base tan before a tropical vacation, exposing themselves to a little bit of artificial rays before undergoing the closer proximity of the equator's sun. I just needed a base tan, a base tan of drinks, so I didn't burn with Glen.

"Cheers," we shoot, throwing back the first round. It was good.

"Damn, girl, where'd you learn how to make drinks like this?" Rachel applauds, while Beth rolls her eyes and turns away.

"Whoopee, it's a drink." Beth's amused, as she stares out at the crowd like a predator.

"We'll take another round and Beth, could you take that stick out of your ass?"

Beth doesn't respond, instead continues her resting bitch face, as I attempt to lighten the mood with spirits.

I pour drinks and chat with my new friends and the rest of the bar. Which was packed with college students. Everyone squeezed inside standing around the wobbly metal highboy tables. Locking down the bar stools and the good corner booths. Jocks with their matching T-shirts gathered over pitchers of beer, while girls with flat-ironed hair and glossed lips sipped sangrias and other fruity beverages.

"Ugh, I hate frat boys," Beth says loudly.

"I certainly don't. Come on over here, baby, Maxine will find you a spot." Maxine responds while staring at a group of guys and rubbing the top of her thigh. Rachel and Beth laughed as one of the boys steps further away.

"Oh, he's playing hard to get. I love them so fresh and young, they don't even know what they want yet."

Beth speaks back up, "Actually, it looks like he knows just what he wants."

We all watch as the young guy grabs the backside of a blonde girl. I could vaguely read her lips, "That's not yours," but the look in her eyes said differently.

Beth continues, "I'm not taking any of these guys home—they look like douche bags."

"Stop being such a sour puss. I need to get laid and you're throwing off my game."

"Scratch that, maybe him—I'd take him home. Excuse me, girls." Beth skips off with the more perk in her step I'd seen all night.

"Beth has fire, but so do these drinks. I'll take another, but this time I want a traditional hurricane. Can you make that, baby? Rachel told us you weren't from around here—Yankee, right?"

"Yankee, yes, but I can make any drink, including your hurricane."

"Damn, this doll has confidence. I like her."

Rachel laughs, "I told you, she's just like us."

A few minutes pass when I saw some girls gathering across the room with commotion rising in the center.

"Shit, looks like Beth's at it again."

I scan the room for our door guys as the tension escalates. The guard moves through the crowd toward the center. Just missing the drink Beth pours out, soaking all one girl's brown hair.

"That's it," the bodyguard yells, "you're out of here."

He grabs the girl's arm dripping with remnants of Beth's lemon drop and escorts the girls to the exit, as the music stops and the crowd quiets.

"What? It's not *my* fault! You think I'd pour a drink on my own head? She should be kicked out!"

"Sorry, girls, but I didn't see who spilled what. Your voice was the only thing I heard. Come back some other time."

"This is ridiculous! I'm never coming back here, ever."

I glance over to Beth—she is laughing and waving her hand, "Bye, bye," completely amused. The guard motions to me and I walk over.

"Look, Iris, I know that girl's here with you, but if you're going to have your friends here, they need to stay respectable."

"Yes, of course, I'm so sorry for the trouble." I'm so embarrassed—I've never gotten in trouble at work before. I hate when people cause a scene.

Rachel looks to me, "I need a cigarette—you want one, Iris?"

"No, I don't smoke."

"Yeah, me either—come on. Now's a good time."

I find myself shouting to one of the other bartenders to cover my end and step outside with Rachel and Maxine following.

It is raining when we get outside, the streetlights shining like a spotlight to the gutters, lining the road with streams of filthy water.

Maxine speaks up, "Looks like that kappa-kappa something would have gotten her hair wet tonight anyways."

I don't respond, but nod my head yes. Beth steps outside trumping the sound of the rain, "Where's my invite?"

"Beth, why do you have to act like such an asshole?"

"What? That little girl got what she deserved, y'all take shit too personal."

"Iris works here—we're not trying to get her fired, because you can't play well with others."

"It's fine, guys." Trying not to make the situation anymore awkward.

"I only smoke when I drink." Rachel says as she exhales a cloud of smoke and hands the cigarette to me.

With all the embarrassment, I don't have the heart to say no thank you, so I attempt to blend in, "Me, too."

"I can tell when I'm not wanted." Beth turns back inside and slams the door before anyone stops her.

"I'm so sorry, Iris. We didn't mean to cause you any trouble, Beth can get a little crazy. I'll talk to her."

"It's not a big deal. I doubt the guard will even mention it to my boss—he's pretty cool with me."

"She just needs a little Xanax to calm her down," Maxine says.

"Xanax? Does she have anxiety? I thought you shouldn't take that if you're drinking."

"Oh, Iris, you are too cute. Where'd you hear a thing like that, the warning label?"

Rachel asks, "Iris, have you never taken Xanax before?"

I didn't have the heart to tell them this was my first cigarette, let alone Xanax. I thought of Vera, and how she would take just about anything. Maxine speaks before I answer—apparently I didn't need to say anything.

"Tonight is your lucky night, this is gonna help take the edge off."

"I don't know. I've never taken anything like that—not really my thing."

"It's good, you're safe with us."

Safe with us, something about it sounded nice. I really liked Rachel and Maxine. I could pass on Beth, but this was the first group I really felt like I fit in. How bad could it be—technically, I did have doctors prescribe me meds for anxiety—maybe I should give it a try.

Maxine jumps in, "Oh, we got ourselves a virgin, here's to firsts."

Rachel pulls out a small Ziploc with a piece of paper wrapped inside from her purse. Inside the paper was a handful of rectangular bars. They were tinged yellow with a strange symbol and a few numbers, the opposite side blank. My examination over the drugs interrupted by Maxine pouting, "Damn raindrops keep putting out my cigarette."

I almost change my mind, but it's not like it's illegal. It's a prescription. I'm not going to do it all the time, pushing down my thoughts of Vera. Maybe just this once, see if I even like it.

"All right, hit me."

"Well, hang on now, baby, it's not blackjack."

Rachel takes my hand placing the medication between my fingers saying, "Here, start with half a bar."

"And you just tell Momma Maxine when you're ready for more."

I look closely at the half, like Rose on the Titanic. I let it go from my fingers, choking back its sharp edges down my throat. It's swallowed, no chance of return.

The metal side door swings open with a bang and my heart starts racing with fear, like we've been caught.

"Whatever, guys, it sucks in there. Everyone's leaving. Iris, I'm sorry about the girl. I can't help myself sometimes." Beth takes sips from her glass and I'm guessing this is as sincere as she gets.

"It's OK, really—thanks though, Beth."

"Everything's good now, we got candy bars." Maxine smiles

"So, what's the plan, what are we doing tonight? And please tell me it's not sitting out here on these wet steps."

"Oh, Iris got me thinking about slot machines, y'all want to do a little gambling?"

"Slot machines, like at the casino?"

Maxine speaks back up, "Please tell me you have been to our city's finest, Harrah's?"

"No, I haven't really had much time."

"Well, this is your lucky night, Ms. Iris. First Xanax, then the casino, who knows what's next, maybe the moon!"

"Casino nights are the best, you gotta come, won't ya?"

"I don't know, I probably won't be able to leave here till three."

Maxine smiles "Perfect, baby, that's just when the place is warming up."

I had a neon pink band around my wrist when I woke, the

smooth paper prize from our wild escapade. Although I would have plenty of evidence after peeling my eyes open to blurred vision and cottonmouth. The only thing clear is my loss of memory. I must have blacked out again. I scramble for my phone to piece together my evening. I look down to see my last text message to Glen at 3:08 am. *I'm going to the casino with some of my girlfriends, good luck on the test!*

Thank God I didn't write anything crazy, years of observing Vera, a fine teacher. Oh my God, I just compared myself to Vera. OK, breathe. Wait—the test, shit today's the exam! I was going to see him off in the morning. Noting my clothes, wrinkled and musty from the bar, sticking to my body from night sweats. What the heck is wrong with me, why can't I remember anything from last night? I'm completely blank, two times in a row. Although the last time was like six weeks ago.

I force myself to a seated position. I look around the room, hoping to figure out where I am. My back aches as I lean forward from sleeping on an uneven wooden floor. I don't know whose place this is ... Rachel, Beth or maybe Maxine's? Searching for a clue, I spot a blonde curly wig hanging on the back of the door and framed a Queen album. It looks likes the most eclectic music for a gay cross-dressing man. Maxine's, we're definitely at Maxine's apartment.

Rachel's voice cracks from the opposite end of the room.

"Good morning, early riser."

"Aw, my head hurts—what all happened last night? I can't remember anything."

"I'm not surprised, you were giving those cocktail waitresses a run. Down like sweet pixie sticks."

I set my phone down and close my eyes, rubbing my temples in a circular motion. She continues, "I wasn't sure if you'd be able to keep up with us, but you proved your place."

"Great, I feel like shit. I'm so thirsty ... and hot. What's the temperature in here, are we competing with Hades?"

"Ha! I'll get you some water, hold tight."

I hate this feeling, the clammy sensation that rests in your skin after a big night of drinking. My blood boils and my mouth feels like an ashtray. Gross, I will not do that again. Rachel steps back into the room holding two glasses of water, for her and me.

"I haven't drank since New Year's, my tolerance is low. I'm so embarrassed."

"Don't be sorry, there's nothing to be ashamed of—you're a trip, baby. I'd go out with you anytime."

My head pounds as I sip the cool water. I can hear myself breathing into the glass and the loudness of my swallow. Like a caveman with no social skills, I set down the glass, resisting further embarrassment (even though I could drink the whole thing in one gulp).

"Besides, Iris, I don't think it has anything to do with your tolerance. Any of us would feel like shit if we drank as much as you did, and we have. Not to mention the Xanax."

"Ugh," I moan. "The Xanax, I forgot about it, like the rest of the night. I don't know what got into me."

"Rachel, I should probably head back to my place."

"Me, too, I have a ten o'clock highlight. I'll walk out with you."

I stand to my feet, whining and groaning at the same time, "Ugh, if I can walk."

Rachel laughs, "Take a bite from the hair of the dog."

"If you think I'm popping another Xanax, you're crazy."

"No, not that. Grab a little Irish coffee with me."

"No, I need to get back, I've got a long day."

"The more the reason—there's a coffee shop downstairs, you'll be good as new. You can take it to-go."

"They'll do that?"

"This is the Crescent City, they'll do just about anything here."

We walk down the stairs and I can feel every step. Jolting my feet as if I am climbing a mountain changing elevations, the air hard to breathe. I swear my ears pop from the altitude of one flight. Today is going to suck.

We turn the corner and I follow Rachel into the café—maybe a latte would help. Plus, I could chug a bottle of water in private as I walk home.

"Last chance, lady." Rachel says to me as she turns to the bistro behind the counter. "One medium Irish coffee, please."

It's tempting, something to take away this forceful pounding.

"I shouldn't."

"Suit yourself, but I know what I'm getting ... Exhibit A."

She holds the steaming cup in her hands, baiting me like catnip to a cat. She lifts the lid for it to cool. I can see the pretty cream and white swirl, it smells incredible. I ponder the thought of not feeling like shit, "Well, make it a small."

CHAPTER 15

Dinner - damsels in distress.

~IH

"One glass of cabernet, and I believe he's having the same." I finish fussing with my dress and set my hand to the counter, placing it on top of Glen's. I was lucky to slip a nap in before our outing tonight. Collecting myself, attempting another try. Tonight I will control myself. Anxious in my graceful shell, we wait for the ordered pleasure inside the lounge. I love lounges, the people, the music, the energy—the drinks.

A long-stemmed wine glass slides across the black marble counter. The wine is smooth, with a hint of cherry and oak. I sip more. No, mostly oak. The dry liquid warms my mouth. *Pace yourself, Iris. One for one in drinks, we're tied.* I sip, listen, nod, and respond. I think of fellow classmates drinking at dive bars or house parties from their plastic red solo cups, while my fingers press the smooth glass. I draw the liquid to my mouth, pausing properly while listening to Glen.

He's a wordsmith in conversation, reiterating the day and questions throughout his test (followed with his answers) —I already knew he would pass. His enthusiasm and sentences push fluently from the breath of his lungs forward to his lips. The lips I lean in to kiss softly, like fireworks, though I draw back into the supported high-back stool. It's tufted and the cold buttons press slightly to my exposed skin, but it's soft and I don't mind. Everything is perfect—Glen, the people watching, along with my full-bodied drink. I stay engaged in conversation with him as we share our dreams to pursue in the future.

"May we get a dozen of your raw oysters, the medium-sized boutiques from Cape Cod?"

It's like he reads my mind, I just saw the tri-fold brochure on the counter, featuring specialty dishes and cocktails. The only thing that could make the oysters better would be a small glass of tomato juice, mixed with Stoli. Kerplunking the slippery morsel into an oversized shot glass, maybe stirred with a stick of celery. No, not tonight. I swallow the fermented grape juice instead, fearing its end.

The bartender spots me and with a nod of his head, makes way to us asking, "May I get you another glass?"

As if uncertain, I turn to Glen, his drink closer to the halfway point. He could go either way. *If he passes, I will, too.*

"Why not," he responds, "we can bring it to the table."

Nonchalantly I add, "Sure," just as carefree. *Two for two, still tied.*

We head over to the dining room, sitting cozy at a booth in the corner. We order our meals a la carte. Sipping and chatting, and pacing. Some dishes are brought over, including the Mayflower Point oysters that were rung in when we were still at the lounge. I mix the horseradish with crystal hot sauce for a fiery concoction, tear open the saltine wrapper and layer the oyster, it's good, but would be better with a Bloody Mary. I pick at the appetizers, filling up mostly on red. Still pacing myself, I notice my beverage getting low again. I'll need another before dinner, but he's still at two, and his is nearly full. There's nothing wrong with three. Maybe he'll want another, we're celebrating. The waiter checks in, "Can I get you another drink, ma'am?"

Ugh, why is he so specific, calling me out. I look to Glen's face searching for a clue on how to respond. He's hard to read, he seems happy and I don't want to ruin the night.

"No, thank you," I respond painfully.

"And you, sir, anything for you?"

"I'm good, thanks," Glen smiles and continues chewing.

Well, I did it. I passed. I did the right thing. The thing a girl who goes out to fancy dinners would do, simple, modest in consumption. Two drinks with dinner. But it's almost gone and my scallops haven't even arrived. I can't. I wonder if the waiter will come back, if he'll give me another chance or if I lost my opportunity for the entire evening. No, too dramatic. Maybe there is something to being a regular college student at a regular party. They could funnel large quantities upside down and no one would think twice. That's what people my age do.

No, I'll be the girl who has two. Content with two drinks, I'll switch to water. The ice is refreshing and cold on my gums compared to the wine. I can do this, it's beautiful here. I take in the enchanting drool-worthy ambiance. The chandeliers dance their dim lights down to the intimacy below. Casting moods into romance, like the one I have with Glen.

I continue looking around the room, observing the others, taking notice of a couple sitting across from our booth. A table with four chairs, two of them occupied. A woman sits the same as me, with love in her eyes. She is dragging her closed-toe pump up the side of the man's pant leg, below the table. Holding composure above with a smile as she sips from her glass, also red. I wonder if it's the same as mine, if she also has chosen the bold cabernet. A fine choice—even the waiter said so. Effortlessly she sips, modestly she pauses, and rests her glass on the table. Taking turns in conversation and beverage, just like me.

For a brief moment, a strange thought comes over me. Does everyone use such measurement to gauge his or her consumption? Surely, yes, this is how it's done. An image of Vera pops into my head. I picture her at a table, wearing one of her horrible cheetah-print dresses with a bra strap showing, possibly in a shade of turquoise. Drinking her beer. Which, at a place like this, would at least be poured into a tall glass, with many empty others lined up across the table. No, the

136

waiters would clear them, but she could never do this, moderation. Alcoholics can't help it, people like her have no control. My thoughts venture back to the table, enjoying Glen on the other side.

Our food arrives, "Please be careful the plates are hot. May I get you anything else to complement your dinner?"

Glen clears his throat, "I'm good—Iris, did you need anything, a wine?"

This is my chance, wine! I pause as if to ponder the consequences, the consequences of being without. "Yes, I'll have one more cab, please."

I'll stay at three. I am a college student. Two to three, it will go nicely with my dinner. Some liquid with flavor to help wash down the food. Pacing myself, sipping, laughing, enjoying each other over the delicacy of the meal. As we near the end, our bellies are full, but my glass is not.

"Can I entice you with dessert?"

Glen looks at me now for direction, I look to his glass and it's finally empty.

"We have flourless chocolate cake and specialty drinks?"

Oh, after dinner drinks sound lovely.

"Chocolate cake, it's hard to pass up a good chocolate cake."

I laugh as we share the same feelings. We both have interest, though to different options. The waiter seems uncertain with my lack of response. He recites the crème brûlée and a few others, but then turns to the last page of the menu, highlighting ports and spiked coffees. A port, I should try a port. That sounds sophisticated. A taste I haven't acquired yet, but I'd be willing to work on it.

"The port here in the middle, is that one good?" I ask sheepishly to soften the request for more alcohol.

"Yes, nice choice, ma'am."

Glen speaks up and I fear he may question yet another beverage.

"Also, bring a slice of the chocolate cake, and one more glass of red."

Red, he's ordering another drink? This is perfect—I have been worried all night for no reason.

"Actually, I'll take another glass of red as well, in case I don't do well with the port," I justify.

Three to four—well, five. No, the port only counts as half a drink. They're so small.

The treats arrive, pleasant bold and full of zing. I could definitely become a port consumer. My cab remains lovely, just like the first and it still goes down smooth. We laugh and I nibble a few bites from the cake. It's thick with chocolate, I swallow a larger gulp to push down its consuming flavor. Glen enjoys the cake and I continue sipping my dessert, I'm not really into sweets.

The bill arrives and I swallow faster. Holding tightly to the long stem, twirling the glass between my fingers, the gravity rocks the liquid back and forth inside the goblet.

"Tonight was wonderful, Iris, and you have been, too. I want to thank you for putting up with me these past few months with me getting ready for the bar."

"Glen, you're no trouble. And your work ethic is inspiring."

"I'm afraid it's consumed me, but I want you to know I'm ready to put more focus on you."

I smile, though I'm not really sure what to say. I'm sure he means it politely, but I can't help but wonder if he still thinks about my little New Year's debacle. I'll have to be even more careful.

I take a final long sip, slowly emptying the glass until every drip has dropped. Standing to leave, I note Glen's cabernet still almost full on the table, he barely touched it. All the same, final count remains, three to four and a half. *I wonder if he will want another round when we get home.* I'll wait a bit to bring it up, or maybe until he goes to sleep.

CHAPTER 16

The windows to the balcony open,
Along with so much more.

~IH

Sophomore year, I officially left the dorms to live with Glen. It made more sense seeing that most evenings I crashed at his place anyway. I was able to save a little bit of money and drop a shift at the Cove, covering only two nights a week. Opening time to work on my art, study, and play (a smidge).

Glen's schedule seemed busier than ever. Between the long hours he put in at the office and the even earlier mornings, he stayed faithful to the gym. Sometimes he was sent to different cities for depositions and such. I'm pretty comfortable in solitude and often used my time wisely, painting and growing my collections. Rachel wasn't Glen's number one fan, but he liked that I had someone to hang with all the time that he was away.

"Rachel will be here soon."

"Thanks for the warning, I'll be sure to stay in my hiding spot."

"She's not that bad." I turn to face him with a disapproving look.

"I know, there's just something about her. I feel like I should be taking her statement or something—she reminds me of my clients."

"Be nice, she has a good heart. Besides sometimes you have good clients."

He looks at me with a one eyebrow raised.

"You say it all the time, sometimes good people make bad choices."

"Why don't you get more friends like Allie? She seems so genuine."

"Allie is one in a million, you can't just pick those up anywhere."

The doorbell rings and I buzz Rachel up.

"Be polite."

"I'm always polite. Just don't get too loud tonight, OK? I've got an early morning."

"As usual."

"I'm sorry, not everyone gets to start their day at 11 am."

"That's not fair, sometimes I have to work till 5 am!"

Just then the door swings open, "What's up, bitch?" Rachel is holding a shiny new bottle of tequila high into the air. "Oh, hey, Glen, I didn't know you were here."

"Well, it would be hard to miss me."

"Sorry, I was just so excited to see my girl." She squeals and runs over to give me a hug before walking the bottle to the kitchen.

"You girls have fun tonight, it looks like you will."

Glen leans in to kiss me, but now I have an eyebrow raised, so he plants one on my forehead.

"Thanks for playing nice," I whisper as he walks back to the bedroom.

"Rachel, watch out for the bartender, she has a strong pour."

"That's one of my favorite things about her."

Glen laughs, but I think mostly because she almost proves his point. Rachel is a good person, full of bad choices.

Rachel and I step outside to my favorite nesting spot in all the quarter with our drinks in hand. The balcony. Perched high above the small garden and streets busy with people below. The wrought iron balcony leaves little room for furniture, but I cram in two chairs and one ottoman. I often bring my canvases outside to paint. I breathe in the mixture of smells, anything from turpentine and solvents, exhaust from pipes, spilt drinks on the pavement, even hints of urine. I don't necessarily love them all, but it triggers something within me. My muse comes forward with a bow and takes my brush. The canvas fills with graffiti, covered in emotion and hues.

Rachel and I curl up into our chairs to watch the evening's shenanigans.

"I hope I didn't upset Glen, I thought he was already out of town."

"No, you're fine and he leaves tomorrow."

"Well, I don't think he likes me too well."

"What? No, he does. He just has a big case coming up—you may have heard about it on the news. The guy who ran his wife over in the driveway?"

"Well, don't stop there, give me all the details."

"Oh, I don't know much from an inside scoop, Glen never gives up information, but they say the guy was married for like fifteen years and he and the wife had two kids in high school. The husband kept getting sick and the doctors couldn't figure out what was going on. After extensive testing, the man was told he had a condition that he never knew about, but it's something he was born with. It helped to explain his symptoms, but it created even bigger problems because one of the side effects was infertility."

"No shit, but the kids!"

"That's what he said. Naturally, he and his wife got into a huge fight. By time they got home, the husband lost it and ran her over three times after she got out of the car."

"Once for each kid and one more for revenge."

"Yeah, something like that. The wife didn't die and Glen's trying to get a plea for brief insanity, but you never know what the court's going to rule."

"That's messed up! I hope Glen can work his magic, I'd run her over ten times, if it were me. I need to stay on Glen's good side in case I ever need him."

I laugh, but can't help but think of Glen saying Rachel reminds him of his clients.

"Crazy people out there, Iris. Real crazy people."

With that, Rachel sets down her drink and raises her black converse sneakers to the chair. She slides her hand beneath her sock and retrieves a small clear bag of white powder.

"What the heck is that?" I ask, fearing I don't need to.

"You're such a prude! Come on, darling, just a little cocaine."

An image of my mother and Jake flashes to mind—he was always getting her to take drugs with him. God I hate him, everything about him, the way he talks, the way he moves, the way he used to look at me. He was disgusting and I immediately feel ill just thinking about him.

"What are you doing? Put that away—Glen would lose his shit."

"He's not going to come out here. I'm here and that would mean he would have to talk to me."

Without correcting her, I skip to the point, "Why do you even have cocaine?"

"It's not a big deal. That story was depressing and I'm whipped from working all day."

"So you take it when you're tired?"

"Sometimes. A lot of people do, it's not like I do it all the time."

I watch in awe as she raises a small scoop to her nose and sniffs. I've seen it in the movies—just never up close in person. It's always seemed so dangerous until now.

"Now I can stay out here and drink with you, without falling asleep."

Rachel has a way of making things seem not so bad. I was looking forward to our balcony people watching tonight, I'd kinda be disappointed if she went to bed early. Still, though … cocaine. It just has that next-level feel.

"Don't worry, I always share. If you'd like some, that is."

For a moment, I find myself thinking about trying it. I could never, and what would Glen say?"

"No, thanks, I'm good."

"No pressure, darling. You do you, that's one of your greatest qualities."

She seals the bag tightly and slips it back beneath her sock. Good as gone to the world's eye. It's strange to see something for the first time—never again will it have the same sting. The intensity lowers and your mind wraps around the concept. But like Rachel says, in small doses.

CHAPTER 17

So close but ...

~IH

The Meeting

A loud sound rings out from the corner towers behind us. One sharp shooter stationed at the top stands on point with heightened intensity. The CO's gun now drawn, with his eyes locked on the target, as he finely tunes his lens. We could faintly hear the shuffle of women and yelling voices. Assumable just beyond this wall, a fight had broken out in the yard. Tear gas clouds float above the walls as the guards attempt to gain control.

I look back to my sister, April, and Glen, "This doesn't look promising. Going out on a limb—this is going to add a good hour to Vera's release—so much for morning."

"Figures," April adds.

Glen remains optimistic, "Vera will leave today and there's still plenty of time in the day. I'll go inside and see what I can do."

I've visited Vera a handful of times over the years. None of which included a real fight breaking out, although they happen regularly. Once I was inside during a real lockdown. Technically most visits include a sixty-minute lockdown procedure, but this one wasn't a practice.

I took my place at Table Number 11, a stationary chair opposite a U-shaped counter. Really I suppose it was more of a W shape, as the loop continued to hump out again behind me. The inmates sat on the inside and the visitors across. Each station had a low glass partition that barely reached the top of my head level as I sat. It seemed pretty pointless, unless it was assigned to protect against bad breath. Not that I was worried about Vera's, but on second thought, it seemed likely that an inmate may have poor hygiene.

The beginning of the visit was awkward. Like meeting a pen pal you feel like you know so well, but it's different when you're not communicating with paper. The images you hold in your mind of the person and what they would look like in a jumpsuit. Seeing it, it's different.

"You look good." Vera breaks the silence as she sits directly across from me.

"You do, too," I lie. Vera's gray roots have grown out and are tickling her eyelashes.

"I look like shit, Iris. I must have aged a hundred years in the first six months."

I can't help but think how old she does look—maybe not one hundred, but definitely older than I remember her.

"How are your sisters? They must hate me."

"They're fine, they're coming along. It's going to take time." I decide not to lie this time.

"Well, I got plenty of that. Time, time, time, time. Maybe the only thing I have."

"Vera."

We sit silently for a moment. It's strange to have to talk on command, it feels unnatural to just start talking. Like about what, the weather, sports, my vacation plans next summer? I feel shy, nervous. There's a lot I want to say, most of which I don't know how. I wanted to make my first amends to Vera, after all, I feel I'm the real reason she got here.

"I'm glad you're here, it's nice to see an old familiar face. Most of the people here blend together—I try to keep to myself."

Just then a young woman walks in, about thirty, and heads to a seat across from her visitor (presumably her mother, given the older woman's resembling features). She catches eyes with Vera and nods with a smile, the acceptable *Hello* with guards patrolling.

"That's Sami, she's a sweetheart."

I turn my head with caution to steal another look. Her straight brown hair is parted down the center. She looks to be about a size 8 and perfectly average, minus she's sitting on the wrong side of the glass.

"She said she had a visit this week. Poor thing has life."

"Life!" I say surprised and yet as quiet and natural as possible. *Vera got like twenty years and she killed a guy, what the heck did this girl do?*

"Well, she had been taking some pain killers from an accident she was in and went out drinking with some friends. At some point in the night, she found out one of her *friends* was sleeping with her husband. She took her outside to the parking lot and beat the shit out of the girl. Then she drove home and stabbed her sleeping husband thirty-seven times."

I am on the edge of my plastic seat and suddenly feel extremely uncomfortable with *sweetheart Sami* sitting behind nearly five feet away.

"She then hopped into the shower and went to bed. When she woke up, she found blood and her dead husband next to her in bed. She doesn't remember any of it—she completely blacked out."

I stare at Vera who seems completely unaffected by this story or her sweet friend's wildly crazy behavior. I have no words.

"The girl in the parking lot was taken to a hospital for a few weeks, I think she became deaf and is blind in one eye. Or maybe deaf in one ear and both eyes blind, something like that."

My chest feels tight and I suddenly feel hot all over. It's hard to believe my mother is telling me this story about her *friend*.

"Sami actually got two life sentences, but her attorney got it reduced to one."

"Good, that should be helpful, if humans ever start getting multiple lives. Maybe she could make better choices in her next one."

"There's not much to choose for friends in here. I don't talk to many people, but she's one of the girls that walks the grounds with me in the afternoons."

Holy shit, Sami is my mom's walking buddy. This is so fucked up.

Another inmate walks into the visiting room, but she heads to the second loop of the W, Table 28. I can see her clearly, so I have to turn my head intentionally not to make eye contact.

"Now she's crazy—Laney Smithson. Do you remember reading about her in the papers?"

"I don't know, should I?"

"Well, she was known as the Dungeon Queen. She was caught with men handcuffed in her basement and … "

"You know I'm good, I brought my imagination today, so …."

"Iris, I'm sorry. I didn't mean to upset you. It's weird what becomes normal in here."

"It's fine, Vera." But my heart is racing and I need to stand up or something. I slide my hand into my pocket and I can feel the sweat as my palms rub my jeans. I feel the quarters—lots of them. Vera already wrote and told me the vending machines aren't good at giving back change from the dollars. Neither are the guards, so bring exact change.

"You want a pop or something?"

"Oh, yeah!" She was as giddy as a rat with a Nicotine drip.

"Orange. No. Dr. Pepper. No, Orange, do Orange!"

"Orange, it is." I stand and see the mixture of Orange shirts scattered among the inmate's side of the tables, lots of orange.

I sit back down to our table marked 11. Just as we twist open our soda, a buzz fills the air, not just from the bottle. The guards stiffen up, chests out, making eye contact with each other. The inmates casually glance at one another as well.

"Vera, what's happening?"

"Lockdown."

"But it's not even ten o'clock?" I confirm with the large clock hanging on the block wall.

"This one's not practice—something must have happened. I'll find out later at chow."

She must have noticed the panic I was trying to hide, obviously not very well.

Vera laughs. "Relax, this happens all the time. They probably just found weapons—usually knives or some other contraband like that. I think the COs were doing some random cell searches this morning. I could hear the guards talking when I was walking up here."

As if finding a weapon from societies most dangerous was supposed to be comforting, I decided to try harder at playing it cool. Clearly something Vera was able to do. There's a lot of talk here, lots of cat fights, not as much action—well, sometimes action."

The whistles from behind the walls of prison interrupt my memories. We can hear the guards continue to try and gain control. Yes, sometimes action, even on Release Day. I look around noticing April on the grass playing with my girls in a round of hand games. Glen walks back with news.

"Turns out, we're going to have to wait a little longer. Vera is in a holding room, she finished exit procedures, but the guards are all on deck right now. The building is not surprisingly in lockdown."

My girls sigh like little girls do, so does April.

"Vera will be leaving today, but we need to be patient a little longer. Probably three hours."

CHAPTER 18

I flip through the television channels, and spot a purple cow and
 say,
"Wow, a purple cow, I've never seen a purple cow!"
I flip some more and the cow appears. I stare with uncertainty.
Again flipping, the screen pops up and I think,
"There's that purple cow again."
Soon, I hardly notice.

~IH

G len was moving up the ranks in business and so was I. My detailed works of art were being requested frequently, I created custom pieces for homes and offices. I was making a name for myself and I was filled with confidence (plus paint underneath my manicured nails). Setting time aside for manicure sessions at least once a week, staying true to the promise I made in my youth. After three long years of late nights tending bar, I decided it was time to leave The Cove.

The usual suspects, friends, and coworkers all came out for my final hurrah behind the bar in true college fashion. The ceiling fans wobbled and circulated the stale air, both occupancy and humidity reaching one hundred percent. As honoree, we sipped all the drinks we could handle, which was a lot. Glen popped in for his last evening to be served, but with the weight of yet another upcoming trial, he wasn't able to stay long.

"You going to miss this?" Glen asks as he finishes his drink.

"Miss what? The smell of chicken wings, po'boys, and Jager on my clothes? I can hang out at the public library if I need a fix."

"I meant waiting on me." His smile is delicious, I could leave now, if the excitement of saying good-bye properly didn't keep me here.

"Oh, yes, darling, now I'll have more time to be at your beck and call."

"That would be the day—you at my call."

We laugh and I take note of some regulars sitting down for service.

"Have fun tonight, Iris, call me if you need anything, OK?"

"You got it, boss." I pivot turn as if I were on the runway and head toward my guests. Glancing back to blow a kiss in his direction.

I was passing out bittersweet goodbyes, promising to stop by frequently. "I'm sure you'll be back often," stated the head manager.

I found myself pondering his words. What did he mean by often— how often would often be? What was he implying and why does this bother me so? I wonder how many others contemplate their return to business past.

Rachel and Maxine arrived just after midnight, pulling me away from my nagging thoughts.

"Well, hello, doll face, we're looking for the retirement party, could you point us in the right direction?" Rachel is beaming and now I am, too.

"Ladies, you made it, this means so much!"

"It would take the fucking national guard to keep us from coming here, sugar!" Maxine adjusts her head and stuffed push-up bra, exemplifying her importance. "We're drinking Patron tonight, ladies!"

"Now you're speaking my love language," Rachel pipes in.

The garage door style walls are raised following freedom to the outdoors. But the heat off the streets is as intoxicating as the drinks, which are being consumed at a faster pace than usual. The manager pulls out our once a month karaoke machine for tonight's send-off. I could see Maxine eyeing the stage. A natural born performer, unlike her female sex, I knew she'd be singing by night's end.

"Iris, I'd also like a glass of courage in the shape of a Long Island, please." Maxine was taken off guard as a hand with red-painted fingernails squeezed her shoulder from behind.

"Liquid courage, you mean for the microphone?"

Beth emerges following her hand, and also notices Maxine's stage interest.

"Whatever, Beth, no one asked you. And you're late."

"Looks like I made it just in time."

Maxine stands, taking her drink in hand. "Come, ladies, time to serenade the room."

"No thanks, I'm good, Max." I say wiping the counter with a sticky rag.

"Me, too." Rachel sips more from her Crown on the rocks.

"Stop it, I am not taking no for an answer—except you, Beth— you're not invited."

Maxine walks off on a mission.

"Come on, doll or Max will never forgive us." Rachel stands, grabbing my arm with hers, leading me out from the hinged-bar countertop, through the crowd.

"I can't sing, Rachel."

"Neither can I—don't worry about it."

"I've never done this before."

"That's what she said." Rachel laughs as we walk through the crowd.

"What? No, really."

"Iris, it's not a big deal, no one can really sing. That's why it's called karaoke—not a record deal."

I'm so nervous I could pass out. I don't know why it feels like such a big deal to go up on stage. I can entertain just fine from behind the bar. This feels different, intimidating. Even the dim lights seem to be blaring in our direction, lighting us like spotlights. Maybe they are. Maxine is busy talking with the MC for the night, I have no idea what song she is choosing. She nods to us with her Long Island in one hand and a microphone already in the other. Before I know it, the MC is talking over the noise of the bar.

"Ladies and gentlemen, you are in for a treat. We have our very own Ms. Iris with her friends Rachel and Maxine for their very first and likely last performance at the Cove. Give it up ... "

The crowd is cheering and everyone inside and out is facing the stage, which we are now standing on, in the center. I need another drink—I didn't have time to grab one before being pulled from the bar. The MC hands the second mic to Rachel for us to share—she holds it in her hands, mine are shaking. I notice Beth comfortable from the stool in the crowd and for the first time, I wish I could be sitting with her. Pushing the microphone down, I look to Rachel. "I can't do this."

"Too late, you're not leaving me up here with her."

A deep seductive tune charges from the speakers, low notes on a piano mixed with a promiscuous familiar melody. I recognize it—most of the crowd does and they cheer loudly with approval. Maxine grabs her microphone tight like a baseball bat, closes her eyes, and opens her lips.

"I've been a bad, bad girl." The crowd roars, Maxine's Adam's-apple pushes forward with her words. "I've been careless with a delicate man."

Shit, she's good, a talent Rachel and I both lack, but Rachel pulls me in by the waist and we both proceed to mouth the words like backup singers. Slowly increasing my volume as I gain a hint of stability. Breaking in at the chorus with confidence building, "What I need is a good defense, 'cause I'm feeling like a criminal."

It's surprisingly fun, almost addicting—maybe the liquor kicking in, but I like it. Before I know it, I'm splitting center stage with Maxine who shares generously. I am belting at the top of my lungs "but I keep living this day, like the next will never come." Whistling and applause rings throughout the bar. I sing louder, even Beth has her hands cupped around her mouth cheering with our performance. It's a rush—in a euphoric moment the three of us lock arms, I'm in the middle. Singing our hearts out as if the song was made for us, as if we wrote it. A coworker passes a bottle of Patron to the stage, Rachel takes hold and gently pushes me backward over a wooden barstool on stage. Maxine continues solo while Rachel lifts my shirt up to my bra line, my head dangles back and I stare to the exposed black pipes across the ceiling. Rachel bends to her knees and pours the drink from my chest bone, collecting the liquid just below my navel with her mouth, some splashes onto the top of my jeans. The crowd explodes with cheer, the men especially pleased.

"This is crazy," I shout, but everyone loves it and for some reason, I do, too!

I propel my body from the backbend to a forward position, sticking the landing like an Olympian just in time for our collective big finish. The bar guests stand to their feet that haven't already—even the outside bystanders are cheering and hollering from the street.

"Well done, ladies." Maxine stays on stage longest, taking a final bow.

"That was fucking awesome!" Beth meets us handing us fresh shots, which we take fast like the need for oxygen.

Looking down to my disheveled shirt and wet jeans, "I need to run to the bathroom and pull myself back together."

Everyone agrees and we head for the long line at the ladies room. The restroom is small and littered with toilet paper, only three stalls and the first door that opens is the slightly larger handicap at the end. The four of us pile in, rotating the toilet in turn. Beth pulls out a small clear bag from her purse along with her key ring. She holds her metal house key with a skull at the end. I'm not as naive as I used to be, so I refrain from gasping.

"Ladies, your reward." She smiles and scoops a small pile of white powder, leveling it off inside the bag, the same I would with sugar, if I were baking banana bread. The product disappears up her nose and she passes it around like a manager handing out paychecks. Maxine innocently hands it to me for a turn. I grab the bag and key chain intuitively, like a basketball flying to my face, though I have no intentions of using it. Strangely, it doesn't feel nearly as uncomfortable in my hand as the microphone did a few minutes ago on stage.

Rachel speaks up on my behalf, "Here, doll, I'll take yours."

"No, she's a big girl, she can handle it," Beth interjects.

"She doesn't do this shit, leave her alone."

"What? She some kind of goodie-two-shoes—you think you're better than us, Iris?"

"No, nothing like that." Holding the bag in my hands it doesn't feel as offensive as I imagined. The weight of guilt slips away with Fiona Apple's *Criminal* song still playing in my head. Maybe it's not that bad—after all, Rachel and Max are good people. I feel open to trying new things, I never thought I would belt my lungs out in front of a crowd of people and that turned out fine, too.

"I'll try it."

"No, Iris, you don't have to, not everyone's as fucked up as us, Beth." Rachel gives Beth a dirty look.

"Yeah, no pressure, Iris," Maxine confirms.

But all I can hear are Rachel's words "as fucked up as us." Every dark detail of my life flashes before me. My friend's car accident and their funerals, Janus stuck in a wheelchair getting through her day with pain meds, Vera's drunken escapades, and all the times I've found her passed out, and Jake. Fucking Jake. I'm just as fucked up, maybe worse.

"It's OK, I want to." The words leave my mouth easily, although I may still be convincing myself.

Holding the key, I dig into the bag and lift, clearing off the extra granules before pulling out the scoop. It's soft and feels lighter than sand, like pushing through whipped cream. I lean my body slightly forward, my head meets the key halfway. Mimicking the girls, I press my French manicured fingers to the left side of my nose and breathe in. One quick, strong inhale.

Just as fast, I cough in reflex, my nose burns, and my eyes water.

"Shhh!" Beth kicks the handle of the toilet with her boot, drowning out the noises from our stall. The flushing muffles the sound and my disappointments. I watch the water swirl as my expectations go down the drain with the water.

I stand, face the mirror, and wipe the white residue under my nostril, then cough some more. I can see my mistake screaming from my reflection. Talking myself down, telling my conscious it's OK— I've been through a lot. Turning away from my image to face the girls, mustering a smile to greet them.

"You good?" Rachel asks, concerned.

"Yeah, I'm good," I lie. What the fuck did I just do? My head begins to spin—it's either my nerves or the drugs. Glen would die if he knew, he can never find out about this. I contemplate my bad choices, I realize it took more courage for me to try karaoke than cocaine.

Maxine cheers, "Let's get some more tequila, bitches!"

Yes, tequila. I need to wash down the guilt—lots and lots of tequila.

CHAPTER 19

Walking through the past.

~IH

I would recognize her long dark-brown hair anywhere. I beam with joy and shout from across the baggage claim of the airport, "Allie, you're here!"

She was visiting me for our final spring break. Our school breaks didn't line up (mine was a few weeks ago), but I was treating hers as if it were my own. In order to function this early, I started with a strong cup of coffee and a splash of whiskey—the way I prefer to take my coffee. It's been a long time since I woke before the sun. This hour is usually only seen if I were already up from the night before.

"Senior year, baby! How is this possible? We are going to be done with school forever in less than a month!" I begin to feel more awake from the excitement of our reunion.

"I know, right, it's crazy!"

"Gosh, I've missed you, Iris!"

"The feeling is mutual! I have lots of fun adventures for us while we play catch up."

I burp unexpectedly, "Excuse me!" A cinnamon flavor permeates my mouth, I swallow hard to push it away. I've lost my appetite for tequila, the taste of cocaine, and lines I thought I would never cross. I've switched to whiskey with a bold spiced flavor unlike tequila. Plus, it pairs well with coffee, which feels appropriate for the first day of vacation. "My sorry body isn't used to being up this time of day."

"You should, mornings look good on you!"

I ponder the shot of Crown after Glen left the house, I don't know how people do mornings on coffee alone.

First stop on the list was a graveyard tour in the Garden District, one of my favorite touristy attractions. I've never been on a real tour, but I've overheard stories being told from the past. It's easy to miss out on the local stuff when you're a local. I like to walk through for inspiration, a nice place to stroll on my way home from the gallery.

The wiry grass struggles to hold its green color, showing defeat in paler yellowing-brown patches. Skinny cracked sidewalks, occasional narrower sections from plots over-measured cutting into the walkways. Elaborate marble headstones mixed in with less ornate markers lined side by side. Plots of family or friends going back many generations, sometimes with intentions for future loved ones. I often think of Wesley and Sean, I feel closer to them on hallowed ground. It's serene equally with no one and everyone around.

I turn to Allie, "Do you want me to grab us some coffees from across the street before it starts? Chicory coffee or ... Bailey's?"

"Ha, I'm not sure about the Bailey's yet, but a little chicory to set the stage."

Inside the café, the floors creak and the building smells musty—it was a lot like being in the cemetery. The line was short, thank god, because the barista was slow and I wondered if I'd make it back for the tour on time. She must have thought she was hired to host her own little ghost show, telling one long epilogue after the next.

At last my turn had come.

"Two medium chicory coffees, with room for cream, please."

"Is that all you need room for—how 'bout a splash of Amaretto?"

Amaretto sounds good, the subtle almond taste allowing me to save the Crown in my flask for later. All the girls carry flasks here, and today was a perfect day to put it to use.

Rachel gave me this flask—it's beautiful and covered in a perfect shade of fawn leather. The leather acts as a bonus, because it keeps the clinking sounds from ringing inside my purse. *OK, no Amaretto. Allie doesn't want liquor, I'll stay on pace with her.*

"Um, yeah—well, no. Just cream and sugar."

"Are you sure? You don't seem too confident."

What the heck—is she some kind of graveyard fortuneteller? The voodoo tables are usually saved for the Quarter.

"No, ma'am, I should be good."

"Should be and being are two different things. How 'bout a little something extra? I reckon you're a tourist on a ghost hunt, this makes it more exciting."

Now, I am the one holding up the line. I'd love a little and this would be a great opportunity to start off without Allie noticing—she's not used to the ways of this city. My flask's prepared but I'll have to find the right opportunities until she's ready, hopefully by noon.

"What'll it be, darling?"

I glance out the window to the cemetery's front gate. I can see a small group gathering with a guide checking her clipboard, probably for attendance.

"Sure, but put the Amaretto just in one coffee."

"You got it!"

Allie won't notice. I don't feel the need to explain to the barista that I'm not actually a tourist because I live in New Orleans. She was right about me being on break, sort of.

⁓ॐ

Our tour guide, Clara, was vibrantly authentic. Silver hairs pulled back into a once tightly wrapped bun. She was a Louisiana native with her family having Creole and Cajun ancestors dating back to the 1720s. Creole and Cajun she explained were two different things. Her stories were genuine and vivid, almost as if they were her own, like she was telling past bedtime stories from her youth. The aboveground tombs create the perfect setting to her master's degree in drama tales.

As Clara takes stage, I stare at the boldly etched names. New Orleans burials are beautiful, truly a celebration of life. The graveyards spare no expense with old school mausoleum and gigantic monuments in hopes to capture one's greatness. Clara tells us their most famous ghost is a little girl named Sarah, whose family had come to visit friends that resided in the now Garden District one summer in the 1820s. Back then, the land was mostly sugar cane fields, so when Sarah wandered away from the house and got lost, it took over a week before they could find her body in a field. Nowadays, large handfuls of unrelated people have come forward saying that they have seen Sarah. She walks through many of the Garden District houses, interestingly enough only making daytime appearances. Clara's voice is gentle and I wonder if she's personally ever seen this little girl.

She continues to another popular ghost, a man named Henri. With dark skin, hazel eye, and reddish-brown curly hair. Henri was a womanizer, with wine and cigars being a close second. It was his love affair with two of his passions that killed him. After one of his many drunken nights, smoking his cigars, he passed out. The lit cigar fell from his mouth lighting the carpet, quickly spreading fire throughout the home. Over the years, women have come forward with stories of Henri prodding and pinching inappropriately in his deviant ways. One woman even claiming he caressed her body while she was lying in bed—a pervert till the end and beyond.

My stomach turns, I envision this Henri with a grimy mustache and think of one person.

"Ugh, Henri reminds me of Jake. We could only be so lucky for him to take himself out."

"I'm surprised he hasn't had some kind of accident yet. Play with fire long enough and, you'll become Henri." I haven't thought about Jake, let alone said his name out loud in so long. But there's something nice about having a friend from your past already know a person and their story without having to explain.

"Henri and Jake would have gotten along nicely—drugs, sex, being inappropriate. Maybe they could have played together." I can almost hear his words from years ago when he told Allie and I to work at strip club. He is disgusting.

"No way, even for two repulsive males, they would notice if they were messing around with another dude!"

"Maybe, but I do know two men that have sex and one doesn't know he's with a guy. They're married and everything." I look to see Allie's eyes widen.

"What, that's crazy. How much Bailey's did you put in that cup?"

"Ha, you noticed, we're on vacation and it's Amaretto." I put on my best-surprised face—it's hard to disguise things from your best friend.

"I notice everything and yes, enjoy your stay-cation. But tell me about these fictitious married gay men you know."

"Well, I don't really know them, but Max from Rachel's salon— ya know the one who cross-dresses?"

"Yes, the wild escapades of you, Rachel, and is it Maxine?"

"Exactly. So, Maxine has a client, and he's done her hair for years. I saw her once when she was leaving. Pretty, slender, well-dressed woman in her late fifties or so. Her name is Patricia, but years ago she was a man."

"Let me guess her name was Patrick?"

"No, James, but she always loved the name, Patricia. Anyway, Patricia went through the long process of changing her gender, taking hormones, adding breasts, and turned her James inside."

"No, kahunas," Allie listens as we walk slowly, following the group in last place.

"You got it. Patricia never had any children or really even a family. When he met the love of his life, or shall I say, her life, she never told the man."

"Wait, so James, now Patricia, fell in love with a man."

"Yup."

"Then got married to a man, but didn't tell the guy she used to be one?"

"You got it."

"That's crazy—no way." Allie looks skeptical, I can tell she's thinking the same implausible thoughts I had when I first heard this story.

"Well, it gets crazier. So Patricia got sick last year, after running tests, they found out she had cancer. Prostate cancer."

"Shut up." Allie stops in place and her mouth drops.

"No lie. And because of the patient doctor privacy rules, the doctors couldn't tell the husband that his wife has prostate cancer."

"Wait, so the husband still doesn't know—what kind of cancer does he think she has?"

"Who knows? Some kind of ovarian/woman parts cancer."

Allie is thrown, I can feel her pondering the details looking for a hole. "I don't believe you, that can't be true. So the doctors and nurses talk to them both about this devastating cancer and its treatments, without disclosing the type?"

"Something like that."

"I couldn't do it, be her doctor—I would totally slip up. Prostate cancer! I mean change your parts, fine, but not tell your lover?"

"Come on, Allie, let's catch up to the group. I've heard the garden homes section are the best part of the tour."

"Why bother—you've got plenty tales of your own. I could have just hired you."

"And miss out on Ms. Clara—no way."

We walk alongside the ornate mansions, the beautiful homes I'd seen on TV as a little girl. Painted in muted historically approved colors. Scattered with tall grand oaks springing from the ground around the properties, the oaks draped in swaying southern moss. The air seems to taste sweeter, like scenes from a secret garden. Almost all the homes are equipped with guest homes that stand one larger than the next.

"This is our dream. Glen and I want to live here one day, in the Garden District." I search Allie's face for approval. This is the most serious conversation I've ever had with her about my future with Glen, actually my future with anyone.

"Wow, business must be good!"

"Well, not that good. He's been saving for a while though—we've both been saving. His parents want nothing to do with it, they're still a little bitter *Fievel* hasn't gone west."

"That's awesome, a house—a mansion—you deserve it, Iris!"

I swallow down some guilt, feeling less worthy in myself than usual from recent adventurous behaviors. Deserving is a strong word.

"Don't get too excited, so far we could probably afford that small garage." I point to the only house on the block that has a dilapidated shed, overgrown with vines from its overgrown garden.

Allie laughs then says, "So a house? That's pretty serious."

Here it comes, I was wondering when she was going to press for details. "What other plans have you guys talked about?"

With a snarky tone, "Oh, ya know, marriage, three kids, white picket fence around our Garden District shed. Right after I open my own art studio, which by the way is actually happening later this year, after graduation!"

Allie screams with excitement, "Really, yay! Well, not the shed part, but Iris—that's huge! And your own studio—I've never heard you talk like this before … let's see, Mrs. Iris Hawthorne. I like it."

"And I'd happily take it, better than having ties to Vera." Like a past secret I'd rather leave in the closet.

We continue as caboose in the group, missing almost all the tour details. My drink has long been gone, but my hand clings to the cup like a security blanket.

"How's she doing, Vera?" Allie asks.

"Oh the same, living out her adolescence. Who knows, I barely hear from her." I find myself longing for the flask filled with Crown. I wish part of the trip included a stop at bar. It's been a while since I've had to talk in detail to anyone who actually knows Vera. It feels strange—I can usually cover family background with a simple, she's busy or it's complicated type of answer. Satisfying the random outside interests, but not with Allie. I clear my throat "The girls are good. April's still working and Janus is doing better, again."

My hands begin to flutter, it's a strange shake, but I'm not cold. I stare at the shake in awe—must be nerves. I need a shot and some privacy from Allie. She isn't used to the ease of the South and I don't want her to worry. I notice a public garbage can one street over, at a trolley line station.

"Hang on, I'm going to toss my coffee cup," I call out to Allie as I find myself jogging to the can. I feel every step, as I dispose of the used cup, taking a quick secretive swallow from my flask. I've gotten good at being discreet, I return to her with my hands inside my pockets and shallow breath.

"Are you OK?" Allie laughs, "You know I specialize in nutrition. I could make up a plan for you, maybe add an exercise routine?"

"Funny, but no thank you."

"OK, but what do you mean by Janus being good again, what happened?" Allie presses back in to our conversation.

"Nothing really unusual. Her catheter causes infections, she gets UTI's easily. Her weakened immune system makes things more dangerous."

"That's terrible."

I close my eyes for a moment recalling my panic a few weeks ago when I couldn't reach her by phone. Janus always answers, I'm constantly telling her how nice it is to call her, because she picks up every time. Janus jokes that she has nowhere else to be. April filled me in after she left Janus in the hospital, April's phone had died and basically Janus was given a long list of antibiotics.

Janus tries to get used to it, although I'm not sure she ever will, or anyone ever does. I can feel heat climb inside my body, I need a drink, a real drink, but I keep talking. "She has a great nurse, Janus loves her nurse."

"That's good—well, don't forget if you ever need anything."

"I know, Allie, thanks."

We walk further and listen to Clara tell us the who's who to some of the beautiful homes, a Saint's football player, a recognized author, and other Hollywood celebrities.

"Sooooo, do you think Glen will be popping the question any time soon?"

"Allie!"

"What? You guys talk about buying a mansion together, marriage seems likely." Allie is giddy with the topic. I have to admit it's a much more pleasant one.

"I don't know, not anytime soon. I still have to finish school and get my gallery running." She smiles, but I can tell she wants more, "What about you—you and your boyfriend getting married soon?"

Allie laughs, "No way, not anytime soon, I don't know about him sometimes. He can be a little over the top, but I love how creative he is, he reminds of you sometimes."

"Gee, thanks, glad your over-the-top boyfriend reminds you of me!"

We both laugh and stroll onward. *I place my hand inside my bag to feel the flask and wonder when our next stop will be.*

CHAPTER 20

The build of inception.

~IH

In 1872 the American Athletic organization founded the NOAC. Making it the second-oldest athletic institution of its kind and a major draw for Glen's attendance, his first stop before slaving away at the office every day. The exclusive gym has a presence of importance—the physical building and its members. It's intimidating—a séance I'm still getting used to, the distinction of people and the physical activity.

The athletic mecca houses plenty of equipment and an extensive number of exercise rooms. A brass balcony loft holds an old-fashioned boxing ring with a perfect view to the floor below featuring an Olympic-size indoor pool. Rows of giant columns stretch alongside the lengthy pool—it's like swimming through an ancient Greek romance. It's finished with a full-length rooftop basketball court and a traditional ballroom that drips with crystals hung from chandeliers. All these lovely features mean very little to me. However, I do regularly take part in one of its great amenities, the spa.

I knew with Allie's interest for a healthy lifestyle, she would appreciate such a facility. Glen was happy to hear we would be joining him, probably hoping her health-conscious way would wear off on me.

I fit in nicely as spectator to Allie's yoga class—I lasted about three minutes before opting for the steam room. Nothing beats sweating out toxins, followed with a cool shower. Then I headed downstairs to find Glen. He was climbing the StairMaster at top speed.

I walk over with pride, "I've built myself up to fourteen minutes in the sweat room."

But Glen's in the zone, he won't speak. Beads of sweat drip down his bare chest and back, he looks determined and hot.

"How long do you think you're going to be?"

The corner of his mouth turns up, as if he were winking with his lips. This is his way of acknowledging our conversation, or lack thereof. He'll be a while, I just like to attempt distraction.

"This is fun. Allie's going to meet me upstairs for our nail appointments when she's done nama-staying."

He stays focused, his eyes stare straight ahead.

"Yup, always a treat to gab when you're working out. By the way, I don't have any panties on."

"IRIS!"

"Oh there is someone in there? Weird, I thought I was talking to myself. I'll see ya in about an hour."

I head to the juice bar to kill some time. Offering juice and full bar, I glance over the specials. Daily Mean wheat grass, Life Force with kale and lime, Beet Blast with parsley, and one catching my interest called Champagne of Gods. I have a hard time accepting the Gods would like cilantro, lemon grass, and spinach in their sparkling beverages. The bar (like the rest of the gym) feels out of place, rich with elegance. Traditional furniture dresses the dark cherry floors, a room colored in amber and cognac tones with flat screens. One wall is lined with shelves covered in books, like a library instead of a gym.

I see Allie wandering down the hallway.

"Allie," she turns, looking a bit lost inside this gymnasium labyrinth. "How was class?"

"It was incredible!"

"Good, glad you liked it."

"Liked it, I would live at a place like this in NY, if I could afford the membership. I see you've completed your grueling rummaging."

"Yes, as a matter of fact, I've moved on to the lacquer and beverage session. And you're welcome, I put your name on the list for a manicure, too. What do you want to drink?"

The menu is written in perfect cursive on the black chalkboard behind the counter. Allie reads out loud. "Oh, they have wheatgrass shots … are they good here?"

"I honestly have no idea. I usually refrain from eating or drinking grass."

"It's so good for you, try one with me."

"I'd take a shot, but not with that!"

"Come on, pressed wheatgrass with an orange slice to suck at the end."

"So good—the orange is free?" My face twists like a child being told to eat vegetables.

"Here, do one with me, what else are you getting?"

"Berries and bubbles is my favorite. One of the few girly drinks I like. They use fresh berries, swirled with a sugar cane stick, and a splash of Prosecco champagne."

"Oh, heck no, I would be sick if I drank champagne right now. You really drink that after being in the steam room?"

A nervous awareness from being judged rushes over me, a feeling I've been sensing from Allie. I try to redeem myself, "I get a bottle of water, too. The berries are refreshing, they use four different kinds."

"Iris, you need to hydrate after a workout."

"I would hardly call what I do a workout."

"Still, this early in the day?"

"Sometimes I'm here in the evening," I lie, but it makes for a better case.

"I don't know—it feels strange at a gym."

"What's so strange? We're in a reinvented mansion, which happens to be a fitness center!"

"I guess, what does Glen think?"

Shit, why does she want to know what Glen thinks? It's not like I paraded my drinks around—I hope she doesn't ask him.

"He doesn't seem bothered," I lie again. He probably wouldn't mind, I try convincing myself. I pay with cash to clear the tab, seems fair since he pays for our membership.

"Sometimes I go home and paint after I leave the gym—the bubbles leave me inspired. And the brushes look great between my freshly painted fingernails."

"All right, but you're still taking a wheat grass shot with me."

"Fine, then make my bubbles a double!"

The swivel chair turns easily as I reach my outstretched hands. The nail girl files and rounds the corners.

"Allie, I cannot believe you drink that green stuff willingly. And on a regular basis?"

"Oh yeah, much worse than the stuff you seem to be drinking."

"Touché, my friend." I look down to my nails as the dust falls from the file.

"Iris, when did you start drinking so frequently?"

"Frequently, I wouldn't say frequently."

"I've been here four days and you have had morning, noon, and evening cocktails during all of them."

"I don't usually," I say, but question my own routine. *Do I really drink every day?* I haven't given it much thought. Self-conscious now towards my actions, I clarify, "It's only because you're here—I'm enjoying our vacation. Besides not everyone is a vegetarian."

Allie burst into laughter, "Your drinking has nothing to do with eating or not eating meat!" But her mood shifts back to concern, "I worry about you, I don't want to you to turn into ... Vera."

I could die—Vera? Me turn into Vera? "I would never."

"I know, maybe not that bad, but still, you should slow down a bit. I studied a whole chapter on alcoholism for one of my classes. They say it's a disease, passed on genetically or from environmental conditions."

How did this happen—are we really having this conversation? I feel so self-conscious.

"You're at a greater risk with your background and harsh situations. It's a fine line you don't want to cross."

Allie's voice is soft, non-threatening—she seems genuinely concerned for me. I sip my bubbles, but it's lost its spark—the appeal melts away with her words. I stay silent but listen.

"Just be careful, Iris."

"I know, I am careful."

I can't help but think of the many times I've blacked out and then to the time in the bathroom stall. I can almost taste the burn of cocaine dripping into my throat. But I'm nothing like Vera, I'm not out buying cheap beer or finishing handles. My subconscious feels better already. I drink top shelf and hold the love of a man with whom I have a very consistent relationship. I will be a college graduate soon. I am nothing like Vera.

I continue with my defense, "It's the city, the culture. I don't drink any more than my friends."

"Some of your friends are questionable."

Allie is beginning to sound like Glen.

"Just remember, there's a whole other world outside of New Orleans. Your body needs a break once in a while."

"I usually only drink on the weekends or if I have an exhibit, it's kind of expected. But that's all." I think of my rules, although something is telling me, I don't follow them as closely anymore.

Allie pauses and looks for the perfect nude polish, my bubbles have gone completely flat from time and conversation. We switch chairs and I feel relieved that the topic has passed. My white tips dry under the fan lamps and Allie's cuticles are pushed back. I can hear Allie's voice from behind, "A friend of mine's brother, back in New York, started drinking heavily … "

Shit, she's still on it, I had no idea she even noticed. I've never given it this much thought. I've gotten so used to Rachel and … all my friends.

She's still talking, "He lost his job, girlfriend, and became dependent on drinking. He ended up in AA and got his life back on track. Matter of fact, he just started a new business, and it's expanding nationwide next month."

She's talking about AA? I'm not that bad. I think the holistic world has warped her mind. She finishes with, "You should look into it, see what it's all about."

"Allie I don't think I need AA or anything extreme like that. I can control it when I want." My tone is firm, but I'm not angry with her—it's me that I'm annoyed with. Annoyed that this conversation is taking place. I know Allie means well, she's my best friend.

"I didn't mean to upset you. I just want you to know I'm here for you, if you ever need to talk. You've been through so much."

I forget sometimes, or try to block it out on purpose. Being with Allie conjures up images of Wesley and Sean. I look down to my French manicure under the lamp and hear Wesley's words: he liked it when girls kept up their nails. That's the reason I subconsciously notice hands polished or not, the reason I polish mine. The pain that filled me when I pulled my chipped polish away from Wesley's chest as he lay dying in the hospital. I think of Janus' agile, strong body bouncing like the tennis ball across the court. Now it's her body being tossed from bed to wheelchair with the help of her aid and large medical equipment that sits in the room. Vera and the agony I've been pulled through from her and Jake—fucking Jake. I can't think of him.

"Iris, if you ever did want to go, I'd sit with you."

Tears fill behind my lids—I close my eyes not to let them drop. I attempt to regain my composure. Allie continues, "Or we could go to a wellness camp, I know a few really good ones out west."

Now she's lost me, I blink the wetness away from my eyes. The laughter comes fast from unstable emotions, "Wellness camp … like fat camp?"

"No, you'd have to be fat for fat camp. Wellness camps or retreats are empowering for nutritional, emotional, and physical guidance. They have yoga and sometimes massages."

"Now you're talking." We laugh, Allie's the best. I've never met anyone quite as loving as her.

"You should try it, we could go together. I could use a break from the city. Who knows—maybe yoga could become part of your routine, before you polish and drink bubbles or anything else."

"I'll make a mental note and let you know if I change my mind, but I think you're reading much too far into this."

"The offers on the table anytime."

Glen was spoiling Allie and I on her last evening in the Crescent City. We were dining at the new hot spot with a full spread of impressive foods paired with different wines. I couldn't shake Allie's words, looming over me from our earlier conversation. *Does she think I'm an alcoholic?* The expensive wines were hard to swallow, they didn't hold their usual appeal or flavor. I found it sour on my tongue— instead, I stuck close to the appetizers throughout the evening.

I used caution with Allie, more so than I do with Glen, or maybe it was caution from me. I feel uneasy tonight and Glen seems off, too. *I wonder if Allie mention our conversation at the gym? What if Glen was the one who had her ask? Maybe they both think I'm an alcoholic? No, she wouldn't tell him that and Glen would never. He would have no reason, he's always gone so early and doesn't get home till late, I'm so careful around him. But why would Allie say such a thing? She doesn't want me to turn out like Vera—she really doesn't get this city. I fit in fine with my friends here. Sure Glen has thrown a discouraging look when I've indulged in a glass too many, but he's never recommended AA! For God's sakes—AA!* Glen waves to a waiter and a fancy bottle of champagne is brought to our table.

Glen raises his glass, "Tonight calls for a celebration. It's not every day we get to enjoy such good friends." Allie and I smile and she tilts her head while Glen continues, "Allie, I am always telling Iris that she needs to find more friends like you!"

Oh shit, he knows, she told him how much I've been drinking this week. "You are definitely my favorite of Iris' friends—I wish she had more like you."

"Aw, thanks Glen, I just love her!"

"Me, too." Glen and Allie lift their glass, but mine feels heavy, I push it forward and remind myself to stay present, participate.

I try to speak from the heart, "Allie, I don't know where I'd be without you."

"The feeling is mutual." We all clink our glasses together, I am exhausted from racing emotions all day.

Glen lifts his glass again with another lecture as if making a case before a judge, his words are smooth and my feelings shift back to joy, comforted with two of my favorite people.

"Since we're on the topic of lasting relationships, I have been wanting to discuss something with you, Iris."

Shit! He knows, he definitely knows.

"You are the most amazing person I've ever met. I love your carefree style, your generous heart, your witty charm and talents."

Wow, he's really laying it on thick—the ball is going to drop hard.

"You complete me, filling places I didn't even know were missing.

Changing the way I view life, your drive to persevere even through darker times. I am a better person because of you."

This is seriously intense, borderline awkward, I wish he would just jump to the chase and tell me to go to rehab already. Glen sets his glass down, stands from his chair and proceeds to bend down on one knee. He pulls a small black box from his sport jacket pocket. Cracking it open, revealing a gorgeous sparkling diamond ring, he stares back up at me.

Holy shit, he's proposing! I did not see this coming.

"Iris, will you marry me?"

Tears slide down my face quickly from the nervous emotion I've held onto all day, especially during the course of this dinner.

"Are you serious?" The diamond solitaire shines its brilliance, lighting the entire room, which I realize both dinner guests and Glen await a formal answer.

"Yes, oh my God, yes! Glen, I'll marry you!"

Allie and the rest of the restaurant cheer loudly. With her camera ready, Allie snaps pictures, while Glen stands to his feet and slides the ring onto my freshly manicured finger.

"Congratulation, you love birds!" Allie squeals.

I am jubilant, wiping happy tears, careful not to scratch my face with the new radiant adornment.

"Allie, holy crap, did you know?"

She is beaming with pride, "Yes, Glen wanted to see if you had any idea. I told him you had no clue!"

You could say that again. Definitely an extremely pleasant turn of events, I don't think I could be happier! I kiss Glen repeatedly and I wave my sparkling hand high over our heads and shout, "We're engaged!"

CHAPTER 21

Titles are powerful.
Graduate. Engaged. Boss.
The higher the success, the greater the fall.

~IH

I was folding a load of whites, the fresh linen scent of Downy permeates throughout the penthouse. Domestication and the radiant-cut diamond look good on me, the sparkle catching my eye as I pull the warm clothes from the dryer. My art studio opened quicker than I expected, and it has consumed a large portion of my time, but I couldn't be more proud. Most days I feel like I am floating and someone should pull me back down to Earth. I get to be a business owner. Selling my own work and other local up-and-coming artists. My fiancé occasionally drops by for lunch and it's just about then I have to pinch myself.

I love the way men's undershirts stack up neat. The shirts piled high like a tower of cotton perfectly in their rectangular shapes. Glen walks into the narrow laundry room twirling his wrists in circles, he pauses only to stretch his fingers back. One at a time he cracks his fingers, a trait I find him doing to release tension, usually when he is preparing for a trial. But he's not prepping for anything special right now.

"Getting warmed up to help me fold?" Glen shakes his head no and keeps his gaze to the ground. His behavior seems off, accompanying his weird finger-cracking practice.

"Everything OK?"

"Everyone's fine, I just have a lot on my plate right now." His tone is sharp.

"OK, well, I'm glad *everyone's* fine, but I was only asking about you. Should I be asking about someone else?"

"Iris, you never know when to stop. I'm under a lot of pressure right now."

Wow, I've never heard Glen talk like this, completely out of character.

"Sorry, I didn't mean to upset you. Forget I asked." I grab another shirt from the dryer to appear as busy as one can in a laundry room.

"I'm going to take a walk, I need some air. I'll be back late."

He storms off and I pondered over his peculiar behavior. Replaying the conversation as I try to figure out what he could be so upset about. I thought I heard him on the phone with his mother earlier—she's probably pressuring him again about our wedding plans.

The extravagant festivities Glen's parents have in mind for us back in Texas. Four hundred and fifty of their closest friends, family, and professional acquaintances. Like the harmonious formalities of the Westminster Abby setting the backdrop. I picture Vera full of emotion and booze stumbling down the aisle, while April attempts to tame her, missing my sweet Janus. Sadly there are many obstacles that come along with getting her and her wheelchair, her meds, and her aide across the country. My hands clam up and my chest feels tight. My thoughts and his parents are overbearing, and now, the laundry is, too.

I pull out an open bottle of red from the fridge. Glen hates that I don't put the bottles back in the wine cooler. But I like the convenience of the kitchen. The wine goes down quick, but I remain unsettled. I hate this feeling, the feeling of conflict. I sip the last drops and decide that I also no longer want to be here. I trade my T-shirt for a silk blouse, toss on a pair of pumps and head to my favorite spot.

Bottega—my place, my sanctuary, my home away from home, where I go to commemorate achievements and/or let worries slip away. Glen and I are regulars, I'm more consistent than him, since I have the luxury of flexibility.

The front wooden doors are heavy with fancy brass pulls. I walk through the lobby to the receptionist post, but veer to the left and slip into the lounge. Unnoticed by the remainder of the swanky restaurant. I liked the relaxed ambiance of the bar scene, the amber glow from the dim lights. Half-circle leather booths line the perimeter of the lounge with a few highboy tables speckled in-between. One cherry oak rectangular bar sits in the center of the room, like a stage with crushed velvet stools. That's where I sit. Perched high, looking over the grounds from my chair. Observing the action of the bartenders practicing patience as they fill glasses for the customers. I recall the days not long ago, when I was on the other side.

My newest drink of choice, Moet and Chandon Rose. I love it as a cocktail with a splash of Elderflower. Its salmon hue sparkles from the long sleek glass. Successfully bottling the taste of vintage in a liquid format. The bubbles caress the back of my tongue, warming my belly and cheeks. The Bottega servers know my art, face, name, and more importantly … my drink. Even when the lounge is bustling with people, standing room only, I simply slide my drink beyond the invisible line across the bar and my once empty glass, no longer is.

I sip and sip and sip and find the sensation awakens my mouth less. Like a science experiment with too much baking soda, losing the volcanic action. I don't remember when or how, but I find myself back home on the balcony, resting in my chair. My vision and thoughts blur back into the evening. The awkward conversation with Glen before he left, I think that was tonight—it must have been. I try to remember how I got home from Bottega, but I am blank. I have nothing, but I do have this glass of white in my hand. I take a swallow—chardonnay, good choice. Although deep down I wonder if I can really tell the difference. How terrible to think such a thing of my own self. My mind is totally fucking with me, disapproving messages and lack of memory.

Just then I hear the front door shut, Glen's home. I must have missed him walking through the garden, but I'm also missing part of my night. I have to pull myself together. I take a final swallow, slide the door open, and step into the living room. He still seems conflicted, but he's calm.

"What's going on, Glen? Something is definitely wrong."

The seven-mile stare is not frequent to his face.

"Glen, talk to me. I'm here for you, whatever it is, we can get through it together."

"I have to leave town for a little while, Iris."

"OK, why are you leaving?

"I just got a call from my mother and I have to go help my parents."

I knew this was his parent's doing, they must be spreading the wedding plans on thick. Glen continues, "I have to help them find my sister."

"Sister, what sister?" *What the heck is he talking about, he's an only child.* "Where do you have to go to find this mystery sister?"

"I have a sister, Iris. She's not well, she's lived most of her life between boarding schools, psychiatric hospitals, and apartments with the promise that our family has little interaction—her request. My parents agreed, as long as she stays medicated. She hasn't picked up her meds and her roommate said she hasn't been home for days. I have to find her, I have to make sure she's OK."

⁓ᵇ

I can feel my blood pressure rising, my hands are clammy holding the empty wine glass. What the fuck just happened? This so much information, I don't know where to begin.

"Glen we have been together for almost four years, we are engaged to be married. It never occurred to you to mention that you have a sister!"

He exhales slowly as he contemplates pondering his next move. I can tell he is trying to find the words to redeem himself.

"How could you lie about being an only child, why? Do you not trust me, do you think I would judge you?"

"No, nothing like that."

Heat sweeps through my body. I am uneasy on my feet, so I sit on the couch setting my glass to the table. "What else have you been lying about?" *I feel like I don't even know him. Like my whole life, my whole adult life is uncertain.*

"Iris, wait, I can explain."

"Explain, explain that you have a secret sister? Our entire relationship, I have talked about my sisters and how close we are. They are my world. At any point, you could have mentioned, 'Hey, I have a sister, too. I like her, I don't like her. I don't give a shit'— bringing her up would have been nice!"

He looks down, I can tell he hadn't taken into account the importance of my own sisters, hiding them would be inconceivable, my holy grail. Even Vera and the complications that surround us with our strange mother/ daughter relationship, I would never dismiss her pure existence.

"Iris, I am so sorry. I've wanted to tell you. I've been telling this version for so long, I guess I started to believe it myself. I know you're upset, but that was never my intention."

I am silent while I stare at the empty glass. I need a drink—this is way too much, but I can't stand up, so I let him continue.

"I love my sister dearly, but it's complicated. My whole life my parents have been hiding her, uncertain with what to do with her. They can fix almost any problem and if they can't, they usually can find someone who can—but not her. I was very young when they sent her away to boarding school. I used to walk into her bedroom hoping she would be back, but she never was. She switched around through different academies until she was fifteen."

Glen's eyes had become glossy, I feel bad for him, but mostly for his sister. A young girl shelpt off, deprived of parental guidance and love. The loss Glen must have felt from missing a sibling. I was still angry, but interested.

"She was diagnosed with a severe case of bipolar schizophrenia. She has spent most of her life switching back and forth to different private faculties and hospitals. Nothing changes, not permanently. She'll do really well—take her meds, and collect an array of friends and degrees. She's fascinating, incredibly kind, and smart. She has a background in the arts."

Glen sentences become choppy, I can hear the heartache through his words. He sits on the other side of the couch with one cushion in between us.

"Then she takes a break from school or jobs and her medicine. She has to go back to the hospitals and treatment centers—she ends up under forced admission. You can't love someone to health, you can't cure mental disorders, it doesn't matter how many degrees."

"That sounds terrible, Glen. I'm so sorry you've had to go through this, but why didn't you tell me?"

"My parents don't know how to handle her. She's become an embarrassment, hunting down their delusional daughter that sometimes gets into trouble. They stopped talking about her years ago and asked that I do the same. At some point, I was put into conversations as an only child and it started to feel real, normal, like it was the truth."

I reach my hand across the cushion and hold his, both of us warm.

"I never meant to keep it a secret this long—I just didn't know how to bring it up and now she's missing."

"Well, you need to go. Go find your sister. I can let this all sink in."

He nods, and I squeeze his hand tightly.

"We're going to get through this, but we have to be honest with each other, if we want this relationship to work."

He nods again and I slide closer to him. I am still mad, but I can feel his pain—it is greater than my disappointment.

"She is sick and needs your help. I would do anything for my sisters, so you go find yours!"

CHAPTER 22

Water doesn't mix with fire and I fear I am both.

~IH

Glen got a flight out to Portland early the next morning, where his older sister lives. Her name, I found out was Carolyn, and she certainly sounded fascinating. She worked as a curator at the Portland Art Museum. Holding great responsibility and incredible amount of knowledge to the many historical artifacts and touring exhibits, along with three master's degrees in art history, archeology, and political science.

Carolyn had a formal contract with her parents, allocating her to financial help in exchange for consistent medication and doctor check-ins. The parents were contacted when she skipped her psychology appointment and was not responding to phone calls. The plan was for Glen to go to her apartment to look for clues, possibly post-it notes, for which she was apparently famous, to see if anything made sense as to her whereabouts.

I wrestled with sleep and stayed in a funk well into the afternoon, bringing on *Law and Order* episodes. Paying extra attention to the missing person's programs for ideas. I noticed my phone lighting up from the coffee table. It was Rachel, again. I had a dozen missed calls from her since last night, this time with a voicemail. I pull some energy together and listen.

"Oh my God, Iris, you have to call me back right away! I was stabbed in the back, literally. Call me right away, it's an emergency!"

I think I'm going to need to have a conversation with Rachel about the word "literally." But then again, coming from Rachel, you never know.

"What's going on, Rachel?"

"Oh, Iris," she sobs into the phone, "Mark cheated on me."

I didn't dare ask when she and Mark got back together—last I knew they were off, but it doesn't mean this week they were.

"Rachel, honey, when? How do you know for sure?"

"That's the best part. He cheated on me with, wait for it … Beth. Fucking Beth!"

"That's terrible, Beth! She's your friend."

Despite the fact that I've never really cared much for Beth, I can imagine how upsetting it would be to get cheated on. Especially with someone who's your friend.

"She *was* my friend." She cries harder into the phone. "I can't believe she would do this—I trusted her."

It sounded awful. Losing trust. A feeling I too am struggling with at the moment, but with Glen hiding his sister.

"How did you find out?"

"Beth was sending him naked pictures, some of which she must have been taking while they were in action. That bitch!"

"Ah, so you saw them having sex?"

"Well, I saw her naked ass bent over, and her mouth on … " She stops to blow her nose, I can hear the ugly cry through the receiver.

"So I gather, he admitted it—right?"

"Fuck, yeah, he did. I made him tell me everything. They've been seeing each other for almost four months now! Apparently the first time they got together, we weren't. But then when we got back together, they never stopped."

"Rachel, I'm so sorry."

"Fucking whore. Anyway, I need a drink, can you meet me?"

I look down to my sweatpants, then to the clock reading 3:45pm.

I notice the hunger pains in my stomach from not eating or doing anything all day, plus I could use a drink, too.

"OK, meet me at Drago's, I need some food."

"Sure, but I think I'll drink my calories today."

"Can you be there in an hour? I probably should change from bum."

"Yeah, one hour, but I'm going as is. Dressed with dark circles and heartache."

I decided not to address Rachel's overly dramatic expression. I was pulling myself together when I got a call from Glen. He had arrived safely in Oregon after his four-and-a-half-hour flight. Glen had been contacted by one of his sister's old friends, Janie.

Glen explained Janie's story. Janie and Carolyn had become friends during an extended stay at a prestigious psychiatric hospital. I learned that Janie was being treated for anorexia and a suicide attempt. She had been battling an eating disorder from the ripe age of twelve when she hit a low point and was placed on feeding tubes. Which was when her enthusiasm to eat and live left her completely and she decided it was time to die. She attempted an extremely painful death by infection and stopped cleaning her feeding tubes to cause a more sympathetic exit. After suffering with the infection for almost a month, she got impatient and followed up with a bottle of pills. It wasn't until she was sent to the psychiatric center that her family learned her feeding tube infection was actually self-inflicted.

After a year of treatment, Janie left the facility, graduated from a finishing school, and went on to become a motivational speaker. She shares her story and offers encouragement to others who struggle and has always remained a friend to Carolyn.

Glen's voice charges through the speakerphone. "So Janie told me that Carolyn called her and asked if she could crash at her place."

"Good, you found your sister!"

"Not exactly. Carolyn is definitely off her meds. When Carolyn arrived at Janie's, she kept talking about an invasion over the water. Janie got my sister to sleep, but when she woke up this morning, Carolyn had already left without her phone. Janie went through her contacts and called me to let me know what happened."

"OK, so where do you think Carolyn went?"

"Well for starters, Janie lives in Seattle. There's no flights tonight, so I rented a car and I'm driving up now."

"Seattle, wow! How far is that from Portland?"

"About three-and-a-half hours, but I think I can make it in three. I've got to find her—I don't want her wandering the streets through the night."

"OK, be safe. I want you both to get home."

"Me, too, Iris. Thank you for your support."

I walk inside Drago's, which connects to the Riverside Hilton Hotel. It's brightly lit and packed with people. Rachel's wide-frame sunglasses cover most of her face and she chooses not to take them off, as we find a seat along the countertop. Giving us a perfect view to the kitchen's open flames and the barrels of garlic butter. The tub of savory butter is poured over their signature dish, charbroiled oysters, before being tossed into the fire.

We start with whiskey and a dozen charbroiled oysters each.

"Glad to see you're eating." I turn my head to Rachel sitting on my left. I wonder if she plans to wear her sunglasses the entire time, although I really don't care. We both have bigger things to worry about.

"I wasn't hungry on the phone, but it's hard to sit here and smell garlic and parsley without indulging," said Rachel. "I'm going to be on that skinny and hot girl diet tomorrow, and he is going to wonder what the fuck he was thinking, jumping to Beth."

I laugh, "Rachel, you already are skinny and damn fine, if I may add."

I can see the corners of her mouth turn up in a smile.

"You think I'm fine?"

"No, I said damn fine! Come on, sip up, I've got to tell you some things, too."

I fill her in on all the crazy details from the last forty-eight hours of my life. She lowers her sunglasses to the countertop, as if taking them off would somehow change the reality.

"That is some shit, Iris! How the heck have you sat there and not said something?"

"Rachel, you're upset. I mean, I am, too, but you just seemed emotionally more unstable." I poke at her sunglasses sitting on the counter and laugh.

"I didn't think Glen had it in him, a man of mystery. Welcome to the dark side, Glen!"

She lifts her whiskey to cheers, but I do not meet my glass to hers.

"Rachel!"

"What, it's not that bad. You could have found out he's been cheating on you … with your friend."

I look at her sympathetically. She says the words sarcastically, but her eyes fill with tears again. It's too soon for jokes, even if it's her punch line.

I proceed, "I know. It's just I thought we were closer. I thought we told each other everything."

"Well, not for nothing, but did you ever tell Glen about your mother's DUI a couple months ago … her second—or was it the third?"

"No, but that's different. It's just another stupid mistake, of *hers*. And it's not like I've hidden Vera's entire existence, just some of her stories."

"Whatever you want to tell yourself, but I bet it's the same feeling Glen has, a feeling he's been taught. Shame. This is all he knows, hiding her."

"I guess."

"Everyone has some shit in their closet—to be honest, I was starting to worry about Glen, like he's *too* perfect, you know. The kind that snaps one day and kills you in your sleep."

"And I thought I was obsessed with criminal TV shows."

"OK, maybe not that extreme, but my point is, he's fine and he was doing what he thought was best. Most importantly, he loves you."

Now my eyes fill with tears. I think to Vera's DUI that I have avoided in telling Glen, the many secretive stories from my youth that I have avoided sharing.

Rachel orders us another round of whiskey tonics. Its rich golden taste is as comforting as its warm color. I swallow a large gulp, clearing my pallet from the thick butter that seems to have coated my mouth.

Truth is, when I'm brave with myself, it's not Vera, or Glen's secret sister that bothers me. A strange feeling comes over me, one I've been trying to shake since Allie's visit. My own conscience turns against me and repeats Allie's concern–she doesn't want me to turn into Vera. Her nagging words circle my head like an unwanted guest. *Should I check out an AA meeting? Maybe I do drink too much—could I be an alcoholic?* But I don't ask out loud or maybe I'm scared of the answer. Or maybe by saying it out loud, it could be true. Questions that I can't take back after it leaves my lips and enters the universe.

I drain the remainder of my drink just in time to see another placed in front of us, forgetting Rachel told the waiter to keep them coming. I stare at my empty glass leaving the counter and then to the full one placed before me. It's our third, or is it fourth? No, we had shots before the oysters came, two of them, so technically—

fuck it, I don't know. We're both dealing with serious issues, broken trust. Anyone in my shoes would drink a lot with these cards. I'm an engaged, successful artist and business owner ... who moonlights as a drunk in the evenings. *Fuck, no, that's not true—or is it? Where is this coming from?*

Maybe it's the comfort of Rachel—she's just like me. With the whiskey still burning the back of my throat, the words sneak out.

"Rachel, do you ever wonder if we drink too much?"

"What? Iris, please."

"No really, do you think *I* could be alcoholic?"

She sets down her fork, grabs her napkin, and wipes away the grease from her face. "Listen, do I think we drink more than the average person—maybe. Do I think we're alcoholics? No, no, I don't. We're just people who know how to have a good time."

"So it never crosses your mind?"

"No, Iris, we both know about alcoholics first-hand. When you start punching holes in the walls, then we'll talk. Where is this coming from anyway?"

"I don't know, I've just been thinking about things." Rachel feels safe, free from judgment. Or maybe I just wanted reassurance.

"Maybe it's the stress from the wedding planning or lack thereof. I wrack my brain trying to figure out all the logistics. I wish there was a way to just be married and not have to do the formal crap."

"Y'all could elope."

"Elope? That sounds like a dream, Glen's parents would never go for it."

"Screw his parents, look what they did to his sister, sending her away. What the fuck do they know?"

Rachel actually makes a lot of sense right now, given the situation. But deep down, I know they're sweet, caring people who didn't make the best decision. I'm familiar with poor parental choices. I don't want to let them down, but I don't want to start our marriage off on the wrong foot.

Rachel finishes clearing her plate and both our drinks. My eyes are heavy and my body slumps into my chair.

"I'm whipped, time to go home and pass out. Maybe when I wake up, it will all be a dream."

"Sleep no, come on! Glen's out of town, you're coming with me, so I can work all my anger out."

"Tonight? No way, Rachel I'd sleep here if it were acceptable."

"I've got a better idea."

"No, I'm going to bed."

"Iris!"

We paid the bill and I found myself following Rachel to her car parked in the garage. She had to grab something out before we called a taxi. I went half-thinking I could convince her to head home, but intrigued as to what could make things better.

"Get in." Rachel's car beeps as she opens the door.

"I'm not riding anywhere with you, Ms. Crown Royal."

"Shut up, we're not going anywhere. Just get in the car."

I get inside Rachel's Red Rover Corolla, or simply Red Rover, as we liked to call her and sit in the very worn passenger seat. Rachel ruffles through her bag.

"Ah, ah! This should do the trick."

She holds a pack of Marlboro's, although it is not cigarettes that she pulls out. Instead she has a small bag of cellophane with white powder. A lump seems to be stuck in my throat.

"No, I can't, Rachel."

"Oh, now you don't want to—you were pretty confident last time. This will help, we both need an upper right now."

She was right about that, something to lift me up was appealing. But, no, I'm not going to be one of those people.

"I can't Rachel, I need to be ready if Glen calls—he's a real mess right now."

"Well, I can't think of anything better to get you ready. Otherwise, you're just going to pass out—you said it yourself. Come on, this will help snap you out of it."

I watch as Rachel flips the lid of her broken center console, placing it into her lap. "I was so pissed when this thing broke at first." Rachel was focused yet calm, like she could do this in her sleep. "But then I realized it made for a perfect tray."

The tray has four screw holes in the corners, littered with dustings of weed and remnants of other powders. A drug dog would go berserk with her car. She opens the bag and gently shakes the powder into the tray. Grabbing her credit card from her wallet, she presses quickly in a chopping motion through the pile and forms two lines. Looking back through her wallet for a dollar. I can't stop staring, not even to blink, like being under a trance. It's a process I've never seen in person (making lines), just in the movies.

"Shit! All I have are ones—got anything bigger?"

"What?"

"Oh, come on, Rachel, it's better to use large bills—they're less circulated. Less germs."

"So now you're worried about germs?" I question, but find myself searching through my wallet, grabbing a crisp hundred dollar bill.

"Damn girl, this is perfect!"

Rachel rolls the bill into a thin straw-like shape and holds one end to the line on the tray and the other to her nose. I look around the parking lot nervously, but I don't see anyone. In a fairly quick motion, I watch as the powder vanishes up the bill. Rachel throws her head back and coughs—a lot.

"That's the shit" More coughing "Here, Iris, your turn."

She hands me the bill. Strangely, I grab it just as naturally as the last time I swore it off. This line seems more intense. I said I wouldn't make the same mistake again, but the touch of the curled bill brings other feelings to mind. It's not like I haven't done it before—nothing bad happened last time. I thought about Glen and how disappointed he would be. Screw it, he's playing search party in Portland, no Seattle, for a sister he's never bothered to mention. The pain of lost trust punches me back in the chest, to my heart.

I look back over to Rachel, "Hand me the tray."

"Atta girl!"

The dollar bill becomes loose and I watch as Rachel re-rolls it for me.

"You'll want this tight," she says as she places the bill back in my fingers.

I glance around for people in the parking lot once more. There is no one. I bend toward my lap and the tray. The white line disappears, along with my will power.

CHAPTER 23

The world changes when my eyes meet yours.

~IH

I wake early the next morning in sweat. I could see Rachel's body draped over my couch through the open door to my living room, still asleep. My eyes attempt to focus, but my vision is blurred and so are my thoughts. I am blank from the night before. Another blackout, something I'm getting used to. A tickle reaches my nose and I sneeze. I can feel the burn from cocaine wash over me, I liked it better when I didn't remember.

What the fuck is wrong with me? A few moments from the night flash though my mind, escaping the blank blackness. Coloring in the night with shades of gray. Oysters, cocaine, casino, and fuck it, I'd rather not fill it in. I look to my phone and see a message from Glen. Shit, Glen's still in Portland, no Seattle, and he's looking for his sister. It's so early and it's only earlier in Seattle. I decided to wait to call Glen, I don't want to wake him if he's sleeping. Heat fills my body and I can feel a droplet of sweat drip down my chest.

I pull the duvet away from my body—I am drenched, as apparently more than one droplet has dripped. It must be ninety degrees in here. I stand to my feet and walk over to adjust the thermostat. My hand shakes as I reach for the buttons. I stare at the trembling in my fingers in awe. I'm certainly not cold, the shaking is strange and unintentional. I watch closely, unable to steal away from the movement, as if it were someone else's hand. I trace up the fingers with my eyes, to the palm, past the wrist, and above the elbow, to the shoulder of my body. It is mine. My arm. My hands. Shaking. I look back to the thermostat—it reads seventy-two degrees. This thing must be broken, but I fear it is not. The sweating increases as I ponder the shakes. *I* am broken. I am an alcoholic.

Fuck it, no I'm not. I'm in the middle of a crisis. Life is fucking hard and this is a crazy situation, anyone would drink in the middle of this. I can't deal with this right now, I need to get a little glass of wine to clear my head.

I walk quietly past the couch with Rachel to the kitchen and open the refrigerator. There's three bottles of wine open, the two red are almost gone, while the white is filled to the top of the label. White should be the most refreshing for this early hour, although it may be the most appealing, because it has the most inside. I pull the cork out and drink some straight from the bottle. It's too hot in here to search for a glass and I don't want to wake Rachel. I pause to catch a breath of air before returning the bottle to my mouth. My lips hold the thick bottle tightly as my hand lightly shakes the liquid out. I sip until the bottle is drained. I toss the bottle to the trash, as if it never happened and walk back to the bedroom to finish my sleep.

Rachel is gone when I wake. It's already eleven thirty, so I'm sure she went back to her apartment to get ready for work. This day feels so long already, I could go for supper instead of breakfast or lunch. Shit, I need to call Glen, see how he is doing. I should shower first, wash away the film of dirt I feel covered in. I would love a steam room right now. Sweat out everything from the inside. There's no way I would walk into the NOAC looking like this.

I grab three aspirin and a bottle of water before heading to the shower. I shut the bathroom door and crank the hot water as high as it can go. The shower puffs up in minutes with smoke—it would scald my skin if it touched me. I lower the temperature a bit and step in, sitting in the back on the built-in stool. My head lowers and I watch the things I hate about myself drip out of me. This is it—I'm done living like this. I'm going to stop it all, cold turkey.

The water rushes over my feet. Quietly in my head I think, *God, if there is a God, I'm starting my life over today. I promise I'll never drink again.*

I stay in the shower for nearly twenty-five minutes before stepping onto the bath mat—I feel like new person. I tell myself, I am not going to drink, and I believe it. I put on a T-shirt dress and comb my wet hair into a low bun away from my face. Feeling confident and fresh, I decided I'm ready to call Glen.

"Hello," His voice is raspy, like he's been awake all night.

"Glen, how's it going?"

"Iris, I'm sorry—I wanted to call, but I didn't get in until late—or was it early? I didn't want to wake you. I didn't think you'd be in the mood to talk to me."

"Don't beat yourself up, nobody's perfect." The words are suffocating in my chest as I say them. I swallow hard and try to continue, "Did you find your sister?"

"Surprisingly, yes. I found her last night."

"That's great, where was she?"

"She was wandering along the walkway near Pier 57. She staged herself as a fortuneteller besides Pikes Place Market."

"What, a fortuneteller, really?"

"Unfortunately, yes. She had a bucket for tips with a lot of takers. She's always had a creative mind, plus her artistic historical background—Carolyn's a natural storyteller. Mix that with the schizophrenia and she becomes a fortuneteller, or at least that's what she and the onlookers believed."

"Wow!" I can picture it, her and her stories. I visualize her wearing a loose flowing dress, probably scraping her toes. I suppose she has long sandy brown hair, maybe like her mother's. Her eyes, a piercing light blue, like her brother Glen. Telling stories with ease, a trait common to their family, another wordsmith. Captivating her audience with details.

"She made a ton of money, I just feel bad it took me so long to find her. Anything could have happened to her. I could never forgive myself."

I listen to Glen and feel a whole new meaning to *Sleepless in Seattle.*

"You did the right thing and you found her, you should be proud of yourself."

"I don't know about that, I'm not proud of keeping her from you."

I let the phone go silent for a moment and take in the apology. It feels good to have someone say words that they mean, and I can tell that he does.

"My parents are flying in this morning—we're all meeting at the hospital."

"Good, they should be there with you and for her."

"Yeah, I'll probably stay a couple of days before I head back. I want to make sure she transitions OK. She's usually confused for a little while when she's been off her meds."

"I bet."

"I love you, Iris, and thank you for understanding."

"I love you, too, Glen."

"And I promise no more secrets. I don't want anything to ever come between us."

"Yes, no more secrets," I promise. Assuring myself that we both mean from this day forward. Starting *today* we share everything and I feel better about the promise knowing I won't be drinking or doing cocaine ever again. We hang up the phone and I repeat the words out loud, this time just for me, "No more secrets."

Glen got back to New Orleans Tuesday evening, but took the remainder of the week off work to decompress from the wild goose chase. The mental drain and pressure he placed on himself had exhausted him. However, I was feeling alive, better than I had felt in a long time. I hadn't drank since the night with Rachel, well, technically the next morning, but nothing has entered my body since I made my promise.

I crawl across the bed to Glen still sleeping, hiding from the sun and the world.

"Come on, Glen, it's Friday. Time to get out of bed."

"Ugh, not yet. I'm not ready."

"Yes, you are, you've laid in bed all week. Today you need to get up." I reach my hand on his chest by his heart. His muscles are strong beneath his shirt, even without a physical workout.

"No, two days. I checked out for two days, and I'm planning on taking a third."

"Glen, come on—I hate to see you like this. The doctor's said your sister is doing good. You've got to move on, get back into life."

"I don't want to yet."

I stretch my hands lower to his waist line and feel his girth bellow his boxers. "Your body says differently."

"Oh, well, you never mentioned getting up for you, I could make an exception."

"OK, mister, but you have to promise to get up for real today. Meet me at the Gallery at noon, we'll grab lunch."

"But first ... "

Glen arrived at my studio at five minutes till noon. There was an unseasonably cool breeze in the air from a topical depression out in the bay. "Let's walk," I said as Glen headed to his parked car, "It's actually a nice day ... for August."

"Nice? The sky is gray and looks like it's going to rain."

"So let it. Who cares, do you melt?"

"No, but I'm not in the business of getting drenched."

"It will be good for you. Besides sometimes I like gray days. It feels like home, like New York ten months of the year. As for the rain, it might not."

I won and we walked. And walked and walked. We passed restaurants and churches, businesses and oak trees. I really wasn't hungry, it didn't matter, if we had time to eat. I just wanted him. I wanted Glen to feel better, to get back to his usual self. We wound up strolling into the Garden District. The breeze had blown a few leaves off their limbs and they crackled under our feet. Side by side we walked.

"I don't even know where to begin, Iris. I let you down. I want to fix things, go back to the way things were."

"Not this again—you've got to stop beating yourself up."

"I just don't want people to hurt her, I don't want *her* to hurt. She's incredible, Iris."

"I'm sure she is."

"You'll have to meet her, I know you'll like her, too. Sometimes you remind me of her, not the schizophrenia part, but your energy and creativity."

"Oh, thanks, I guess."

"Not like that, I mean y'all would have a lot in common."

They say a man marries his mother. I have very little in common with Glen's mother, but I wonder if it's his sister that makes me fit the bill, a part of me that fills the void.

"Glen, if she's anything like you, I love her already."

As we pass the homes, they become larger and larger. I think to my own sisters. I miss them so much right now, I wish they could be here, both of them. Even Vera, I miss her, too. I think of our deep conversations at the kitchen table and I long for New York. The gray clouds illuminate my memories with the overcast sky. I wonder if Vera is in her garden, or if she will jar tomatoes this weekend? I can almost taste her sauce, the acidic flavor minimalized with a pinch of sugar.

A sharp chill runs over me as a thought of Jake enters my mind. His timberland work boots and foul language. I quiver—there's no place like home, but I don't want to be there. I look over to Glen and reach for his hand, happy to be here in the Garden District with him. Everyone has something they want to keep behind closed doors and some doors seem heavier than others.

"Oh, look at that house, Glen, isn't she a vision?"

"She's something all right." We stop and pause at the foot of a typical Garden District home, but this home looks to be entering her season of winter.

"Glen, seriously."

"I am serious, it's a beautiful mansion. A mansion that looks forgotten for a long, long time. It could use some work."

Work would be an understatement. A black wrought iron fence with sharp pointed gold tips stretched across the perimeter of the corner lot, most of the gold flaked off. Overgrown vines and branches weaving in and out, cascading onto the roof of a matching carport. A few missing shutters around the many windows, one window has an orange and white slip taped to the glass. It's a massive two-story traditional Victorian style home, painted in a faded dingy tan shade.

"This home has so much potential."

"Potential! Potential to cost a lot of money."

"It needs work and, yes, probably money, but not as much money, if it was already fixed up. This could be our chance. She just needs a little paint."

Two large grand oak trees stand tall next to the driveway on the right, framing the lot perfectly.

"I don't know, Iris, it looks like this house needs more than paint. Who knows what kind of shape it's in on the inside."

"Let's look!"

"What! You're kidding. We can't break in and look."

"We're not breaking in. Come on, we can look through the windows, the curtains are open."

I walk up the creaking wooden steps of the gorgeous wraparound porch, complete with a wooden swing facing the corner-crossing street. It feels as if I were coming home. I envision myself caring a tray full of tall glasses holding sweet tea, or maybe Long Islands—no, not Long Islands anymore. Lemonade—I could be carrying lemonade over to our wooden rocking chairs, with our unborn children running around in the front yard.

The yellow door has an oval-shaped stained glass cutout in the center. I could justify buying one of those oversized and overpriced wreaths from the market with a door this big.

"We don't even know if it's for sale, Iris, they don't have a sign in the yard."

"Oh, of course, it's for sale, Glen. For the right price, anything and everything is for sale."

"You said it—the right price! Just because this mansion is a little broken down doesn't mean we could afford this place."

I peek into the window. Dark burgundy wallpaper covers the formal dining room, it's peeling around the edges of the very high ceiling. Two columns are at the back of the room with an archway that extends into what looks like a butler pantry. I rush across the porch to the windows on the other side of the house. It's the remnant of a formal living room, four boxes and a dilapidated couch that has a sheet draped over the cushion.

"Look Glen, we wouldn't even have to move our couch, they're preserving the fabric with that sheet."

"Good, because we certainly won't be able to buy any new furniture. I could say to our visitors, 'Please have a seat in our mansion on our sheet-covered couch.'"

"Could be worse, could be wrapped in visqueen."

"This place would a crime scene if they used visqueen. I'd be surprised if there wasn't a dead body inside as it is."

"You're just talking out of jealousy."

"Yes, this is jealousy."

We both step back down and head to the sidewalk.

"A girl can dream."

"Yes, dream, but this house looks more like a nightmare, my love."

You don't want to see my nightmares, but I don't say the words out loud.

We continue to walk, passing picket fences and more gorgeous homes.

"I want to keep a closer eye on my sister from now on. I don't want her to feel alone, abandoned."

"You should, you need to visit her. Carolyn deserves to see her family."

"I know—it's just, we have to finish up details for our wedding. I don't want you to feel stuck with everything."

"Ugh, the wedding—remind me, did your mother decided on a band or was it the linen vendor she wasn't sure about?" I look away as I talk, I don't want Glen to see my disappointment. This is what we want after all.

"Iris, yes the band. I thought you talked with her. Why do you sound so down?"

I attempt to perk my voice and mood. "I'm not down—it's just the wedding, I find it very intimidating. Overwhelming at times."

"Really? You haven't mentioned it, I thought you were excited?"

"Yes, well, no. I mean I am excited to marry you. I can't wait to be your wife. It's the wedding part—I never thought I'd have a big wedding. I have so much anxiety about getting my sister here, and then there's my mother, I don't want to worry about her the whole time. Sometimes I feel like it's hard to breathe when I think about it."

"Wow, Iris! You should have said something."

"I did, or I tried—I wanted to try. You and your parents seemed excited, I didn't want to spoil things."

"Iris, I could care less about having a wedding, not if it's not what you want. I just don't want you to regret not having a big wedding. Besides, maybe your mother will surprise you?"

"I doubt it. April said Vera just got another DUI."

"Really? We have a good family friend who practices up there—he could probably help. He's like an uncle to me."

"No, don't waste your time. She'll never learn, we're lucky it wasn't worse."

"I'm sorry to hear all this, I had no idea all this was going on."

"Well, it's pretty embarrassing to tell your criminal law fiancé that your mother just earned her third DUI."

Glen is silent, but not mad. There is compassion from him and the family secrets we both failed to shed light on. We continue to walk. The sidewalk squares pass like the distance we've been keeping between us—the further we go, the closer we become.

"My parents are going to be busy with this new transition for my sister. I bet they wish we could just skip the whole wedding now, too!"

I smile—it feels good to finally come clean about so much, including about my mother.

Glen stops in his tracks and faces me, "That's it, let's skip the wedding!"

"Skip the wedding … what and elope?"

"Yes, it would be perfect! Just you and me and no more planning for my parents."

"We would save so much money! But what about the deposits? We would lose those."

"It's not nearly as much as we would spend … we could look into a house, our dream house, maybe the mansion on the corner?"

My whole face lights up.

"Pretty please, Iris?" Glen laughs with an overly fake grin. I want to jump at the chance, but I want to make sure he's not going to regret this decision, and I don't want to piss off his parents. He continues, but now a little more serious, "If we don't have a big wedding, it doesn't mean we can necessarily afford to fix up that mansion. We don't know what's going on with that house. But we could look for a different house, any house. And we won't have to worry about stressful wedding plans."

I can't believe it, this is like my dream come true, marrying Glen without the hassle of a wedding.

Glen stops and runs his hands though his hair, his eyes seem extra blue with the cloud coverage, steely blue. Then he reaches his hands to mine.

"Are you sure, Glen, no wedding?"

"One hundred percent—you're sure you'd be OK?"

"I'm in, one hundred percent!" *I could cry I'm so happy.* We embrace in a hug and an abundant amount of weight lifts from my shoulders. We begin walking down the sidewalk again.

"All right, Iris, when do you suggest we do this … eloping?" Glen says this like his heart and his words could be smiling.

I look down to my watch, it's a quarter to three. "I'm free now."

"Now! You want to get married right now? You would just get married right now?"

"Yup, let's do it!"

"Holy crap, this is crazy! Iris, really, you're ready now?" I smile—he looks to be contemplating the option.

"Iris, if we catch the ferry to Algiers, we could speed up the process. They don't have the three-day waiting rule at that court house, for tourists' sake."

Oh my God, he's serious—I don't think I could be any happier!

"That's why I'm marrying you, you're good with the laws!"

"Let's do it, let's get married!"

And that is exactly what we did. Sober, happy, with both of us in jeans. After we jumped into a second line and pretended it was our own. Stopping at a bakery for a mini-strawberry-filled cake and spent the night in the penthouse hotel room of the Ritz Carlton. It was perfect, our first night as Mr. and Mrs. Hawthorne.

CHAPTER 24

Becoming anonymous.

~IH

G len was gone on business for the week and I was carefully packing up decorations. *Mr. & Mrs. First Christmas* engraved into the star-shaped crystal ornament. Glen's parents and his sister, Carolyn, came into New Orleans for the holidays. It was wonderful finally getting to meet Carolyn. She was exactly what I was picturing, a beautiful female version of her brother, only with lighter brown hair. I was drawn to her conversation and enthusiastic passion for fine art and history. She was the skeleton we weren't allowing to go back into the closet.

Everyone ate and chatted night after night, as we all sat by the light of tree. The crystal star came in addition to a substantial amount of money. Glen's mother gave it to us saying, "The ornament is for you and Glen. A keepsake for annual holiday memories, the money is for the home in which you will make them." I cried as we thanked them graciously for their generosity. We were thrilled finally to have their blessing and approval for our marriage, if only the bank could do the same with the house.

We had been waiting crossing our fingers, hoping our offer would be accepted for my Victorian dream house in the Garden District. We started the process of buying the foreclosure immediately after getting hitched, but the months have slipped by and we haven't heard anything. The money from his parents would be more than enough for us to begin the remodel, if everything goes through.

It's painful, waiting. All good things take time, but it gives me anxiety. And I haven't had anything to drink since pledging our vows and continued to avoid alcohol through the holidays with Glen's family around. It's been challenging to deal with so many changes, like I'm white-knuckling life.

I place another ornament carefully into a box, sent from Janus. She sent me an apple painted with traditional Mardi Gras colors of yellow, green, and purple. She had attached a note that said, *"Your heart belongs to New Orleans, but your soul will always be crisp from New York."* I missed Janus. I missed April and Vera. I was feeling sorry for myself, lonely. Glen would be gone for three more days, so I decided my abstinence had gone on for long enough. No one was here to govern me and a little Vue Clute would comfort me while taking the Christmas decorations down.

And so, I drank the first sip of alcohol after being dry for almost four months—it was delicious. I sipped until the glass was empty, and then I did it again and again and again. I popped another bottle, this time, Patron. I cut a lime and my finger.

"Shit!" I walk to the bathroom for a bandage. When I got back to the kitchen, my finger stung from the citrus, so I drank more. This continued for a while, but I'm not exactly sure how long.

I woke the next day and I was blank. Blank but with a pounding headache, reminding me of my behaviors before finding the empty bottles—not that I needed evidence. It looked like I broke open the vodka at some point, too, along with a bottle of cabernet. Reflections of poor choices, and the Christmas decorations still dressed the apartment. Everything sat exactly where I had left them untouched, only messier then when I started. My head pounded and my finger throbbed. I look down and see the bandage with blood soaked through. I must have cut myself deeper than I realized.

"Crap, what is wrong with me!" The words slipped out my mouth, but for no one to hear except myself. I swallowed three aspirin and decided to leave for some breakfast. This mess will be here when I get back.

I felt better after a cheeseburger with bacon, I would have opted for eggs, but they had already stopped serving items from that menu. Bacon made the meal feel more appropriate—bacon always feels right. I had plans with Rachel later and decided I was being too hard on myself about the night before. Basically, I had become a virgin to drinking after avoiding it for so long—what did I expect?

I brought home a new pack of bandages (knowing I would need a healthy amount for a while) and dressed for a long overdue girls' night. I had two more days until Glen would be home, the decorations would come down by then.

Rachel and I hit the night and bottles hard. Dancing, drinking, dancing, drinking, and more drinking. Patron, Crown, Patron, Patron, Stoli, Patron, cocaine, more Patron, more dancing. Then a little more cocaine, but I only used the powder to hang longer with Rachel. We were having an excellent time in the center of the dance floor. LMFAO beating throughout the club and my body, it felt like the soundtrack to my life.

"Now where are my alcoholics, let me see your hands up."

Rachael and I proudly shoot our hands high over our head, like filming a music video.

"I love this song," I scream over the pulsing beat. "This is our fucking jam!"

And it was true, alcohol brings forward the truth, the way it can. The truth I will deny tomorrow, but in this moment, I let go of judgment. I dance my ass off, owning the music and the amount of alcohol I am capable of consuming, especially with the aid of another key bump.

The following morning was awful. The melody still throbs through my head, the rhythm of my headache … "Everybody shots, shots, shots, shots, shots!" Then nothing, another black out.

I look over to Rachel through the open door, passed out in my living room, which is still a mess of red and green. My nose feels like it's going to drip. I grab a tissue, but find blood. My nose stings and a droplet of blood drips down to the bandage wrapped around my finger. So much for the tissue, I have blood residue on the bandage both inside and out. "What the fuck, why do I do this to myself?" I need water and a shower and a new bandage.

I stand with the water pouring over my head, *Why is this happening? I haven't had a drink in months and I'm fucking worse than I was before I stopped. I thought I just needed a break, but the time away has helped me none. I need to fix this, I need …*

Allie's voice pops into my head, her words coming back like being trapped in a car with a mosquito, "Check out AA, go to AA."

No I don't want to do that, I don't need that. But another droplet of blood slips out my nose to the shower floor, it blends with the water and I watch it go down the drain, like my spirit. Maybe. Maybe, one meeting.

I look up AA meetings in the area for the evening and decide on the farthest one away. I don't want anyone to see me, I can't let anyone know. I pull up to the address that doubles as a church. Swarms of people are walking through the parking lot, tons of them. Some are even bussed in from rehab centers. It looks like I may have picked the fucking Mecca of AA meetings. Almost everyone is talking or laughing. *I'm not sure what everyone's so happy about. I feel like they can see me in my car—they are closing in on me. I think they are going to pull me out of my car like crazy zombies or something.* My chest tightens and a shooting pain charges through my left arm. *I'm having a heart attack. No, I'm twenty-three years old, this is not a heart attack.* But the anxiety feels the same.

I look around the parking lot again and take a deep breath. This time I notice that I parked directly in front of the main entrance. Apparently no one was closing in on me after all. *What am I doing here, I have nothing in common with these people.*

I step out of my Silver 5 Series, I could choke on nicotine. The smokers are all stationed across the street with a giant orange plastic bin. It has a big cardboard label with black marker across the front, declaring "butt bucket." The smokers gather together waiting out to their final minutes before entering, soaking up every last drop of their expectable bad habit. I decided I want one, too, but not if it means I need to stand with them.

I climb three granite stairs of the church before opening one of the double doors. Two overly friendly faces wait like Wal-Mart greeters, "Welcome, we're glad you could make it!"

I bet. They don't even know me—fucking weirdoes ... but I say nothing and politely nod before heading to the back of the room. I don't want to be seen. I can't let anyone recognize me—my Lacoste hoodie isn't big enough to hide my face. I would pull the strings tight to close the gap, if it was acceptable. I'd wear a mask if it was allowed, but it's a long ways away from Halloween. My eyes, nose, lips exposed, even my loose jeans seem to be giving away my figure. Surely someone will know who I am.

I take an open seat at one of the round tables and gaze upon my surroundings. It's loud with chatter. The majority of people are already sitting while others continue arriving. A smaller group congregates by the coffee and lemonade stand, some of the people are hoarding a tray of off-brand Oreo cookies, including the vanilla flavor. I haven't seen those kinds of snacks since elementary school, the taste of Big Lots.

I continue my scan of the room—it's huge. The meeting is taking place inside the church's gymnasium. The sealed wooden floor has painted stripes for a basketball court and two undescended hoops near the celling. The hoops wait for other special events inside the room, other than fucking AA meetings.

I can't help but think, how can there be so many? So many alcoholics—there must be a hundred people in here. At least thirty large round tables and dozens of extra chairs are filled with willing bodies. I look down to my phone to avoid eye contact with these people. A brave young woman walks to the front where a podium resides, she taps the microphone.

"Hello, everyone, and welcome to Alcoholics Anonymous."

She speaks loud and clear, her voice projects across the room over the sound system.

"My name is Beverly and I am an Alcoholic."

In unison like programed robots the whole room responds, "Hi, Beverly."

Holy shit, it's a cult!

"I am the chairperson for the meeting and I would like to ask everyone to turn off their cell phones as we begin with a moment of silence, followed by the serenity prayer."

There goes my distraction, I place my phone back into my newer Louis Vuitton satchel. I probably should have changed my purse before tonight. My bag and Lacoste hoodie are probably the nicest things in this room.

The silence begins with the sounds of a few shuffling of feet and late arrivals walking to their seats. Then hundreds of voices join together including mic girl, "God, grant me the serenity to accept the things I cannot change, the courage to change the things I can, and the wisdom to know the difference."

It's powerful and less weird this time. All the voices sound like fan participation with the national anthem at a baseball game or something. I find out that the meeting is being recorded and CDs can be purchased to take home later. Back to weird—definitely fucking weird. Like I want to remember any of this shit after I leave. Do people still use CDs?

A few other people stand up and read pages from what's called *The Big Book* along with light housework announcements.

I squirm in my seat, the familiar sensation of uneasiness comes over me once again. Looking around the room, I spot a clock—we're nearing the five-minute mark. Wow, this is going to take forever. I look around some more. The guy next to me is young—even younger than me. He doesn't actually look old enough to drink, wearing jeans and New England Patriot's jersey, his hair is a little long on the sides from a grown-out fad, but nothing unusual pointing that he would be an alcoholic. He's sitting with his friend, I know they are friends, because I saw them talking earlier and they look like they would be friends. They are dressed similarly, but his friend has on the hometown's Saints jersey.

There's a group of older ladies siting at the table in front of me. I feel like they would be holding hands in a circle with or without the round table. They are excited about something—very excited. Each one of them has a decent amount of glitter and a ton of eye shadow. They're decked out with sparkling bracelets, shoes, and purses—this is a big outing for them.

Farther over, a very polished young woman sits and patiently listens to every word the chairperson depicts. She has long brown hair with soft side bangs framing her face, which is pretty, very pretty. She reminds me of Allie, but Allie would never be here, she could never have problems like this. Pretty people like Allie aren't alcoholic. Her brows are manicured and so are her nails. She looks like a J-Crew advertisement. What the fuck is that girl doing here? Maybe she's a parish member making sure the drunks don't destroy the place.

I look over to the front door as a couple walks in very late. Their arms interlocked like a trailer on a hitch. Their physical appearances seem to have morphed together like a midget walking his Chihuahua. Unless they're twin brother and sister, which by the way they are grabbing each other, I would hope not. They're probably going out after this, and definitely fucking, lots of fucking. I bet they used to get fucked up together. Do people do that? Get fucked up together, and then get sober together? No, they must have met afterwards, there's no way a couple could make it through that much fuckery.

The guy sitting on my right looks angry and washed out, like the tattoos along his arms, a man with lines around his eyes, and a black leather vest with a Rough Riders patch on the chest pocket. He should have used a good sunscreen riding his Harley. He looks about seventy, but he could be in his forties. I bet his story's good. I bet it's full of warrants, fights, lots alcohol, and lots of cocaine.

The chairperson, Beverly, is back up front with a "friend." I feel like the other girl is not her friend, they would never hang together outside this place. Beverly pulls out a plastic flat caboodle thing, like the kind I used when I was young to make string bracelets. It's filled with pirate-looking coins, but I'm too far away to make out anything for sure.

Beverly hands over the clear plastic treasure box and proceeds to the microphone.

"OK, now we're going to offer out the coins representing our sobriety. Anyone here want to be free and pick up a white chip?"

Wow, out of the gate! There's no way I'm going up there, not in front of all these people. I don't need them judging me. I've been here for almost seven minutes playing a solo game of *Guess Who*, figuring out who should or shouldn't be here, and what mistakes everyone has made. I look around and see a guy scrolling through his phone—great idea, surely I have some important messages. I glance at my inbox, but not one message. I proceed to scroll through anyways, certainly I should be handling something.

No one stands, Beverly and her friend continue going down a list.

"Thirty days?" An older guy briskly walks to the front. The women hands him a chip and offers a handshake. He whispers something to the chairlady, "That's Fred with thirty days."

Everyone claps. What the fuck, they just blasted his name over the speakers? I thought this was an anonymous program.

"Ninety days?" This time three people stand and walk to the front, two of them go in for very personal hugs, one holds onto her safe space with a handshake. Again Beverly reads off all three first names, and the crowd claps.

"One year?" Nothing

"Two years?" A heavier built guy stands and approaches the ladies, they all hug it out, he accepts his coin, and his name is announced, followed with applause. This cycle continues. The years, chips, handshake or hugs, names, and clapping.

"Five years?" If my eyes were closed I would have thought I went to BINGO tonight. I would have thought I was inside a hall with the jackpot winner. The cluster of women decked out in sparkles, stand to their feet and begin roaring with approval. A woman from the sequin party walks to the front to collect her prize, while her cronies cheer.

"That's Stacy with five years."

No surprise, Stacy went in with a hug.

At this point pretty much all the people collecting coins are huggers. I wonder if it's twelve steps, and a hug. Everyone is happy, hopeful, cheering, laughing, and hugging. No one seems to mind the attention and no one seems to be judging anyone, just me. The one who is miserable, the one who hates what I've become—a drunk and apparently someone who doesn't mind cocaine either. And the blackouts and even after my four-month break. The break, what good did it even do? I'm right back where I left off—no worse, I feel worse than where I left off. I hate it, the way I feel in the morning, the guilt. The guilt I hold until I can't stand myself so much that I drink again to numb out and to fill the void. Repeat, repeat, and repeat.

If I could just stop, I wouldn't have to worry about turning into her, into Vera. But how could it be? I have so much, my career, a husband, and a fucking offer on a mansion. It's like I'm drowning in shallow water—I just need to stand up. I'm sick, sick of this. I'm sick of myself, of my shit choices. My thoughts are interrupted with loud cheering as I hear Beverly recapping, "Thirty-four years of sobriety, thank you, Stan! Well done."

Some people are standing, the applause is strong, and impressive, like the time Stan has accumulated. Wow, thirty-four years, that's more time in sobriety than I am old. Maybe I could do it. Maybe one day everyone would be standing for me as I walk up, I'd plunge into a deep gripped hug and take my thirty-fourth coin. Stan returns to his seat as the room settles down again.

Beverly asks, "Anyone have any birthdays greater then thirty-four years?" but the room stays still, silent.

I think that is it, I missed it, my opportunity, I'll stay like this forever.

Beverly speaks again. "This is the last time I'm going to offer the very first white chip. Anyone want to stop living in their miserable ways and join us?"

I'm not exactly sure what came over me, but I rose to my feet and found myself walking up to the front of the room. With the room and my head spinning, I was suffocated with applause. I searched for the front as I walked through the labyrinth of humans, my body felt like it was carried to the chairperson.

Beverly held the white chip in hand and her arms out for a hug, I didn't mind, it was done. I allowed my body and mind to collapse into her.

She held me close and said, "Welcome."

I turn back and take my seat, my mind finally at peace, as if I truly surrendered. Maybe I did, I think that I did. The problem I've been trying to hide, mostly from myself, is lifted. This will be me—maybe I could do this sober thing. All you have to do is go to a few meetings here and there. I can handle that.

Shit! I have that art exhibit next weekend. I have to go and I always drink—it's expected. How will I make it through something like that without at least one glass of champagne? Maybe one glass wouldn't hurt. Now that I have these meetings, I could charge up on AA beforehand. I'll control my drinking, just one.

I feel the smooth circular coin between my fingers. I spin it around and around. My thumb runs over the etched triangle on the surface. No, no drinks. No drinking next weekend at the show.

Everyone here has heard my name, but an uncomfortable feeling crawls back inside. My discomfort wants me to hide, disappear—maybe my cover hasn't been blown. There could be a dozen girls named Iris here today. If I leave now, I could probably make it to the door without anyone coming up to ask questions. I stand quietly from the table and push the four-legged chair back. To my horror, the metal legs create a loud screech. At least ten people turn their heads, annoyed.

"Sorry," I whisper and the disapproving faces turn back to the front speaker. I step away from the table and slip out the front door without any more disruptions.

I didn't need to worry about the art show the following weekend, because I started the morning with a mimosa. There was a bottle left opened in the refrigerator—it was waiting for me to finish. I don't know what came over me last night. I've ended up at some strange places before, but last night's adventure may take the lead. I have nothing in common with those people. Thank God, Glen wasn't home to find out about my little pit stop. He'd probably be annoyed that I'm having a drink this morning and I would die if he knew I picked up a white chip. Ridiculous, like a chip has some special power—there was something about power last night. Oh yeah, I think it was a *Higher Power Chip*. Those crazy people need a hobby.

I must have been pretty heavy-handed with the orange juice, there's barely any champagne in my mimosa. I sip the glass down and fill it back with equal parts—I may as well just have been drinking orange juice. The stove clock read 7:05 am. Wow, it's fucking early, I can't remember the last time I was up this early. A fleeting thought hits me—most people would be drinking *just* orange juice at this hour.

Ugh, what the fuck, where did that come from? I sound like one of those weirdoes from last night. It's like they're still in my head, spoiling the taste. Taking the last sip from my glass, I decide I've had plenty of vitamin C for the day. I tilt the bottle vertical, pouring the final drops into my glass. This time, I refill with just champagne—that's the best part anyway.

CHAPTER 25

I will only drink one.
I will only drink two.
I will only drink with friends.
I will only drink alone.
I will only drink on weekends.
I will only drink on weekends and Thursdays, and sometimes
   Mondays—because they suck.
I will only drink in the evening, unless it's Friday, Friday
   afternoon.
I will only drink wine.
I will only drink liquor.
I will never do cocaine.
I will never do cocaine regularly.

~IH

We were hit hard with past due HOA fees and unpaid property taxes, but after bending over for the bank with negotiations, we finally closed on our Victorian dream. Dream used loosely (at least until the reconstruction is finished). Luckily Glen had a buddy that works as a general contractor, and he put together a crew and plans for our house right away.

We put our place in the quarter on the market to free up assets, though we didn't expect it to sell in a week. Difficult to live out of boxes, many that we didn't want to unpack, due to the dust in the air with the renovations. Existing in closed-off quarters of visqueen made rooms unpleasant, but that doesn't even begin to describe the living arrangements.

I have to wake before eight am daily to let the workers inside. It's horrible and only the beginning of a projected ten-week project, which in construction land equals about six months. I keep one special brown moving box inside my walk-in closet, camouflaged with the other moving boxes. It holds a few bottles of wine for days when my early morning doorbell rings, but just *too* early. I didn't indulge every morning, it was comforting to know it was there, should I choose. We didn't bother unpacking our glassware with the kitchen renovation starting next week and I didn't mind sipping out of the bottle—I can rough it. I would have preferred it chilled, but I thought a minifridge would give way to the hiding spot in my closet.

Glen was wrapping up a big case and wouldn't be home until later tonight. I decided to take the afternoon off to run a few errands and make our supper before the kitchen demo. The downstairs bathrooms and front half of the house was already underway.

Two banks, the art supply store, grocery store, and post office (my Mother's Day card would never make it by Sunday, but it was better than nothing). Maybe it was Hallmark's catchy phrases looming in my mind, but I missed my mother. I missed Vera especially during cooking preparations, the fond memories with her in the kitchen.

The grocery store was surprisingly busy—I suppose that's where it's happening on a Thursday afternoon. Filled with fresh-delivered produce and moms pushing carts, little ones anticipating their prize—a free cookie at the bakery. I get it, I love grocery shopping, the cheese and wine section. I love when they have samples and today there is no shortage of vendors. Testing different varieties before perusing the aisles, the best way to shop.

I arrive back home and notice a table saw set up out on our front porch by the workers. I grab as many bags as possible to avoid passing through the debris multiple times, but I still need to make a second trip. Feeling accomplished from all the tasks I've completed, I decide to treat myself before venturing back out to the car. I open a new Cakebread chardonnay. It's nice, smooth, but a little warm, like the wine in my bedroom. I set the warm bottle in the fridge and open a different white already chilled—much better.

I slice carrots, onions, garlic, and potatoes, and finish the preparations for dinner. Turning on the oven lights, I finish both bottles of chardonnay and opt for a cabernet. It will go well with the roast, the deep oaky flavors are strong, and I pour a little into the baking pan before closing the door to the oven and setting the timer. I sit down at the table, raise my feet and rest my eyes.

I wake with a start, as Glen walks through the door, "Iris, I'm home."

I toss my feet back to the floor and stand. A little wobbly, I sit back down to catch my balance.

"Glen, I'm in the kitchen." I look at the stove clock—seven forty-five. I must have been more tired than I thought. The kitchen's a mess, littered with food scraps and dirty dishes. My eyes narrow to the empty bottles across the counter. I can hear his footsteps through the creaking floors waiting to be refinished.

"Shit, I've got to get rid of these."

"Sorry, what did you say, Iris? I can't hear through our plastic walls."

"Oh nothing, just … "

His steps are closer—he zips the temporary plastic door containing the drywall dust behind him.

I speak louder, "I made us a special dinner, so I hope you're hungry!"

"You have no idea, I've had a ginger ale and two bags of almonds since noon."

I place two of the empty bottles toward the back of the fridge. I don't want him to see or hear all the bottles clink together in the garbage.

"What's for dinner?"

Glen sees me drop just one empty bottle into the trash.

"We're having a roast with carrots and potatoes."

"Fantastic, when will it be ready? I'm starving.

"The timer should be going off any minute now." I smile with my arms stretched out to embrace him in a hug. I lean in close for a kiss, but stumble hitting his chin with my forehead.

"Ouch, you OK?" he asks.

I sturdy my feet and laugh it off. "Yeah, sorry. You make my knees go weak!" I turn my head back for a second try, but Glen leans away.

"Whoa, how much have you had to drink today? You smell like a barrel of wine—are you drunk?"

"What? No, no, I have been cleaning, and cooking, and I went to the grocery store earlier. I got your favorite roasted peppers and ricotta cheese, plus a new cheese they were featuring. The girl at the store said if you like ricotta, you will love this one."

"Thanks, that was thoughtful, but Iris, are you OK? You really don't look so good. Are you still on that cleanse?"

Shit, the cleanse! I forgot I was supposed to be doing that juicing cleanse Allie told me about. Every time I hear wellness, I wonder if she means rehab or AA. Fuck. AA, I still can't believe I went to that. Ugh, Glen can never know about that.

"No, I decided I would restart the juices next month. I think I'll need real calories with the extra work from our move." I place my hand to the counter for balance, but miss and nearly fall over.

"Iris, are you OK, you are drunk?"

"No—I mean the recipe called for cabernet, so I had a little of the leftovers, but just a glass. Here sit down and get comfortable. I'll check on the roast—it's going to melt in your mouth."

I walk over to a drawer and pull out the red oven mitts with black grips. I slide each glove over my hand and proudly look into oven.

This will settle him down when he sees how hard I've been working, but as I near the oven I notice the lack of smell. The fragrant aromas of tender meat and garlic should be overpowering.

I pull down the oven door and reach in for my redemption ticket and roast, but neither face nor arms are met with heat. It is in that moment that I realize I never turned on the oven.

"Oh shit!" the words slip out of my mouth before I can prepare an excuse.

"What is it?" Glen stands back to his feet.

There is no excuse, I am loaded and if he had any doubts, he doesn't now.

"I was so busy today." I try, but it's no use. I don't even believe myself. I turn my head to Glen and our eyes lock.

"Iris, you forget to turn on the oven? How much have you really had to drink today?"

Before I have time to answer, he goes to the trash and pulls up the bag. The cabernet bottle sits on top of carrot and onion shavings. Below clinks some additional wine bottles from earlier and last night, along with one empty bottle of Patron.

"This has got to stop—you are out of control."

Thank God two of the empty bottles are in the refrigerator, not that it would matter at this point.

I scramble for words to say.

"Yes. No, I'm in control—I don't drink all the time. I took the day off to recharge from all the stress of moving."

Glen turns and walks back to the table.

"Glen, wait. I'm sorry. I can fix this—I'll call in pizza or I can pick something up?"

"Iris, enough. It's not the food. You know I could care less about the food."

I sigh and look to the floor.

"It's your drinking. It's always your drinking. I make excuses for you, but I thought that it was over. I thought you stopped drinking. But you didn't—you're getting worse."

I think for a response, for an excuse, but there is none.

"If we go out, you don't want to leave—you'll say 'One more round.' We come home and you're pouring yourself 'One more drink.' I try to get you to come to bed, but you're busy making another drink. It's always just one more with you, **One More Iris!**"

I swallow hard and taste the oaky flavors in the back of my throat, I could be sick. The reality of Glen listing my drinking as a problem fills me with disgust. I hate it, I had no idea he even noticed. My eyes fill with tears, but I don't let them drop.

"We're supposed to be creating our dream home, our dream life, but this is not my dream. I don't want to pretend everything's fine—I can't watch any more, Iris."

"Glen, I can explain."

"No Iris, not tonight. I'm tired and there is nothing more I would like to discuss right now." He stands to his feet and pushes in his chair calmly. "I'm going to sleep in the guest room, please don't follow me."

I stand alone in the kitchen, watching as Glen walks away, down the hallway to the stairs. A feeling of Deja vu comes over me—a sight I have seen many times, the men walking away from my mother. All the fights that would break out after a night of Vera drinking too much. Her many men—they all left.

My stomach and heart aches, as I ponder Glen leaving me. What would I do, how would I recover? I hate it that I have hurt him. I hate that my drinking has messed things up. I hate that I have become someone who messes things up from drinking. And that it's true, I drink too much. Am I an alcoholic though? I think about that AA meeting—those people were alcoholics ... not me. He has no idea what an alcoholic looks like—I do. I know how sloppy and out of control they get. The jobs and men they run though, the traffic tickets, arrests, and the DUIs. How could I be an alcoholic? I'm nothing like of that—no tickets or lost jobs, I'm not Vera.

The next morning I wake to the sound of our temporary countertop coffeepot percolating in the kitchen. Glen is standing by the sink, looking out the window, I walk in slowly as not to upset him further. He turns his head in my direction, "Good morning, Iris."

"Morning," cowardly I return.

"I'm sorry about last night—maybe I was a little too hard on you."

"No, you were right. I think you're right to be mad with me. I'm mad with myself. When I drink, I drink too much. I need to slow down—I want to do that. I don't want anything to ever come between us. I'm so sorry, Glen."

Glen shifts his body to face me, his eyes urging him to believe me.

"I'm going to stop drinking," I say. "I think it would be good for me."

"Really, Iris, that's great! I can help you. I won't drink either."

He is sincere and loving as he stands in his pajamas. It's unusually late in the morning for him, eight o'clock on a Friday.

I laugh at his enthusiasm, "Glen, you hardly drink."

"I know, but if you want to stop, I will, too. I'll be there for you not drinking."

"Deal. How did I ever get so lucky to find someone like you?"

"I love you, Iris. You were there for me and I want you to know that I am going to be here for you."

I got a call the following week around noon from Vera. She must have received my late Mother's Day card and felt obligated.

"Vera, good morning!" assuming she's just starting her day.

"Hello, Iris, I don't have time to talk right now, but I figured you would like to know."

My face tightens and I fill with fear—something must have

happened to Janus. Vera proceeds, "Your grandmother is very sick. She was taken to the hospital a few weeks ago and hasn't been able to recover. They are placing her on hospice and your sister insisted that she stay here with us, instead of going back to the nursing home. I can't take care of her the way she needs, even with the aides. April is doing her best and naturally, Janus can't really do much. I was hoping you could come home and help."

I am relieved in a way that it's not my sister, but still saddened with the news of my grandmother dying.

"Grandmother's at your house in New York—is she in pain?"

"She shouldn't be with the meds they have her on, but this is probably it for her—a week, two at most."

"Yes, of course, I'll come home. Why didn't anyone call sooner."

"Well, we knew you were moving and April said you just started construction. We thought it would better to wait. We knew you would drop everything." Vera's voice is clear, compassionate, and comforting, the way a mother's voice should be.

"I'll look for a flight now and see if I can find something by tomorrow."

"That would be good, Iris. It will be good to have your help. We've missed you, I've missed you."

"I've missed you, too, Vera."

As I hang up the phone, I can't help but feel like I was talking to someone else, like my mother was someone else. Vera's name disappears from the screen of my phone and a flood of emotions rush over me. Replaying the fear from thinking again that something happened to my sister. The sadness of losing my grandmother is real, but it is Vera who puzzles me. I can't put my finger on it, but her voice was without booze—maybe I'm not the only one turning over a new leaf.

I hang up the phone and immediately call Glen to tell him I would be leaving to help my family in New York. He offers to could come help. I tell him not to worry—it would be far too crazy in the house with everyone running around. He needs to hold down the fort here, plus he's in the middle of a big case.

I find a flight and head to my closet to pack my bags. I can't stop thinking about Vera, how she sounded. Things seem different over the phone. I have a hard time figuring out what to bring, as most of my clothes are still in boxes. Usually you're safe from snowstorms in the middle of May, but the temperature can still get pretty cold at night. I should grab a few sweaters. My hand reaches my favorite leather flask, normally a staple for a trip to New York. I think—to pack the flask or not? I'd be fine here, not drinking with Glen, but I have a hard time imagining a sober visit home under these conditions. Death is hard to swallow—liquor would help ease the pain. No, I'll leave it. I'm not drinking anymore. I scan the room for a few more items, but my eyes pan back to the box with the flask. It could get really stressful—Glen would understand, given the circumstance. I'll pack it, but I won't use it, except for emergencies. It will be my umbrella, so it doesn't rain.

April picked me up from the airport. I don't know what it is about flying back to New York, but I was almost moved to tears before I even saw April's face. We chatted in the car as I watched the trees pass by in the midst of their change. The buds coming to bloom for the up state's late spring, the new cycle of life while my grandmother completed hers.

April insisted that we stop to eat before going home and I had no complaints, it's been a while since I've been to a chain restaurant. The neighborhood Applebee's made me feel like I was walking through a high school yearbook. It's strange to be in a town where you could run into old friends after getting used to living near no one from your past.

I slide into the red leather booth. The room is tiered like a stadium with the lowest level to the center, highlighting the bar. Which is not where we sit, but I couldn't help but notice it with all its lights and specials.

The perky waitress graces us with a wide smile and the scent of vanilla spray. She lists the signature lunch specials and the buy one, get one deals. I wonder if I should order water, maybe a club soda with a lime, to make it feel like I'm having something fun.

April jumps in "The skinny mojito, please." She looks me in the eye and says "I think we're both going to need a drink when you hear what I've got to say."

Sobriety leaves me without remorse—I could never turn down a drink for my sister.

"In that case, I take the *two for one* mojito as well."

"Also an order of the boneless wings and potato skins, fully loaded."

"You got it, ladies."

The waitress heads back to place our orders and I wonder what disturbing news April could have. I know it's bad, she doesn't rattle easily and her mood has shifted.

April unrolls her silverware and examines the fork, she's nervous.

"OK, Iris, we have to talk—it's Vera. She's been different lately."

"I noticed she sounded different on the phone, serious or something."

"Yeah, well, it's serious all right. She hasn't been drinking much anymore."

"That's great." I think to my recent abstinence pact with Glen and feel guilty for ordering the mojito. I didn't drink it yet—maybe I'll just say I'm not in the mood when it gets here.

"Well, not really. She hasn't been getting drunk because … well, we think she's been getting high."

"What's new, she's always gotten high."

"Not high like this. Serious shit. Janice and I think she's … doing crack."

"Crack, like as in a crackhead?"

"Yeah, like a crackhead. It's bad, Iris, the worst she's ever been."

My mind races through stereotypical crackhead images—gangly teeth, crazy eyes, and scratch marks.

April proceeds, "Her face is sunken-in and she's let her hair go gray. She gets paranoid, so she opens and closes the curtains."

"Seriously? How could this happen? Sure she always drank too much, but crack, fucking crack?"

"That's not even the worst of it. It's Jake, they're back together."

"Of course, they are. That's just perfect."

The waitress places our mojitos on the table and every bit of guilt slips from my body. If I knew it was going to be this bad, I would have ordered Crown. I sip the sugary rum instead.

"Vera was depressed. She's never been able to deal with Janus' accident, with her not being able to walk. It's tormented her and after you left, she lost it."

A new feeling rushes forward—guilt. Not from my drinking, but from leaving.

"When Grandmother got sick, Janus and I thought bringing her here might help Vera, give her some kind of purpose, and maybe another chance for forgiveness." I imagine April and Janus brainstorming plans to fix Vera—it saddens me that I wasn't there to contribute ideas.

"You know Grandmother's health is bad. I'm glad you're going to have a chance to say goodbye. We're just trying to keep her comfortable at this point."

Tears fill my eyes and I swallow a piece of mint leaf that slipped through my straw, it surprises me—the leaf and this conversation.

"Anyway, she's worse. Vera's gotten worse. The plan backfired."

I sip and listen as my straw sucks the last of the liquid, the gurgles of emptiness at the bottom. Like the emptiness that Vera must have felt with me gone and another daughter paralyzed, the emptiness that comes from not being able to do anything to help. The helpless feeling that consumes people, and only gets masked by substances, until you don't feel it anymore. I know the feeling, too, I've felt it. I push the glass to the end of the table for the waitress and proceed to my second.

We sit in silence for a moment. The sun seems to have come out from a cloud and glares thought the window. It is in this light that I notice the aging of my sister. She looks worn and much older than I envision her to be in my head, now a woman flirting with thirty. The lines of stress seem to be pushing her to age beyond her years. It's a look you miss when you see people regularly, but with the gaps of months or sometimes years, the changes become stronger. I swallow hard.

"I hate that I haven't been here for you, for all of you. And Jake, I can't believe he's back. I don't know what's worse … Vera being on crack or Vera being with Jake."

"It was too much for her, she's been broken a long time. I think she just didn't have anything else left to fight. Vera was complaining a lot, then she fell deeper into her depression. We think Jake got sick of hearing it. We think he gave it to her to shut her up and then … she was hooked. Just like that. Well, that's our theory."

I feel sick that I haven't helped Vera, that I never said anything. Maybe if I had spoken up, she would have stopped. It might have been different if it came from me, her baby. Maybe she wouldn't have felt so alone. I sip more of the advertised refreshing drink, but find disappointment in the end.

"Vera's in a different world. Only hints of the woman we used to know."

April slides her tall glass across the table, "Here, looks like you could use mine. I've had more time to process all this. It's a lot."

"You could say that."

I reach for my third drink, but wish I had a shot of patron or two. I wonder if shots are excluded in the buy one, get one lunch-hour specials. This is a lot to take in.

"Be careful though—the last thing we need is another Vera."

My face tightens and so does my chest. Being compared to Vera. I can't deal with this right now, I'm nothing like her, I would never do crack! But April's my sister—I know she doesn't mean anything by it.

"It's the airplane, I'm probably dehydrated." The flying cans suck the life out of you and so does this conversation.

"I'm kidding, Iris, relax."

April eats a couple wings, as I attempt to wrap my head around this visit to Applebee's. I think to April's words when she picked me up, "A lot can happen in a year." *I'd like to up that to: A lot can happen over lunch.*

"We're mostly going to need you to keep Grandmother company and occasionally babysit Vera when she's home. We can take turns."

I nod and attempt to drink my water, still feeling self-conscious being compared to Vera.

"Also, I'll need help with the funeral arrangements, when Grandmother does pass away."

"Whatever you need, I am at your disposal."

"It's good to have you home, Iris. Is Glen OK with you staying for a little while?"

"Oh, you know Glen, the family man. He's glad I'm here to help. If it wasn't for his case, he'd be here, too."

"How is his sister doing?"

"Good, she's good, even went back to work for the museum. She's making real progresses—if only we were making progress, too."

"Who needs to make progress—you and Glen? What do you mean? You guys are like the perfect couple."

"Well, we've kind of hit a rough patch." I contemplate the other night when he slept in the guest room, because I was drunk.

"What possibly could happen between you two?"

A guilty feeling from drinking three of the mojitos at lunch comes over me, I feel hot all over. I don't exactly want to explain our argument of my heavy drinking, especially during this conversation.

"It's nothing, really. Just some difference in opinions with the renovations," I lie. "I think it will be good for me to be here, give him some time to miss me."

I take another bite of potato skin, but the grease creeps up my throat. I need another drink, but there's no way I could order more with April around.

I try switching the conversation back to Vera, "Have you guys looked into … rehab centers?"

I almost said wellness centers. Allie's and her wellness centers give me anxiety. I fear that wellness is really code for fancy rehab. I feel like I'm losing it.

"Not yet. Having Grandmother around hasn't freed up any time. Besides I don't think it's going to be that easy."

CHAPTER 26

The dreams are back or rather, the nightmares.

Returning to me, as I have to New York.

Vivid.

This time in the dream I see clear images of my life, should I have stayed.

The dead-end road where I called home, holding me captive to a crazy scene of madness.

I claw at the windows that I usually stare out of, but I can't break through.

I try to run instead.

I run from a mad man and myself.

A man that I can't see but hate, I know who he is without visual confirmation.

Sometimes you don't need it.

A glass breaks and so does my good will.

In an out-of-body experience, I feel nothing and everything, I am floating.

I look over the house, yard, and street.

The SWAT team covers our grass, the street is roped off, reporters fight for good angles while, the house in the backdrop rages with flames.

I have broken free.

Somehow escaping via a hot air balloon.

I wake up in sweat.

~IH

In a blink of an eye, my grandmother was batting her last. She passed like the month of May. April and I finalized the arrangements, while Vera walked around the funeral parlor with a golden-tinged Aquafina bottle. We were strangely happy to see her drinking, the socially acceptable option and none of the staff seemed to mind. It was genius in a way and I wondered why I hadn't thought of such a clever trick. Skipping the whole finding a place to sip from a flask, it takes the burden of appropriate timing out of the equation. I would opt for a clear liquor to keep the disguise better hidden, of course, Patron or Stoli would be perfect. I wonder if she used a funnel to pour or if that kind of skill sharpens with time.

I pondered the obituary we submitted, the sweet, simplistic sound it held, but thought of other ways to describe her or even the people around her, if I was being honest:

A grandmother, Edie Hunt, was raised in New York on highways and Jameson whiskey. Before giving it all up for her love of gardening, trinkets, and Ohio. Spending her final days back in her home state with her crackhead daughter and struggling granddaughters, who remain stressed, alcoholic, and paralyzed—not necessarily in that order.

The sound was not so sweet, not nearly as charming, when I color in the truth. Instead the paper said:

She left behind her only daughter and three beloved granddaughters and one grandson-in-law. She lived a long and very full life, both in Ohio and in her home state of New York.

The funeral was small, moments of tears and unexpected laughter from reminiscent stories relived. A small collection of friends gathered after reading of her obituary, showing respect. Most of her friends were probably out of state or already deceased.

I noticed a strange feeling as I walked around greeting the strangers—it was coming from my hands and started in my fingers.

Trembling, almost with fear, yet I was not scared. I've had it before, the shakes increasing their frequency. April noticed it, too.

"Iris, you OK? Go take a break, I'll cover for you."

"I'm fine—just a little hungry." I lied, pushing my hands to my sides for pockets that weren't attached to my black dress. I crossed my arms instead, "I haven't eaten a thing all day."

That time it sounded more believable for me. Maybe that's what it was. Hunger and a bit of anxiety mixed together. Funerals are stressful. But I knew better. I needed a drink, bad. I had unintentionally forgotten my flask this morning rushing out of the house, of all days. I need a shot of something, anything, just to take the edge off. I need to get out of here.

April drove Janus in the wheelchair accessible minivan, while I naturally drove Vera and her jeep like usual. Vera insisted on stopping by the liquor store and I didn't fight her, my collection at the house was running low and it was a good way to keep Vera home and safe. Plus I could discreetly grab a swig from one of the bottles before we even get home.

We pull into the parking lot. A few letters were burnt out from the sign Mel's Liquors and Spirits, drained from the hardship of being *on*—like me today. The top tray on the metal trash can was smoking from a cigarette as we walked past the doors. The scent reminding me that I needed smokes, too, but first, alcohol. It was commonplace to go to Mel's, one of Vera's routine stops. Complete with a ding from the doorbell, as familiar as high school homeroom—I believe it was set up the same since then, too. We stocked up on some favorites and few others less expensive because … no need worrying about reputations on Worth Street. I place all my goodies on the counter and look to the store clerk, who was about my age. And she says, "ID, please."

"ID?" I laugh, I hadn't been ID'd in a while. Leave it to New York.

"Sure. Here, it gets stuck in the plastic—do you need it out?" I raise my entire LV wallet eye-level to the girl.

"Yes, I need to scan it into the computer."

"Of course, you do."

"I'm sorry?"

"Nothing. Nothing it's been a long day. Just left a funeral."

The girl stays quiet as I proceed to pry my license away from the clear plastic film listing all my information.

"Here ya go."

"Louisiana, you live there?"

"No, I just like to take pictures in random states and pretend it's home."

The girl stares eyes wide. She must be younger, no idea to the world's cruelty or humor.

"I'm kidding, yes, I live there. I'm just not used to getting ID'd. I'm married." I have no idea what being married has do to with my ID, or why I said that, but I notice the girl searching to find a year, unfamiliar with the state markings.

"Here, it's in the corner, my birthdate. Sorry the license is a little confusing, and bent, and broken—like me."

She says nothing to my comment, but it hits me hard. I don't know what I'm even talking about—why am I talking to this girl? I need to get out of here. I need a fucking drink.

"OK, Mrs. Hawthorne, have a good night."

Mrs. Hawthorne, I almost turn around looking for my mother-in-law, but remember she's addressing me, the grown, married, broken woman, I've so clearly stated for no apparent reason.

I couldn't wait to get a drink. I needed alcohol, lots of it. I hope I bought enough, Vera was still shopping so I stepped outside for relief. The trash can had finished smoldering, I twisted the cap eagerly flushing the liquid into my mouth. It stung, but not nearly as much as my body stung without it. Comfort from the quick swallow hitting my system, but it is brief and leaving me longing for more. I drink more, and more. I can see Vera, finishing up at the register and swallow again before stashing the bags into the jeep. Vera won't notice, the quantity of bottles or my drinking half of one. My sisters will be happy to see the stockpile to keep our mother grounded and away from crack. I would keep Vera company—after all I promised.

It was late and my sisters had both departed to their rightful grounds after a long draining day. I reassured them I would keep a watchful eye on Vera, tucking her in safe and sound with an abundant supply of drinks. Shots, and wine, and shots, some with beer for her and wine to chase for me. Followed with more shots. No judgment, no rules, just drinks. Today was a hard day, a long, hard day. I noticed the collection of cans and bottles lining the counter, waiting for their five-cent deposit, in some cases ten. I begin to sip slower allowing myself to feel bad, to feel the sadness, all the grief.

I look out the window. The moon was high, bright, and full, contrasting the dark black sky. Not even the woods or Janus' studio was visible in the backyard and the infomercials were filling the television. I must have passed out. For some reason, my jeans are wet, just my lap. Did I fucking pee myself? Turns out there is something worse than wet jeans from beer. The kitchen lights shine brightly like spotlights, when I saw him walk inside. Everything had gone as planned until then—until Jake. I wasn't expecting him to come over, not this late, and not tonight after my grandmother's funeral.

He walked straight through the side door like a landlord. An enigma barely nodding to me in recognition, assumedly he must have thought I was April. My stomach tightens as he does a double-take.

"Iris? Whoa, whoa, whoa, little Iris, is that you? All grown up, a full-fledged woman with … look at that body."

I freeze as if I were sixteen all over again. I can't believe it. After all these years, his voice still holds power over me and I am helpless.

"You know it's true—some things do get better with time. Living proof right here." He reaches down to his jeans zipper in a grabbing motion before walking back to Vera's bedroom.

How could he do that, why would he talk to me like that, still, and on the evening of my grandmother's funeral! I feel sick immediately, his words haunt me like the many times when I was young. I can't think, I need a drink, I need to drink his words and gesture away. I have to make a plan, I have to keep Vera here, I can't let her do crack.

I walk over to the liquor cabinet pulling down everything I could find, enticing Vera to stay with the many temptresses. Taking some for myself first, I line the countertop like a commercial display. Stoli, Goldschlager, Jack Daniel's, what's left of the Patron. I slam a shot, a couple shots, then a few more. I pull the glass away from my mouth for the fifth time and place it on the counter. The tension slides from my neck and I take a deep breath. Think, Iris, think. I look back in the cabinet for a solution and pull down my favorite royal-velvet purple bag. One long pour from the last bit of Crown, and the final bit of my dignity. I don't recall drinking much whiskey this week. The empty package even has an essence of recherché. I slide the empty bottle back into its personal packaging, pull the pale yellow ribbon ties together tightly and toss it to the trash. Calmly I sit back to the kitchen table to collect my thoughts.

Banging noises come from Vera's bedroom. I hate it, the noises they make. Yelling mixed with laughter, and screams. I try not to listen and continue to distract myself with whiskey. It's the break of a fight, sex, or their getting high. You can't tell the difference in the beginning, but now with crack, there's a whole new level of danger. I attempt to figure out my plan for her rescue, if she should try to leave with him.

I try to tune them out altogether and take another sip from my drink, but my whiskey comes to an end—there wasn't much to begin with, I need more. I switch back to vodka and pour a splash of tonic to recharge, clearing my pallet from the disgust surrounding me. Think, Iris. I wonder if I should call April, have her come back to help? No, it's three o'clock in the morning, I can handle it, and I can handle him.

I gaze back out the window into the black. Lost in the darkness that surrounds me, both inside and out. Usually I find the darkness comforting, softening the images of my blackouts, but not tonight. Not waking in the middle of what I would normally not remember. I find myself confused and my vision blurs from the nothingness to focus on, everything is one giant smudge of black. I hate that I can't concentrate, its Jake. Jake being here tonight, I feel lost and confused. Acid swells into my mouth and I swallow a gulp of the vodka tonic. The drink is weak and almost gone. Oval bits of melted ice cubes soften the cocktail's normal strength. I light a cigarette from the pack and take a drag. It's good, but not enough.

I slide my hand to my right ankle, underneath the sock and pull out a tiny clear pouch. Holding the bag I confirm there should be enough for a bump. A key bump is just what I need, only for emergencies. Like this. I pour a pile onto the magazine lying on the table. I grab my purse on the floor and scan my wallet for a large bill. This will recharge me—I can't believe I didn't think of it sooner. A line, a small line, or I suppose just one regular line, medium size. Apparently, I've spent more than I thought while I've been up here. I decide the crispest five will do, less circulated when they're crisp. I form two parallel lines and the powder disappears.

There's a loud thud and I can't tell if it's her headboard against the wall or her head. Fuck, they are gross, but maybe I should go back and check on her. How could she be with a man like that—I wonder if she shoots up or smokes it? I can't believe she's let herself fall so low. One more drink before I head back there, for courage.

I pour a splash of Jack Daniel's, it's no Crown but it will do. As I turn my head I catch a glimpse of myself in the window. The window's glass changes like a mirror from the lights of the kitchen and darkness outside, spitting back my reflection. My hair has slipped to a loose ponytail and my lips are stained purple from wine, the way they do sometimes when I drink cabernets. I don't even remember drinking wine. What the fuck is wrong with me? I take a seat again and try to think of what I'll say to Vera.

The banging sounds are back, but louder. A crashing sound from her nightstand or maybe dresser, it's glass I think. Then a strange pause of silence, as they awkwardly attempt to cool off. Glass and screams pierce the air again. I am certain now what type of escapade is taking place. It is violent. She needs my help.

I jump to my feet finding unexpected stability through the chaos. I can hear it in his voice, the lack of control. The fight escalating as I reach the hallway in time to watch Jake slam Vera's head into the wall. Opening a hole right below one already in place. I stop and stare in astonishment, uncertain with my next move or his. He screams to her, "Filthy whore, where's the rest of it?"

My eyes and vision are glossy, but I manage to shout, "Stop it, Jake, leave her alone!"

"Stay out of it, you little cunt." His words are sharp like the kick he thrusts into Vera's stomach. I hate him.

I run back to the kitchen cabinet, pulling the wooden knob like many times tonight. My hand fiddles around until the object I'm searching for is familiar in my palm. I wrestle my fingers to meet the small groves of its surface, like Braille for the blind. It feels heavy, but firm in my grip and I return to the hallway. She's screaming, screaming for her life.

I hold the gun tight in my hands, with my arms locked out in front of me. Stabilizing my aim as the tears collect in my eyes.

"What are you going to do, save your slut mother? You don't have it in you."

Somehow even as I hold a firearm, he holds power over me. The tears are blurring my vision further. I hate him. This is all his fault, if they had never met none of us would be in this situation. Drinking, drugging, all of us are fucking out of control. Vera's on crack! She would never have gotten to this point, if he had just left her alone. My drinking and the cocaine, I wouldn't have turned to cocaine if I didn't feel the need to drink. Drink him and all his cruelty away. All the suffering, all the hurt, all of it started with him. I am just a sheep.

His gaze reaches mine, he looks delighted with his hands wrapped tightly around Vera's neck.

"Stop it, Jake, you're going to kill her!" I yell as my arms shake. I fucking hate him, but I pause to take action. My conscience holds the trigger and me in place.

I wipe the tears falling down my checks—he releases his chokehold, tossing Vera back to the wall. She scurries away, close to me.

"Fucking pussies," Jake turns away to leave, I can barely see.

My eyes and emotions are giving up. The commotion is over and I taste the salt from a tear that falls to my lips when my ears are jolted with the thundering sound from the gun. The jarring noise bounces off the walls trapped from the tight perimeters of a hallway. I can almost feel the gun recoil when I realize that the Smith and Wesson is no longer in my hands. The vibrant thrust of power never reaches my body. The trigger was pulled, but my fingers were no longer attached, at least not for the last four seconds.

I look over to see Vera, arms out, her eyes still locked onto the target, Jake. He falls to the floor, face down and curls into the fetal position. Blood rushes out from the upper left side of his back and pools onto the laminate.

"Fuck!" Vera yells or Jake, maybe both. I can't hear the change in pitch, my ears are still ringing from the gun. Vera is yelling and I am sweating. Beads of sweat are dripping down my chest. I wipe it away and notice a splash of blood across my shirt. I scream and cry and scream, although I can't hear myself do either.

I look to Vera—she is shaking her head and panicked like me. Jake cannot stand, he remains curled up on the floor.

"We have to get out of here," Vera grabs the keys to the jeep.

I follow, but I am lost. I am lost more now than ever before in the darkness of the driveway. Trying to wrap my head around what just happened. The cold air of the night brings forward the urge to vomit—I can almost taste the iron of blood in my mouth. But there is nothing there, it is just on my shirt. Vera hands me the keys and yells, "Let's go!"

"Where are we going?" I scream trying to hear my own voice over the ringing.

"I don't know yet—anywhere. Just shut up and drive, let me think."

My heart races as we resume our usual positions into the vehicle. I peel out of the driveway, without being able to hear or see.

I drive well above the speed limit down dark narrow roads. Avoiding major expressways and streetlights. My high beam lights bounce off the solid white line down the center. I hold the wheel tight as I try to drive as straight as possible. Stay within the lines, stay within the lines. I repeat this like a mantra over and over again.

We are surrounded with tall pine trees clustered close together and the road, without a shoulder. It's like driving through a tunnel of branches and the color black. My view is limited to but a couple of feet, leaving little room for mistakes.

I am focused on the lines and staying in between them, trying to push away the ringing. The speed of the jeep reaches seventy, but I don't think to slow down. I don't notice anything but the lines, until I see Vera making large gestures with her hands. She is speaking to me. What she is saying? I can't tell. It's as if I were wearing earplugs. The sounds and words are distorted. Unable to stop the electrifying ringing noise still charging in my ears.

Her hands and arms are flapping. I study her movements, she appears to be bracing for impact. We become airborne as the lines and road come to an end.

CHAPTER 27

On the wrong side of revenge.

-IH

My eyes open slowly, the darkness is gone. The black has faded to white, bright white. Whiteness so bright it's blinding. I squint and struggle to focus. All I see is white, bright fucking white. My eyelids are heavy, I blink and try again for an object, something to replace the nothingness of the white. It's a ceiling, I find the popcorn texture and soon the fluorescent light panels. There are two long planks of long lights with a white background ceiling. Where the fuck am I?

A woman I do not recognize leans over me. She reaches her hand to my head and adjusts what feels like a bandage across my forehead. I sit up and muster out, "Who are you?"

The pressure is too much on my head, actually my whole body. I lie back.

"Mrs. Hawthorne, my name is Trisha, I'm the head RN on staff. You were in a car accident and I'm going to be taking care of you."

My head pounds and I have a flash of the road and the lines—the road and the lines and the dark woods surrounding the road and that is all.

I reach my hand down to my side and feel the stiffness of a blanket, it catches on my wrist where my hand is taped with a tube.

"Car accident ... where am I?"

"Mrs. Hawthorne, you're at Strong Hospital. It was a pretty bad car accident last night—do you remember?"

The hospital—I'm at a hospital? I attempt to move my feet, but they are restrained from the sheets tucked in tight, so tight I cannot free my legs. I feel trapped, claustrophobic, the whiteness and the walls feel to be closing in on me, suffocating me. The lights are so blinding, I shut my eyes and go back to blank.

My eyelids are pulled open. A different woman dressed in scrubs combs over my motionless body with her instruments. I start to squirm, confused still as to my whereabouts or time of day … or has it been days? She grabs for my arm and scans my wrist like a can of corn at the grocery store.

"Well, hello there, Mrs. Hawthorne, glad you could make it. I'm your nurse, Hillary, and I'm taking care of you today."

Confused, I attempt to sit up and feel the cotton hospital gown fall from my left shoulder. A pounding force of extreme discomfort rushes to my head.

"No, no, no, you need to lie back down, Mrs. Hawthorne, You were in a very severe car accident. You need to rest."

I lie back and cup my hand over my eyes from the bright lights, as if I am staring into noon's fullest sun. The light is overwhelming and a forceful feeling of sickness comes over me.

"We had to pump your stomach, so you may feel nauseous and light-headed today. We found high levels of alcohol in your system, along with opiates."

My head caves over my body and the nurse quickly retrieves a bucket. I vomit in the form of small acidic drops, though it feels like I could fill the whole thing. The lack of memory and emptiness that surrounds me apparently also fills my stomach. I dry heave, producing all that's left of me—nothing.

The nurse continues, "You almost died, you're lucky to be alive."

Another voice pipes in from the other side of the room, this one from a man with a very firm tone.

"Mrs. Iris Hawthorne, correct?"

"Yes." My throat still recovering, the nurse hands me a cup of water and exits the room.

"Do you remember anything about last night?"

I sip the water from the paper cup. The light is still so I bright, I'm having a hard time comprehending the situation, the information—or was it a question? I sip again and try to focus, I can see the outline of a cop in uniform. The man is staring at me. A question, he must have asked a question, he's pausing for my answer.

"Um, ah, I can't."

"Do you remember driving a jeep last night, you were driving a Ms. Vera Hunt—that is your mother, correct?"

My mind shifts slowly into gear, recalling the stick shift of Vera's jeep. Moments from the dark road, the speeding, the lines and the road coming forward. Driving through the blackness, but I can't bring forward any other thoughts. Blackness from another blackout, or maybe I have a concussion this time—either way, I'm blank.

"Mrs. Hawthorne, we have reason to believe you were at the scene of a crime, prior to your accident. Can you tell me anything about that, Mrs. Hawthorne?"

"Crime?" I'm lost.

"Yes, crime. What can you tell me about the shooting of Mr. Rice, more specifically your involvement?"

Shooting, what shooting? Who the hell is Mr. Rice? I don't know any, Mr. Rice. I blink hard as if to reboot my brain, but it fails.

"Well, Mr. Jake Rice was shot in the back at your mother's house on Worth Avenue approximately around four o'clock this morning. You did say your mother is Ms. Vera Hunt, correct?"

Suddenly, it hits me, all of it. Like a New Orleans levee breaking into a flash flood of images. My ears are filled with the ringing once more, taunting me. Jake—Jake is Mr. Rice. In all the time I've known him, I don't believe I've ever heard his last name. *Holy shit, last night—what the fuck did I do?* In that moment, the lights are turned up or so it seems, as if it could be brighter than before. I cannot see or hear except for the sound of the gun suffocating me like the blankets. What was I thinking—I pulled a fucking gun on Jake. *Shit, holy shit! Everyone would be a lot better if I never came here, if I wasn't here now. What's happened to Vera, and Jake, is he alive? Fuck, this is bad. And Glen, what will Glen think?*

My fears consume me, but before drifting back to the big white nothing, I scream in my head or maybe out loud, "I want to die."

—⌀—

It is night, or maybe day—I have no idea. Time is not a part of my thoughts, not to mention how many hours or days have passed. The lights in my room are off and I find it comforting, only the lights from outside the hallway are lit. I'll assume it's night. Only now do I realize the room is different from the last time I woke. Consisting of concrete block walls, no curtains and exactly 97 tiles across the floor. I started counting as soon as my vision returned. Pondering the square footage of the room to escape the horrific nightmare I'm living.

I decide to stand and have a look around. My torso feels tight. No, not tight, sharp, like a broken rib or something. Who knows maybe one is. I am no longer attached to any tubes. My feet are warm from a pair of pale yellow grip socks that reach high up my legs. I peek my head out of the room and notice a common area with tables and chairs, just in front of the nurse's station, along with a security guard monitoring the area by the elevators. The ringing sound returns along with visions of blood splashed on my shirt and hands, I rush back into my room to the sink and scrub. The water and soap wraps my hands the way my chest feels wrapped with pressure, tightness. I stand for almost ten minutes washing, or what seems like ten. There is nothing on them, I'm lost in nothing and everything, this is purgatory. Or, as the staff more commonly refer to it, the psych ward. I return to my bed and collapse.

Later, my strength returns and I walk around the unit to get my bearings. A fellow patient gives me the inside scoop to the ways of the ward. The pale green bracelets are used to help indicate suicide risks for the nurses, doctors, and staff. Like the celadon-colored bracelet around my wrist. I couldn't help but think of Janus and her studio, years ago when she was selecting paint colors. Being a stickler for colors, I have often thought of her words, the faint green tone being calming. I wondered if that was the doctor's intentions as well.

Screams circulate the floor along with a few patients. One man chants, "They're coming for me, the CIA, they're coming for me soon!" Another one stands by the phone in the hallway, a girl. The phone is old fashioned with a very short cord connecting the receiver to the box. Different from most public phones, this one disconnects precisely at midnight. There are no calls in or out after that, not until 8:30 am. The girl stares waiting for it to ring as if it was her personal line, but the phone is never for her. She doesn't seem to mind, she stares just the same, while others roam the halls, lost in or out of their minds like myself. Lost from all the pain, I think I'm dying I tell the doctors. Or maybe it's that I want to die—yes, the latter. I stare off at the nothingness, but the visions keep coming. I can't escape them. Repeating the events over and over again. I grabbed the gun, I killed Jake.

I wake again and the lighting is fresh, like the doctor that walks into my room clearing his throat. I've seen him before. I think.

"How are you doing today, Iris?"

Really, how am I doing today? Probably not too good, seeing that I'm in the psychiatric ward. But I don't say that. I don't care enough—it would take far too much energy.

I manage to tilt my head to the side with a nod, acknowledging his question.

"Well, your eyes are looking a little better. I'm going to run some more tests and see what your body says, OK?"

I don't have the strength to answer. I don't even refuse the wheelchair that they offer for my ride downstairs to do the blood work. I am paired with a guard at my side, only a special section of the hospital gets a security escort. The guilt is overbearing in the common area, these poor people are just sick. I am a criminal—it's not fair for them to be stuck with me. I retreat back to my room when they are done, alone where I belong with my demons. It is too much in my mind, I pull the thin white sheet over my head and wait for sleep to come.

Noon approaches and so do the few visitors. I don't know the day or how many have passed, but the families come during the weekdays at noon, so it must be one of the five. Family members and friends search for their loved ones who may or may not really be there. I glance up to see a tall slender woman without scrubs or a white jacket walk through my door. An image I know well, but was not expecting … Allie. Her face is gentle, yet tired, and her eyes red, presumably from the tears that have fallen. I imagine her image not too distant of my own, though I'm certain I look worse.

She warmly moves to me, embracing me with a long hug. Rocking me slightly in her arms, scurrying her hands around my back. I burst into tears, wailing as she holds me in her loving grasp. Our friendship has lasted through time and tragedy, Allie is here for me in my darkest hours. Showing me the love and friendship that I don't deserve.

I sit back for a moment, "What are you doing here?"

It is the first full sentence I've formed since being here. Lost in the thick fog and the sedative drugs the doctors keep me on. I hardly can tell up or down. Mostly down—mostly down or dead. That's what I fantasize about most, being dead.

"I was going to ask you the same question," Allie manages to say. More tears stream out like rushing falls. I'm actually surprised I have any left.

"I don't know what to say." *My mind plays tricks on me, sometimes I think it was all a nightmare, but then I fall asleep. And it can't be a nightmare, if I'm awake.*

"Allie, you have to tell me what happened? I can't find out anything, except that I have a court date in a couple weeks for a DWI, which means nothing, because I don't know what day it is in here. Where's Vera, what did they do with her?"

"She's fine, Vera's being held at the county jail."

Already guessing, I ask to clarify.

"What is she being charged with?"

"Murder. Second-degree murder."

I shake my head in the disbelief, hearing the words out loud make my terracing thoughts become a reality.

"Murder in the second degree, so Jake is dead." It's not really a question—it's a statement I have to say out loud to make sure I am processing the information correctly, confirmation.

"Yes, he's dead."

"Do they know how he abused her?"

"Yes, they know everything."

"What about me, do they know I was the one who went for the gun? I was going to do it, it's my fault!"

"Yes they know everything. Glen has a close colleague working on it as we speak."

Oh my God, Glen, what does he think? He must think I'm a monster.

"He's here in New York? Oh my God, how is he?"

"Yes, he's here. He's fine and you're going to be fine."

The tears swell up in my eyes as I think of Glen combing through this criminal case, his own wife, the criminal.

"You were acting in self-defense. You were trying to save Vera's life. They know, Glen knows. The alcohol level in your blood makes things a little tricky, but everyone came back high. They also found traces of cocaine in your system, but they're probably going to be able to get that dropped. When did you start doing cocaine?"

I look down, the tears fall to my sheets, the shame sets in further with all my secrets exposed. I couldn't hide it much longer anyway, it was exhausting. I'm exhausted and disgusted with who I have become.

"Never mind, it doesn't matter." Allie changes the subject, "The fire might get complicated, but that one will be for the insurance company to fight about."

"Fire, what fire?"

"You don't know about the fire? Maybe you should lay down and rest. We can do this when you're feeling more up to it."

"No, Allie you have to tell me—what fire, what are you talking about?"

"Apparently there was a cigarette that caught fire in the house. They believe it happened close to the incident with Jake."

If my head could have burst, it would have in that moment. I threw my cigarette down before I went for the gun—it was still lit.

"Oh my God, Allie, I was smoking when we left, I think. I don't know. I was definitely smoking cigarettes that night."

"No, Vera has been very clear about details. She has been taking responsibility for the whole thing. It was her cigarette."

"What—that's crazy, I'm the one who grabbed the gun, and I'm the one who …"

"Iris, you've got to calm down. Vera told everyone the truth—you don't have to worry. You were trying to save her life. She took it a step further and pulled the trigger."

"No. No. She wouldn't have pulled a trigger, if I didn't get the gun."

"Take a breath, big breath."

I'm horrified, Vera's taking full blame and it's my fault. I should be punished. And the fire—where the fuck did that come from?

"How bad is it, the fire?"

"It's not good. Janus woke up from the light of the flames. She called 911 but a good portion of the house was burnt. I haven't gone inside yet, but there's a lot of smoke damage."

It's hard to listen to Allie talk about a fire—mine, the one I caused. I know it must bring up old feelings from her experience as a teen. I hate myself, even more than I thought I ever could.

"It's not your fault."

"No, you're wrong. It was me, it was my stupid cigarette and me. I burned down the house, while poor Janus watched. I'm the reason Jake is dead."

"Stop it, Iris. You can't take on all the blame. Besides they're still finalizing the report, but the fire started in Vera's bedroom. Vera said she was smoking cigarettes and crack. You were never back in her bedroom. Her story only has you as far as the hallway—she said you were in the kitchen most of the night. You couldn't have done it."

"It started in the bedroom, the fire?"

"Yes. It sounds like most of the problems started there."

I am sick thinking of Janus, stuck, unable to escape from her studio. Watching the house burn just feet away. I feel queasy, I doubt anything will come up, but I reach for a bucket just in case.

"Lay back down, you've had a rough week."

"Has it really been a week? I don't know what day it is."

"Just rest, Iris, don't worry about it."

"What does she think, Janus ... what do both my sisters think?"

"They feel terrible for you, for everyone. They feel like it could have been one of them just as easily. They are angry with Vera for asking Jake to come over, for creating the perfect storm, the storm that you were thrown into."

I can't let her take all the credit—I caused this. "But I reached for the gun, Allie, do you hear me? I was aiming it at his head!"

"Yes, Iris, you did, but he was going to kill her—if it wasn't for you, she might not be alive."

"Yeah, alive and facing murder charges."

"That's her bit to deal with—hopefully, the jury will see the big picture and go easy on her, but that will be her trial. Vera killed Jake, not you!"

It's all so painful, I close my eyes and picture Jakes body burning on the floor. I wonder if he died from the bullet, the smoke, or the actual flames. I cover my ears and try to drown out the ringing that has returned.

When the sounds quiet in my head, I find the strength to ask, "What about Glen, what is he saying about all this?"

"You can ask him, he's here. He's right outside the door. He wanted me to go in first, to talk with you."

I see his image appear in the doorway. Standing from a distance as I was brought up to speed, attempting to not actually give me a heart attack. I probably wouldn't have been able to handle this kind of information from him—the shame is thick enough coming from my best friend. I can see the day's events have taken a toll on him as well. The only thing worse than being in a psych ward, is seeing the ones you love while you're a patient.

"I just left the courthouse. You have court date for the DWI in two weeks—we were able to enter a plea on your behalf. They should go easy on you, as this is your first offence. You will most likely end up with probation, a fine, and some kind of mandatory rehab treatment."

It's like a serial, waking up in a psychiatric ward where the man you love and normally call husband explains your legal rights regarding your criminal activity.

"I'm so sorr … "

But I can't get that word to leave my mouth, the word SORRY is too small for the amount of power I need it to hold. It's not worth it—like me, I am not worth it.

"Your lawyer is a good friend, like an uncle. He's going to try to get your charges transferred back down to Louisiana, so you can go home."

"Home?" The tears which were dry are wet again, "Surely you don't want me anywhere near you."

"Honestly, right now, no. No, I don't know what do or think right now. But I'm not going to let you stay in here—you're not crazy, Iris. You need help and I want you to get the best."

The best, because that's what I deserve—I'm a fucking wreck! But I say nothing. Instead I stand at the sink and wash my face. The water is cold and reminds me that I am still alive. I didn't notice the mirror until now, or maybe I was just afraid to look. My eyes are sunken-in with black circles underneath, I appear to have stiches across my temple and forehead. That must have been the bandage I felt a few days ago. My head has been pounding, but I have become so numb to the aftermath of drinking I really haven't thought much about it. This is what crazy looks and feels like. I can feel the tears once more and the salty drops fall back into my mouth. They taste like the gun. I have no control over my body, in so many ways.

Nurse Hillary walks in smiling, she may be the most optimistic thing on this whole floor.

"Time to check your vitals. Oh look, how nice, you have company—not everyone here gets visitors, you're one lucky lady!" she says this without flinching an eye.

"Yes, lucky." It's hard to say without crying harder.

Allie's soft voice breaks my sorrowful moment, "You are lucky, lucky to be alive. When I first heard about the accident, I thought you were …" she stops to collect herself and looks at her watch, "Visiting hours are ending, we can talk more tomorrow."

Allie walks over and kisses my right cheek, the side opposite my stiches. Glen looks torn between both loving and hating me. I get it—I don't want to be affiliated with me either, let alone be married to me. He seems to find some compassion before heading out the door, "Rest up, Iris. You're going to need your strength."

CHAPTER 28

The reporters enter the courtroom ...

*Tripping over the metal detectors, as the man scrambles to get a
 bin for his laptop and a separate bin for his camera, so the lens
 doesn't get scratched, again.*

*Making casual friendly greetings, unenthused by the guards
 scanning for mischief.*

*Looking out the glass windows to the world, the world waiting
 for verdicts like the one he will be first to report.*

The reporters enter the courtroom ...

*With a five-dollar latte in her hand, and a bagged breakfast
 pastry that she won't eat until noon, which she'll feel guilty
 about because of the carbs, failing her diet again.*

*She wears the perfect shade of rose lipstick, a color that doesn't
 wash her out under the lights.*

*With manicured nails and hair, she's a faithful client to her
 appointments that keep her stress and grays from showing.*

*With layers of dry shampoo that give her hair extra hold and
 time to sleep after her late night.*

*The late night she forced herself to go on—the blind date her
 friend made her promise to keep because she's a workaholic
 trying to establish a career.*

The career she pursues, but loses time to finding a husband.

*A husband—like her friends have, each with two children and a
 dog that fill their four-bedroom houses.*

The reporters enter the courtroom ...
*With one hand checking the phone for the final score to the game
    that he couldn't stay awake to watch because mornings start
    early.*
*Wearing a suit from Men's Wearhouse that was in a buy one/
    get one half-off sale, his microphone is already clipped to the
    jacket collar.*
*Worrying about the mortgage and being overextended, especially
    if the roof should need to be replaced. He wonders how bad it
    would be to take out a second mortgage and maybe set a little
    extra money aside for a vacation—*
*the vacation he wants and needs or else he may not last another
    day. He may end up on the news himself, after throwing
    himself over a bridge from the torturous monotony of his life.*
*The monotony of attending therapy, even though it doesn't seem to
    help, still trying to fix his marriage after the affair.*

The reporters enter the courtroom ...
And so does the judge, the court is now in session.

~IH

I t was a blur of weeks and my perception of time, I found myself back in New Orleans living in our Victorian dream home. Neither the home or my life resembled that of a dream, so it was fitting. I had been given a slap on the wrist fine, an ankle bracelet with a clunky monitor, and I had one year's time to complete a thirty-day stay at my choice of a rehabilitation center. My punishment was not fitting, so my mind took it upon itself to do the abuse. Meanwhile Vera waited for the trial of her life in one of New York's county jails.

Glen and I were staying in separate bedrooms. I thought it was generous of him to even allow me to stay in the first place. I would listen to him getting ready in the morning—timely, consistent. He remained respectful to me, although the first few days went by without one word exchanged, at least not to me. He'd give a few hellos to the early arriving workers as he made his way to his car, escaping the chaos of the house and me. With the large amount of demolition already underway, Glen decided to push through with the remodel. The hit we would take for selling a dismantled house would only sharpen the harsh consequences we were living through, losing more than the trust that was already gone between us.

Contractors and working men went about their business throughout our home, much like the rest of the world. The life I knew in New Orleans was unfazed with the events of my mother's high profile case raging in New York. And there was plenty of rage fueling the scene surrounding Vera, *the druggy that was armed and dangerous*. Rumors were flying to make an example of her—I knew in my gut her punishment would be harsh.

I was grateful not to be in prison, but it was horrifying to play the events in my head, like survivor's guilt—I was almost unscratched from the entire incident. I watched daily from the window, as Glen would pull out of the driveway, free from me for a few hours, a thought I fantasied about. No matter where I went, there I was. I couldn't escape the house or me (at least not 300 feet from one of the two).

When the sounds in my head became too much, I moseyed to a room full of distraction. The men wearing masks, with a hat or bandana, ripping away the walls and floors around me. I'd sit trying not to think, but I was consumed with thoughts and my life literally crumbling around me. The gun occasionally sounding through my mind, overpowering the power tools of saw blades and hammers. This is what crazy looks like. I was trapped with my thoughts, fears, and a construction crew.

It was Friday and I had been home for a week, I think, which really meant a whole lot of nothing. My Fridays could just as easily be a Saturday, Tuesday, or Thursday. They were all the same. I had a hard enough time tracing the days from nights or which week we were in—I think July would be here soon, though that didn't matter either. The plague of June looked promising for July. At times it felt like the shooting was an eternity ago, while in others, it seemed as if it were yesterday. I wanted to die. I couldn't keep going like this. Every day was worse than the next, every hour, the guilt and the pain went deeper.

I was sitting on the floor of what should one day be Glen's office, the sanding noises fought over the voices in my head.

"Iris! Iris, are you here?" My disturbance interrupted, but I almost can't tell if it is real or still my head fucking with me.

"Iris, you must be here." I can hear it more clearly—it's familiar. I stand and walk toward the front entrance of the house.

"Rachel?" I walk through the visqueen and zip the closure behind, "What are you doing here?"

"What—no 'Good to see you'?" She's witty as usual, "What's a girl got to do to get a hold of you?"

I look across the room to her eyes, the ones I've looked into so many times before this—her eyes without judgment, the eyes that knew me before, pre-incident. Emotion fills me and my eyes are flooded with tears.. She walks over and holds me.

"Oh, Iris, I'm so sorry."

I sob. And that is all.

"Come on, Iris, you're going to be fine, I heard you didn't end up in all that much trouble. I know plenty of people who've gotten a DUI."

My cry grows louder.

"Come on now, let's find a place to talk."

"We'll have to sit outside for some peace, it's far too loud inside." I refer to my house, though it is equally disturbing in my head.

We walk through to the terrace out back and shut the door behind. The sounds muffle inside the house. I sit curled in my worn wicker chair brought over from our old balcony nights and I light a cigarette like the many times before in this seat. An image of Vera's house burning flashes before me, my demons playing their cruel games again. I shake my head and the flames disappear, I return to the view of my overgrown garden.

"That was when I was 17," Rachel finishes saying.

I must have zoned out—I do a lot of that.

"What was when you were 17?" I ask, feeling sorry for the lack of comprehension to her story.

"When I had to go to a mandatory AA meeting, it was court-ordered." She looks at my hand and I notice my cigarette is almost down to the filter.

"Did you miss the whole story or just the last part?"

"Oh, the last part. I'm having a hard time concentrating."

"Well, it felt like a cult. I hated it—I had nothing in common with anyone there. Everyone walking around trying to shove God down your throat. So I like to drink a little—it's not that bad."

"Maybe it is—for me, I mean. That bad. The drinking. I went to a meeting once, about six months ago. I hated it then, too, but I can't help but think maybe I should have kept going."

"What—no, Iris, this whole situation was a fluke."

"Did you ever think you were wrong? About AA, I mean—you said you were 17?"

"Iris, I admit you got into a good bit of trouble, but nothing really long-term. So you have to go to rehab, no biggie. Lots of celebrities go to rehab—think of it as a mini-vacation from life. A DUI can be expunged, I think. Artists are known to be extreme, so it's not likely it's going to affect your work."

"Rachel, it can't *not* affect me. I'm there if I go, I'll be there when I come back. I can't get away from myself, I'd rather die."

"Now let's not talk like that—cheer up. You just need some time."

She raises her glass to her mouth and swallows. I really must be out of it, because I also have a glass. It's a glass from our kitchen, which I don't actually remember walking through. The glass is filled with a clear liquid and two ice cubes, tequila. I don't know if I've been drinking from it. My barren, broken fingernails press to the glass as I lift it to my lips and swallow. The clear liquid slides down my throat and I feel nothing. No sting, no burn, no taste. It's like water but not.

"That's not even the worst of it—lately I find that the alcohol doesn't even work. It has lost its affect. I fear I am losing the one thing that's aided the pain." I set the glass back down. It is halfway full and stays that way. It is useless, like me.

I am startled awake from a door shutting. Somehow I am back inside my room and Rachel is gone. I have no idea how I got to bed or how long I've been sleeping. My chest tightens the way it does when I wake to my new reality. I break into tears weeping from the agony of still being alive. My body aches for comfort, like my mind. Glen walks into the room in which I lay.

"Iris, what happened?"

"Me! I'm what happened. I hate myself." I sob harder.

"Take a breath, you have to calm down." He walks to me, sitting on the bed and lifts my head to his chest as I wail.

"Iris, my God, have you been drinking?"

"Yes. I've been drinking. And I don't know how much. And it doesn't work—even *it* has given up on me! There's not enough alcohol in the world to help me—I don't know if anything can."

"Shit, Iris! You have a monitor on, they could arrest you for this. You're on probation. Do you understand?"

"No, I don't understand. I don't understand how this happened. I don't understand how I turned out like this! I hate myself, I'm fucked up. Do you hear me, a fuck up! I drink to fill a void, a void that I have always felt. I've turned into the person I always swore I would never become, but here I am, fucked up like my mother."

Glen slides back from the bed and stares, unable to find words.

"I drank today and you know what, I didn't want to. You know why? Because I'm an alcoholic. I'm done—I can't keep living like this. I need to go to rehab. If they can't help me, then no one can."

"Iris, we can call the treatment center Monday. I'll see when they can get you in."

"No! Not Monday, now. I need help now, I won't make it till Monday."

"It's after eight o'clock on a Friday. I doubt anyone will be able to take you right now."

"Tomorrow morning, if I'm still alive. I need to go in the morning, I'm dying, Glen."

"You're not dying, you're going to be fine, just try to relax and breathe. I'll take you when you wake … wait here, I'll get you some water."

As if I had the energy to go anywhere else. He walks downstairs and I find myself alone once more. My crying is unstoppable, painful tears—the sounds bounce off the barren walls of the room. Like echoes from the psychiatry ward, but these screams all come from me. I have no idea what comes over me, but I drop down to my knees beside the window and cry out loud.

"God, I've never prayed like this before, so I don't know the words to say. But I've heard you can save people. Save me. Please. Save. Me."

In just a few moments, the tears stopped. The screams quieted, the room was just a room without noise vibrations. The pain was still there, I was still there. I wasn't sure if the devil was laughing—maybe he finally won. But maybe it *was* God. I was calm. I find my way to the bed and lay down in the quiet of the darkness.

Glen soon returns handing me water. He sits down beside me holds me close, his face mixed with confusion and compassion. I may have been the saddest thing he's ever seen, and he has seen some pretty tragic sights. He held me through the night. It was the first time we touched since before New York. The first and last time I may have the opportunity to hold my husband, should he get rid of me (which he should). But I can't think of any of that now. I surrender.

CHAPTER 29

Getting sober is like walking out of a pool with all your clothes on expecting to be dry. You may be out of the water, but you're still sopping wet.

~IH

August 16th, six weeks or 49 days to be exact, into my stint of rehab. Well, past the usual thirty days, with no desire to go home anytime soon. Anxiously, I pace back and forth in the lobby, cautiously looking over my outfit. It's the first time I've bothered to put on a nice shirt since being here. My good, dark-blue chenille blouse, black leggings, and the dressiest shoes I brought, tan leather sandals.

My hair is neatly brushed, falling nicely to my shoulders, except for the few strands that I have to keep tucking behind my ear. I can feel my hair-tie rubbing on my wrist—no, I want it down. It looks nice and smooth today. It's driving me crazy though. I contemplate pulling it up, as I run my hands through my hair nervously three more times. Its fine down, I washed and dried it today. Looking up at the clock, I can see the big hand crawling closer to the black number nine, so he will be walking in soon. Pulled back, he loves my hair back. Swept away from my face. Smoothing my hair into a low simple ponytail, it is settled.

The lobby's front wall has giant windows, which are fogged with dew around the edges. There is a chill in the air today—I can feel it every time visitors walk through the automatic sliding doors. A storm front moved in causing gray clouds to cover the usually bright summer Louisiana sky.

Jose—that's what they're calling this storm, well, hurricane. It feels appropriate to have a hurricane take place during my stay of rehab. My life surrounded in a literal and metaphorical hurricane. But not today, a day that should have sunshine and cheer. It should be filled with light, laughter, and intimate love. I pick up my card from the counter, *August 16th*, the envelope reads. With one more line below, *Happy One-Year Anniversary.*

Like a cruel joke, *Happy.* Writing that word alone was enough to make me sick. I stepped away from two group therapy meetings before going back to finish the envelope. One year ago, we were skipping off to Algiers, roaming the streets of the quarter after becoming man and wife. Lavishly celebrating with dinner, drinks, and a second-line already taking place. The spontaneous stay at the Ritz-Carlton, where they upgraded us to the penthouse suite. Now I'm staying here, *The Breezy Oak Recovery Center.*

Glen drove in last night to be here for the morning visiting hours. He stayed at the Super 8 with a kelly-green awning and a fair rating of two stars. I saw it on my drive with some other patients when we were getting groceries. Glen has already stayed at the Super 8 twice to visit me. I was able to put a face to the name of the hotel that I had preconceived ideas towards. Not fooling anyone with Super in its title. A step down from the signature linens and feather duvet the year before.

Our visits thus far have been fairly brief with no inclination as to what our future holds. Glen remains respectful, I think he checks on me to make sure I'm alive. My mind is still foggy, I'm unable to cognitively comprehend the situation. The realization of being an addict and the daunting task of becoming clean and sober.

Recently I've been having waves of clarity. I feel more human, like I used to be—well, actually nothing at all like I used to be.

He's here. He walks through the automatic doors wearing jeans and holding a flower. One purple iris, the same flower he brought to the art gallery when he asked me out for our first date. Tears fill my eyes as we step towards each other embracing, he holds me close.

"Happy Anniversary," he whispers in my ear as we hug, and the tears began to drop. Most of the people here are unstable, so crying is nothing new. Tears fall easily, through the halls, lobby—actually all the property grounds, from me especially. I don't have the strength to say it back, instead, I try to make light of the situation, "I saved us the good table."

We walk towards a circular wooden table with two cushioned armchairs, much nicer than some of the other metal chairs. The table closest to the front window is where we take our seats. He looks beautiful, like always.

"How are you feeling, Iris?"

"Good—better. I've been looking forward to seeing you."

"Me, too. You look good, your eyes are clear."

"Yeah, I feel like I'm getting better, I've been crying less."

"Yes. It's a good sign when I only have two spontaneous cries in one day."

"Thanks, Glen, glad I still amuse you."

I smile and realize how strange it feels. Smiling, it almost hurts the unconditioned muscles in my face—something I haven't really done much of lately.

"They promoted me to senior peer, so I was allowed to go on permission to the store this week. It was nice being out."

"I bet."

I place the anniversary card to the table and slide it towards Glen. "I picked this out. It's stupid—they didn't have much of a selection. It was the only card without a spa picture or champagne flutes."

"I'm sure it's fine, Iris." But there's change in his voice, his body language shifts and he seems colder. Maybe I shouldn't have brought up the champagne flutes. The patients have a strange sense of humor around here and we joke a lot about drinking, even though it's not appropriate.

He reaches his hand inside his sport coat, pulling an envelope from his pocket. It's a white small 4x6-ish envelope, too small to be formal divorce papers, I think.

"I have to be honest with you Iris, I bought your card last week. I was feeling bad for you then. My feelings fluctuate from day to day."

"That's fair," I couldn't believe he even bothered to get me a card.

"I'm finding myself more angry than sad this week. I suppose you could say I have less sympathy for all the escapades, from your behavior and the lying."

Bowing my head to the floor I can feel my facial muscles relax, like a dog being scolded by his owner, but he's right. All that I've done, it's horrifying.

"I'm confused with the hiding and sad that you felt like you couldn't talk to anyone, not even me." He rolls his fingers on the table from right to left, the way he does when he's upset. "But this week, right now, I find myself angry. How could you get so out of control? Did you drink yourself into an inebriated mess every night? And the cocaine, how long have you been using cocaine?"

"It wasn't overnight, well, mostly at night—I mean, it happened slowly."

"Wait, Iris, honestly I'm not sure I'm ready yet, I don't want to hear any more lies. I think that's the part that gets me the most—the lying. How could you lie to me after everything we've been through?" He continues without time for me to respond … "All the talks about not keeping secrets from each other, even after the escapade with my sister! How that tore us apart."

His sister! I can't believe I didn't even think of his sister. I was so hard on him for keeping his sister a secret, and he was just trying to protect her. Not like me, and the mess I made. I'm the opposite—the villain, and the antagonist. I was only thinking about myself.

"I'm at a loss. I feel like I lost someone I'm not even sure I ever knew."

His words are strong and relevant. A long awkward silence lingers above our table. I try to put myself in his shoes. Sadness, followed by anger, the natural process of grief. It kills me the pain I've caused him, everyone.

"I'm disgusting. I don't know how I let myself get like this. I can't erase the hurt I've caused, there is no excuse."

Glen's head lifts back up, staring at me. Streams of warm tears fall from my eyes.

"Glen, I am so sorry. I will never be able to make this up to you."

"Iris, stop, rewind—you're not disgusting. Everyone makes mistakes. You just made a lot, a lot of really bad ones. I don't know where to go from here either, but you can't keep torturing yourself. We have to figure this out."

I wipe the moisture from my cheeks and wonder if Glenn is considering staying with me—an idea I hadn't imagined him entertaining.

We remain silent for a moment. In the corner of the room, I spot a woman that I've become friends with. She's hugging her mother and three-year-old son. The boy is far too young to comprehend exactly what's going on. I watch as they walk to a water fountain. The boy is extremely excited, and repeatedly asks for more. Water has never tasted so good, a thought many of us are trying to retrain ourselves to think. It is his enthusiasm for life that I crave most, that zeal. All I am is a body going through the motions—I fear I've lost my thirst for life a long time ago.

Glen's voice interrupts my thoughts, "Come now, we're leaving."

"What, I can't leave!"

"You can't or you won't?"

"I can't, I'm not ready to go yet."

"Actually you can. We're going to get some fresh air and lunch, not from here. I'll have you back by three, before visiting hours are over."

I look down at the table with my nerves getting the best of me. I doze off noticing the grains of wood running somewhat straight except for a few bends and knots. Some of the planks make it look easy and smooth, some not so much. But it gives the table character. The knots and at the end of the day, even the splotched boards make for a great table. The table feels safe, the rooms feel safe, rehab is safe. The outside is the unknown—a scary place full of temptation and … a plastic trash can rolls across the parking lot from the strong winds.

"But the hurricane!"

"*Jose* is flirting between a category one and a tropical storm, so it's a little windy, but I think we can handle it." He pauses and cuts right to the point, his motivation. "Iris, you've been here for almost two months—you can't stay here forever. At some point, you have to start living your life again."

"I don't know if I'll make it. I don't know who I am or what I'm supposed to go back to."

"Then start over. Become the person you were meant to be, the one that's already deep down inside."

He stands from the table and reaches for my hand, I take it and we brave the weather beating down outside. He drives slowly down the narrow drive. I remember the feeling I had when we first pulled up—the fear, the pain, the darkness. It feels similar when you leave, even though we'll only be gone a couple hours. I know that one day soon, the security blanket of rehab will be taken away and it will be for good. The wipers swished back and forth as the rain pours down, but I am safe inside the car.

We reach the main street and Glen accelerates down the isolated roads. The car hugs the pavement and I feel a sensation that I have been lacking—enthusiasm. Glen speeds fast around the curves as music plays over the speakers. Bringing a beat back to my heart, a pulse to my body. Muse sings the complicated lyrics to our lives. Deep passion filled with rage, the sound track for this weather and our love. Madness.

Glen pulls a hard right into a dirt parking lot overlooking a small lake. He stops the car in the vacant lot. He seems angry, but composed, I've seen him like this before, but I can't help but wonder what he's planning to do next. Maybe he'll throw me out to the water and let the alligators dispose of my body. I deserve it.

"This is it, Iris. I'm going to lay it all out for you. If we are going to be together, husband and wife, I have to be able to trust you. No more lies or hiding. No more drinking and drugs. You will go to meetings and take responsibility for your actions. I will not be sticking around for vacations to rehabs. This is not baseball, no three strikes and you're out."

My head and heart may burst at the thought of having another chance to still have Glen. I have lost everything—my word, my mind, my dignity, and my respect.

"Glen, I want to be with you more than anything. I want to change, but I can't promise you my recovery."

His eyebrow raises, confused from my words.

"I will try every day to do my best. I don't want to relapse, but if there's one thing I have learned from being here, it's that I am sober for today. Just today. I can't guarantee tomorrow, I wish I could."

Glen looks puzzled, but not angry, he listens.

"I am sober today and I will try to go to bed every night saying that exact sentence. The days will hopefully turn into weeks, then months, then years." I take a deep breath at the thought of years. Glen and I sit quietly while the storm rages on outside the car. I've never felt so present. Sitting in the passenger seat beside Glen. Though he has full control of both the car and our future. I don't think I gave him the answer he wanted, but it was honest—I gave him the truth.

"Well, Iris ..." after what seemed like hours, "looks like we both have a lot of adjustments to make. It's going to take me some time to trust you again, but I'm not going to hold your past over your head. I'm going to do my best to move forward and I need to know you will, too."

The tears that I thought were dried up return.

"I would love to try."

His arms reach for me and I can feel his strong embrace. The winds howl around us, but I only hear his words of hope.

"I almost forgot, I brought something for you—well, us."

Glen lifts a medium-size cardboard box from the backseat. Carefully he opens it.

"I stopped by the bakery in the quarter before I drove here, the one we went to last year."

He lifts the lid. Inside is a small circular cake with tacky pink and red flowers piped onto the top.

"The baker told me it's custom for couples to eat the top tier or a small replica of their cake on their one-year anniversary. They say its good luck."

I am crying and smiling and laughing, all at the same time. A random ray of sunshine breaks through bands of clouds, while the rain and wind continues through the sun.

"I figured we could use all the luck we can get."

I grab the plastic fork in my hand and push the sugary piece of cake in my mouth. I taste the sweet crumbles of baked flour and the moments of failure from our past. I move the cake around in my mouth, swirling it like the winds whipping outside. It's just a storm—this too shall pass. I was lost in a storm and forgot that it would pass.

These feelings I have towards myself are not all of me, they do not make me who I am, I don't have to be a sheep. I can be more—I will become more than my mistakes.

I swallow hard and lean over the console to kiss his cheek, but he turns to face me and our lips connect. They're plush and sweet, and even better than they look. We pull away slow, I can feel a warm sensation through my stomach inching closer to my inner thighs. I feel alive.

"I'm ready." The words slip off my lips and ours meet again, but this time they stay. Locked into each other, he reaches his hands to my back and lifts my shirt. It creeps up over my head, as I lift my legs over the stick shift and in between his. Our mouths separate for just a moment as he leans his seat back for more room. As I slide my leggings down, I can feel my foot hitting the brake pedal, but we continue to go.

I found myself in the midst of a hurricane. My mind settled while branches lashed around, and I have never felt so anchored to the ground. For the first time in a long time, I felt free.

CHAPTER 30

Hello world, nice to see you again.

~IH

The Meeting

A day of anticipation, like drawing the last number in a competition, but the excitement has worn off … until the moment you're *on deck*. April, her boyfriend, Allie, Glen, our daughters, and I listen to a sound we had gotten used to throughout the day. The slamming pitch from the heavy metal doors opening followed with disappointment, as we watched visitors come and go. I turned my head expecting another false alarm, but then I saw her.

The door was still buzzing, as it jolted shut. The barbed wire coils, stonewall, chain-link fences, the guards, her cell, the maximum-security state prison, and her past all behind her, Vera was outside. Her hair was short and had lost its strawberry hue, replaced with silver strands. Her long stride appeared to be moving in slow motion. She carefully placed one foot in front of the other, like a baby stabilizing herself for the first time. Her eyes squinted as she turned her head into the sunlight. Like stepping out from a long dark film at the movie theater, being greeted with sunshine from the day.

"Oh my God, she's out," April says under her breath.

Her jeans and cream-colored T-shirt are familiar, I had picked them out and sent them to her for her release day a few months ago. The clothes look different on her body. I grabbed the outfit in the store from the sale rack, so I didn't take time to imagine what she would look like with them on. It's been so many years—I hardly remember seeing her in real, outside, citizen clothing. Jeans. She looks crisp, pulled together with her shirt tucked in, and fit. Especially given her mature age now. Most of the inmates stay in pretty good shape—plenty of time for exercise she would say in her letters. Simple diets along with exercise, not drinking or drugging, does a body good. She looks better physically now than before she went in. She would even joke that when she gets out, it will be like stepping out of a Tupperware bin, preserved in her healthiest body ever.

We all stood from the benches where we had been waiting. My girls, who were playing under a pine tree noticed the change in commotion and ran over, looking to me for confirmation. I didn't have the words yet, but I nod once with my head up and down. She hasn't seen us yet.

"Grandma!" My girls shout.

We all stand and stare from a slight distance, watching for her response, but she has none. She doesn't recognize *Grandma*, a name she's never been called before. *Mom* probably wouldn't be much help either. For the last eighteen years she has been referred to by a sequence of numbers and letters.

"Vera," I yell and wave my hand, "We're over here."

She squints her eyes and turns her head from the sun's rays to us, a smile fills her face. As she walks closer, I can see her cheeks a little wrinkled, and wet from the tears that have been falling. Just like mine. I wipe away the sentiment of joy and guilt. I take a deep breath and walk over to meet her.

I reach my arms out to embrace her, and we hug. Her body shakes as she sobs in my arms and I in hers. Holding each other as I experience a flood of emotions I wasn't exactly sure I would be filled with in this moment, all these years later, but turns out to be tears. My eyes pour out with pain. Pain from the incident, the drinking, the drugs, with more tears from the guilt. Vera enduring the severe sentence, while I barely had any consequences. Tears from the items we lost in the fire and even more for the time we lost together.

Vera pulls away, "Is this real, is it really over?"

"Yes, it's over. You're a free woman!" I speak through the tears that taper.

"AHHHHH!!!! Whoaoo!!" She throws her arms over her head.

"Well, free with lots of restrictions, and of course, probation." April chimes in, walking up from behind.

"April, oh goodness, April, you're here! I've missed you so much."

They step in towards each other for yet another long emotional hug.

"Wow, I feel like, like I could fly. Am I flying?"

"I hope not, I'm terrified of heights," April squeals.

"Oh my God, I'm freeeeeee! I've dreamed about this, it's incredible, more than I could imagine. It's here."

She twirls around similar to the way my girls were spinning in the grass just a few minutes ago. She stops before becoming dizzy, high on adrenaline and hope. She spots the others still by the tree.

"Glen, look at you, you look incredible! I don't think I could ever repay you, you've taken such good care of my Iris."

"She's a tough cookie, she's takes care of herself just fine. She's the one to be proud of."

"Oh and I am. I'm proud of both you girls." She looks at me and over to April. "God, I'm so happy you came, April. When Iris told me she would pick me up, I wasn't expecting to see you, too. This is all so much, I can't begin to express."

She wipes a few more tears, we all do.

"And these children!"

My daughter's play-timed out for once and stay near the bench I couldn't get them to sit down on earlier.

"Come over here, girls, I want you to meet … your grandmother."

"Hello."

"Hi," They both respond bashfully, after a full day of talking nonstop.

"Hello, ladies, I'm sorry it's taken me so long to meet you, but I want you to know, I plan on getting to know you better going forward."

"Did you really kill someone?" My daughter asks without warning, the way children do. Apparently not feeling as shy as I thought.

"Well, sadly, yes I did. I've spent a long time paying for the crime that I committed. I will forever hold a heavy heart for my actions. But I'm not the same person I was all those years ago. I've changed."

"That's good, I have a goldfish at home and he's stuck in the tank, too."

"Girls! I think that's enough questions and comments for Grandma right now. Beside I believe you're thinking of a holding tank, which is where people are first taken when they go to jail or maybe they're crazy. Grandma hasn't been sitting in a holding tank for eighteen years."

"Not really a holding tank, but it certainly felt like one sometimes," Vera yells out. "Clearly these girls watch too many true crime shows with their father." I look over to Glen, who is attempting to refrain from laughter.

"I remember a little girl who used to like all those detective shows, too." Vera smiles.

Stepping into the ring of conversation, Allie approaches.

"You remember Allie ..."

"How could I forget Allie? I can't believe you came here, too—it's wonderful to see you!"

"Vera, it's been so long—you look great, really."

"Thanks I've been on a diet for the last eighteen years—it's called prison food. It's all the rage for this side of the ZIP code."

"Just as spunky as ever, I see."

"Oh, I hope so," said Vera. "I feel a little rusty. I could really use a drink."

My lungs grew tight, like I was gasping for air. As if oxygen could somehow be sucked out of the universe. A sharp silence fell over all of us. How could she after all these years, all this time getting to where we are now? She wants a drink. She'll do it again. She'll make a mess of everything, everything we have been waiting for. A drink, she wants a drink, fifteen minutes out. After all my years of sobriety, alcoholics never cease to amaze me.

"A drink?" April speaks up loud and clear. She pauses for a moment, while everyone stares at her.

"No! I'm kidding—tough crowd." Vera laughs, but she laughs alone.

A few pumps of air release back into the atmosphere, I sip the breath cautiously, as Vera continues looking straight into my eyes.

"I've been wanting to tell you for a while now. Shortly after you got sober, Iris, I went to a meeting. Well, they *brought* the meeting here, but I showed up. I started listening to everything they were talking about in AA, and it all became very clear."

My eyes grow wide as I listen, I think my mother just me told she's been going to AA meetings … in prison.

"As if they were telling my story or knew all my tricks—I've never felt like I belonged to anything more. After a couple of months, I knew I was an alcoholic, always have been, always will be."

I glance over to April, Glen, and Allie standing in shock. Their mouths were closed, but they could have fallen open just as easy like mine.

Vera continues, "I didn't want to tell you, because it hasn't seemed fair. Sure I could get alcohol, drugs, or whatever in prison, but it's not the same kind of temptations. I don't run into the corner store to get milk and accidentally buy a case of beer. Or drive home from work, but stop at the bar first. It's not a socially acceptable habit with the COs."

Tears are failing down everyone's checks, including mine. She is serious, this is really happening.

"Now it's up to me. I have to work just as hard to stay sober, the way you have done all along, Iris."

She looks to me as I attempt to collect myself.

"Vera, sobriety is sobriety. Some people get clean and sober, because they want to, some because its court-ordered. It doesn't matter how you get sober—it just matters that you stay sober. We've all done stupid things to earn our membership."

Vera smiles.

"I have to remind myself daily, **if you don't change, your sobriety date will**—it's one of my favorite slogans."

"I like it—I'd like to see a slogan like that for myself."

I look down to my phone, checking my browser for information and note the time.

"Lucky for you I have a local list of AA meetings, and there's one down the street in twenty minutes."

Vera clears her throat, "I would like that very much."

I look to the group and tell them to head into town for dinner, we'll meet up with them after. Vera and I have a very important meeting to attend.

⟶ৡ

The Meeting

My mother and I turn to take our seats in a small room of an old strip mall plaza. The chairperson begins the AA preamble and a small wicker basket is passed. I lean over to Vera and whisper, "I don't know what it was like in there, but out here you have to pay a dollar to see the circus." She laughs as I continue, "I'll spot you this time."

The group begins with the usual introductions. I can feel the words spill off my lips easily like the many times before.

"Hi, my name is Iris, and I'm an alcoholic."

"Hello, Iris," the group returns.

Then my mother speaks. Like a child, I listen to the healing words I have waited a lifetime to hear.

"Hello, my name is Vera, and I'm an alcoholic."

The driveway to nowhere—post fire.

SPECIAL THANKS...

To God. Yup, I'm that person. But if I'm being honest, I wouldn't have been able to overcome all of the obstacles in my life nor formed the words to create this book.

My husband, who encouraged me to pursue my dream of being an author, even though I thought I'd write this novel when our kids got older. Reassuringly saying, "You find the time to work, to run, to yoga, to cook, to volunteer at school, to be a mom and wife. I know if you want to write a novel, you will find time for that too". He insisted for me not to hold back on details, to write without a filter. And the only person that could possibly be happier then me that the book is finally done.

To my children, who were very young when I began the process of writing this novel (my son was 2 years old and my daughter just a new born). Writing the first drafts of chapters while my daughter nursed and my early rising son would tag along on the couch for a sippy cup of milk and cuddles.

To my amazing Mom, whom this book's, Vera, is NOT based on! I am lucky enough to have an incredible mother. She taught me from a young age, Women Can Do Anything. Who's influenced me to try different things, sarcastically stating "Oh no, she has another idea." Thanks for humoring all of them.

My three incredibly sweet big brothers that have all saved me in so many ways. My first role models. Who growing up brought Jackass and fantasy football to life, never miss a birthday (not more then a day or two), and have become very good at calling me back in a time timely manner.

Tara Loop, my childhood friend, who has been such an inspiration to find light though darkness. The person that always believed in me, helping me onto my right road and pushes me to do the things that scare me most. She leads by example, with grace (hand on heart).

My TAMPA core four… Eugene & Celeste Greco, Aunt Josephine & Uncle Al Dato. I don't know where I'd be without you, thank you for accepting me and showing me how a big loving family works. For being there for me before and after you ever had to. For not judging my non-Italian cooking, my intensely detailed photo books, over dressing for holiday parties, giving longer than expected answers to "how's your day?". And look I have more long winded things to say, this time in the form of a novel.

All my family and friends, my old high school crew and especially my clients that have supported my ideas and had to listen to me talk about this endeavor with all the events and characters for much longer then I ever expected.

Dad. Who told me from a young age "Whatever you do, do your best." Also, for survival skills, all my Christmas cards that "birthday" was crossed out and your knowledge of gardening- even if I still don't have a green thumb.

—ℰ

Special thanks to Ann Weydener, who is more then just a client and friend, she is also the very first person to ever read my manuscript. Thank you Ann for seeing my writing potential after receiving my daughter's sip & see thank you card. The passion you had for my poem and enthusiasm to write more was the push I needed. If it wasn't for you offering to help with my first round of edits, I don't think I would have ever had the courage (with my dyslexic self) to ever begin. I would tell her "I have no business writing a novel". To which she would respond "You are a story teller, tell your story. People like me can clean it up later."

Which brings me to my COOL friend Bennie Lazzara, who took interest in my writing early on (which was super fantastic because "BENNIE" liked my writing and introduced me to this publisher Julie Ann, and Ruth my editor- thanks for cleaning this up. Not forgetting my very talented graphic designer and patient friend, the lovely, Kathryn Reina.

To all my newer comedy (fam) friends, thank you for showing me (whether you realized it or not) the art of less. Cutting the fat in sentences to get to the meat. I know there's still a ton I could trim in this 81,504 word count novel, but there actually used to be more.

To Ira Davis- from UF Health Florida Recovery Center "Shands", may you still be enjoying the circus from heaven.

Finally, to any one who is or has a loved one that suffers with addiction, depression and or suicidal thoughts, you are not alone. Get help, keep getting help.

I see you and I love you.